SCREENPLAY

After the death of his parents, eighteen-year-old Alys finds himself rich enough never to have to work. He becomes a dilettante, a connoisseur of French Baroque and Italian Renaissance music—and a devotee of the silent movies of the Twenties. Then Julius Nesselrode, a European émigré film producer from the pioneer days of Hollywood, moves into Alys's mansion. At Nesselrode's instigation, Alys is conducted—literally—through the screen which separates frenetic present-day Los Angeles from Hollywood exactly as it was sixty years ago—with the colour drained out of everything and everybody.

SCREENPLAY

MacDonald Harris

A Lythway Book

CHIVERS PRESS
BATH

First published in Great Britain 1983
by
Jonathan Cape Limited
This Large Print edition published by
Chivers Press
by arrangement with
Jonathan Cape Limited
and in the U.S.A. and Canada with
Atheneum Publishers
1984

ISBN 0 7451 0083 X

British Library Cataloguing in Publication Data

Harris, MacDonald
   Screenplay.—Large print ed.—
   (A Lythway book)
   I. Title
   813'.54[F]   PS3558.E458

   ISBN 0–7451–0083–X

FOR ROBBIE
The onlie begetter of this insuing boke

Bold Lover, never, never canst thou kiss
Though winning near the goal—yet, do not grieve;
She cannot fade, though thou hast not thy bliss,
For ever wilt thou love, and she be fair!

KEATS

CHAPTER ONE

I was born in 1950 in a rather odd part of Los Angeles that not very many people know about. If you are like most people, you probably don't regard Los Angeles as a very enchanting city. But I can assure you that St. Albans Place is a very enchanted street indeed. It is a private drive that you enter through a large and ornate iron gate on Wilshire Boulevard, where a guard is always on duty in a small kiosk like a miniature alpine chalet. From there it winds its way—sending off a number of tributary streets with names as spuriously English as its own—through a park of enormous trees and well-kept lawns, to end at Olympic Boulevard at another iron grille that is never opened, although there is a small pedestrian gate at one side that can be unlocked, if you know of its existence and have the right key.

The park was subdivided and most of its houses built in the Twenties, when the city first left the confines of the downtown area and began moving out to the west. The trees were planted at that time. Now they are huge—elms and sycamores for the most part, with gnarled trunks and thick overarching branches. When you come into it from the traffic of Wilshire Boulevard the place has something of the atmosphere of a bird sanctuary, or a cemetery. The noises of the city are shut out by the trees, and you are conscious only of quiet and isolation, of the pastoral and shady green light that pervades everything, and of the sense of privilege that comes from being very wealthy. The street is broad and curves its way with a kind of negligent magnificence through the sylvan atmosphere of the trees and lawns. The houses on it have only one quality in common— they are all large and expensive. Except for that they are a kind of anthology of all the pretentious and derivative architectures of the time—fake Florentine villas, English country houses, Venetian palazzos, stucco Spanish palaces with tiled roofs, and one house with eaves curled up and stone lions in front of it that vaguely attempts to be Chinese—we always called it the Pagoda. The one I grew up in is a large shingled house with overhanging eaves, a kind of Cape Cod cottage magnified to the dimensions of a mansion. It was built by my grandfather, a Harvard professor who lived most of his life in Cambridge and spent his summers on Martha's Vineyard. He was independently wealthy (the family fortune came from a plumbing manufactory that owned the patent on the flush toilet, in case anyone is curious), and when he was widowed in his fifties, he retired and came to Los Angeles, bringing with him my mother, who was born

2

late in his marriage and still a small child. He acquired a large lot in St. Albans Place, and there he built an exact replica of what he regarded as an ideal habitation, even though it was far too large for a middle-aged professor and a small child—a Cambridge townhouse like those along the winding and shady sanctuary of Brattle Street.

The furnishings of the house, as I remember it from my childhood, were expensive but ill-sorted—some heirlooms, some acquired at a later period. Most of the furniture was that left by my grandfather, whereas the bric-à-brac and small objets d'art had been acquired by my mother and father, or, as I always called them, Astrée and Dirk. (My grandfather was a professor of French literature, and it pleased him, out of a kind of antiquated perversity, to name his only child for a character in a seventeenth-century pastoral.) There was a pair of Sisleys, said to be authentic, on the wall by the mantelpiece, and a photograph of my mother by Man Ray. In the dining room there was an extraordinary piece of furniture: a Louis Quinze sideboard with gilded legs and a large ornate mirror covered with gray splotches, which in my childhood I endowed with all the mystery and significance of a map of an unknown land. I identified continents in it, rivers, and even cities, which I inhabited in the secret reveries of my imagination. The house was full of a clutter of other odd things: a camel saddle, a bronze Pompeiian figurine with a phenomenal erection (when I was small I thought it was only the way he carried his sword), an arquebus which worked and could be fired on the Fourth of July, and a toilet in the downstairs bathroom so old that it might have been the original of the family patent, with a brass chain hanging from the tank on the ceiling and a pattern of stains, in the bowl, almost as complex as those on the tarnished mirror. This we called the Infernal Machine. It had a sound all to itself: a wheeze, a gurgle, a chuckle or two, and then, after a pause, a great rush of water that went on for a long time and left all the pipes in the house humming. Finally it shut itself off with a snap, the gasp of a person suddenly throttled with an iron hand.

My grandfather died when I was still very young, so that I hardly remember him and I think of the house mainly as a place where Astrée and Dirk and I lived together. We must have seemed an odd family to others, although, since we lived almost entirely to ourselves, our way of life seemed to us perfectly natural. Both Astrée and Dirk were exceptionally good-looking and seemed eternally young. They were always blithe and happy and gave the impression somehow that they were living in a romantic comedy rather than a life in the real world. Sometimes they sang to each other,

4

trading lines like characters in a Noel Coward musical as they moved through the house from room to room. 'Many's the time that we feasted...' 'And many's the time that we fasted...' 'Oh well, it was swell while it lasted...' 'We did have fun...' 'And no harm done...' And then, with a look of mock sentiment and a glance through the doorway between them, they would join together in two-part harmony for 'Thanks ... for the memory...' Astrée had difficulty taking things seriously, including her own unique and striking boyish beauty, the wealth she had inherited so effortlessly, and even the house itself. Sometimes, when the three of us came back at night from the noise and traffic of the city and stopped the car in the drive, in the silence and the dank, slightly foreboding shade of the old trees, she would intone in a fakey theatrical voice:

'A savage place! as holy and enchanted
As e'er beneath a waning moon as haunted
By woman wailing for her demon lover!'

They lived their lives almost entirely together and for each other, so in some ways they hardly paid attention to me. They were always going on motor trips, burning the toast, quarreling and making up, trying to outspend each other for clothes, and having disagreements which turned

5

into torrid clinches and then ended in the bedroom. When they went away on trips, often for a week or more, they left me with a sitter, a disagreeable middle-aged woman named Mrs. Bent whom I detested. Mrs. Bent, however, was engaged more to satisfy the legal requirements about child care than out of concern for my own security or welfare. If it hadn't been for the law, they would probably have gone off and left me alone in the house when I was a boy of ten. It wasn't that they were lacking in affection for me or that they were bad parents. It was simply that they had no experience of children and didn't understand them very well. They had no friends who had children, and neither of them had had brothers or sisters. So they hardly knew how to regard me, and they ended by regarding me simply as a person like themselves. It was true that I was physically smaller than other people, so that my chin came only to the edge of the table and my clothes had to be bought in the boys' department at Bullock's, but they saw this as no reason not to treat me exactly as an adult— a friend perhaps of whom they were very fond, and yet didn't mind leaving for a week or two when they went away on a trip. They were aware, of course, that this behavior was unconventional, but rather than address themselves seriously to the question of what childhood was or how a child ought to be brought up they preferred to regard the

6

situation as a joke. '*I* was certainly never ten years old,' said Dirk, regarding me gravely over the dining-room table, 'and neither was anybody on my side of the family.'

Still I had an intimate, if intermittent, relationship with the two of them. Dirk called me 'old fellow' even when I was seven, and had long conversations with me in which he would explain to me, for example, that the reason Astrée was out of sorts today was that she was having her period. Women were difficult at such times, he advised, and it was best to have nothing to do with them. Having married into the family money, he had no need to work and never did so, even though he had a university degree in architecture. He had a single passion, antique cars. He bought and sold at least two dozen of them during my childhood, spending great time and effort searching for rare parts to restore them before, reluctantly, selling them to make room for others. Sometimes there were four or five of them in the enormous garage behind the house. The ones I remember most clearly, from the time of my late adolescence, were three: a rare Invicta three-liter touring car, a 1929 Duesenberg Model J, and a dual-cowl Hudson phaeton of the same period with coachwork by Biddle and Smart. The actual restoration work, of course, was done by professionals. But Dirk was assiduous in his attention to details and meticulous in his taste, sometimes making trips East in search of a rare hood ornament or an authentic magneto—once even to England for a pair of headlamps for the Invicta, the ones on his own car being too rusted to be replated. The Invicta was his favorite: a lean and elegant machine from the period of the mid-Twenties, with long sweeping fenders, a riveted hood with a sharp chine, nickel-plated headlamps mounted on a crossbar, and a thermometer emerging from the nickel-plated radiator cap. It was painted a beautiful rich deep persimmon color. I remember once watching him polish it with a can of Simoniz wax, while he explained to me the aesthetics of automobiles and other things 'It's when you are polishing a car that you are most aware of the beauty of the design,' he told me. 'It's because your hand goes over and follows all the curves, in addition to your eye. You *feel* the body kinetically. The curves, you see, of the fenders, and the place where the hood joins the body.' He demonstrated as he worked the rag into the hollow curve between the fenders and the hood. 'And it's the same,' he went on, 'when you're making love to a woman. It's when your hand follows the curves of the body that you become fully aware of its beauty.' Here he put the lid back on the Simoniz, got out some metal polish, and began polishing the large round headlamps at the front of the car, glancing sideways at me with a little smile.

He was a slender, handsome, courteous, joking, good-natured man who charmed everybody who came into contact with him. When he took off his clothes he had the body of a twenty-year-old. We often took baths together, in an enormous enameled tub that stood on four clawed legs in the bathroom upstairs. 'Always wash your pecker carefully, old fellow,' he advised, while doing so to his own. 'That way, you form the habit and you won't pick up something nasty from some tart later.' I was curious that he had no foreskin. 'It's because I'm Jewish, old fellow,' he told me. At that time I had no very clear notion what a Jew was, and he didn't explain any further. He never mentioned the subject again.

Astrée too was strikingly beautiful, in a style more of the Twenties than of the mid-Fifties when I first became aware of her as a person. She was slim, with a not very pronounced figure, and she emphasized this boyishness by wearing straight clothes with simple short skirts. She had a perfect ivory complexion, a heart-shaped face, and short hair that she tossed carelessly back from her head; she looked something like Mary Pickford. She had only one passion, and that was herself—her own body and her beauty. Yet it could hardly be said that she was vain; taking care of her beauty was simply *what she did*, as Dirk lovingly took care of old cars. She was perfectly objective about

9

herself and would often ask others' opinions about her body—whether the faint rings under her eyes were enough yet to justify cosmetic surgery, or whether she ought to wear the tight turtleneck jerseys that were coming into fashion considering her rather small breasts. ('Yes,' was Dirk's opinion. 'It's the gamine look. My own taste, darling, doesn't incline to the bovine, so be happy about it.') She spent several hours of each day in her dressing room, before a table fitted with a mirror framed in light bulbs, like that of an actress. Yet she was careless of her makeup and clothes, once they were on, and would enthusiastically engage in pillow-fights, wrestle in the straw with Dirk on our visits to the country, or impulsively take off her clothes and throw them into the sand when the three of us, hand-in-hand, strode naked into the Malibu surf at midnight.

It was Astrée who, for reasons best known to herself, decided to name me Alys. Perhaps because she had really wanted a girl, or perhaps because she did not distinguish the two sexes very clearly in her own mind—there was some evidence for this. I was subject to a certain amount of satire on account of this, especially when I was away at school, but it never particularly bothered me. I felt that I too was special, like Astrée and Dirk, and it seemed natural that I should have a special name. After all what other boy had a mother like Astrée? To me she behaved exactly as she did to the rest of her friends; she was affectionate without sentiment, she confided every intimate thought that came to her without hesitating, she often asked my advice on things, and when I came home at the end of the day she embraced me as she did her other friends, male and female, as was the custom in their set—in the French manner, a quick hug and a touch of the lips on both cheeks. I still remember, from the time I was fifteen or so, the soft bittersweet sensation of her small breasts pressing against my own thin and boyish chest. It fixed my notions for a long time, permanently, of what women were like. I was not interested in ordinary girls. There was nothing wrong with me physically; all my male reflexes worked perfectly. It was just that, living with Astrée and Dirk, I had no need of anyone else.

I have said that she was affectionate toward me, and she was, but no more than she was to her other friends; and she didn't care to have me around all the time any more than she wanted the house always full of her friends. I was sent to private day schools, and later for a brief period they sent me away to an exclusive prep school in La Jolla, perhaps as much to get me out of the house as to provide me with the excellent education they could easily afford. It was an excellent school, in a kind of English manor house set in well-kept landscaping at the edge of

11

the sea, and the pseudo-Etonian curriculum, with its classical languages and its emphasis on *mens sana in corpore sano* (we played soccer and even cricket) was also excellent. But I was unhappy there, or so I told Astrée and Dirk; in actual fact I was only bored. I didn't mingle much with the other pupils, most of them the children of wealthy lawyers and physicians. I had no interest in their giggling and goosing, their flatulence jokes, their snobbish gangs and hierarchies. It wasn't that I felt superior to them; it was just that I had nothing in particular to say to them. I couldn't succeed in thinking of myself as someone like them, that is to say as a child, because Astrée and Dirk had never treated me like a child.

So I came home again. It was the end of my formal schooling. After that I did nothing but get up late in the morning, read the books in the house and play records. As a matter of fact I ended up reasonably well educated, even though along slightly old-fashioned lines, because my grandfather had left us his books along with the house. I remember, at the age of seventeen, reading Adam Smith, Proust (my French was excellent), Newton's *Principia*, Krafft-Ebing's *Psychopathia Sexualis*, Sacher-Masoch's *Venus in Furs*, Goethe's *Gespräche mit Eckermann*, and Gibbon's *Decline and Fall*. One of my favorite books, which I found tucked away on a high shelf where my grandfather, evidently, had kept

12

volumes of special interest, was *Une semaine de bonté,* a kind of surrealistic novel in collage by Max Ernst—a book full of odd nudity, scenes of levitation, scissors, sadism, and scenes in which fin-de-siècle maidens were abducted by frock-coated men with birds' heads. It goes without saying that I had no friends my own age, even though there were other families with children in St. Albans Place. I couldn't have discussed *Une semaine de bonté* with them, and their concerns—bicycles, rock music, girls, skateboarding—I viewed with all the contempt of an overrefined adult intellectual.

★   ★   ★

I have said that Astrée and Dirk liked to go away on motor trips leaving me alone in the house, and I have explained too that they engaged Mrs. Bent to take care of me in their absence simply because of the law regarding the supervision of minors. Through consulting an attorney, they found out that this obligation ended when a child became eighteen. As a result, as my eighteenth birthday approached they looked forward with anticipation to the time when I could legally be left in the house alone. Mrs. Bent (who for some time now had been referred to as a 'housekeeper' rather than a 'sitter') was getting rather aged in any case. So, according to a plan that I agreed to quite willingly, they

13

celebrated my eighteenth birthday in a way which might have seemed odd to some people. They went off on a trip to San Francisco to stay at the Mark Hopkins for a few days, go to the opera, shop at Gump's and Abercrombie & Fitch, and dine out in their favorite places like the Blue Fox or the Basque restaurant in North Beach.

The Invicta was too delicate and too unreliable for a long trip, so they went in the Duesenberg. It was a powerful roadster with an enormous long hood, a set of chrome-plated exhaust headers curving down over the side, and a canvas top with a small window in the rear. They put their bags in the rear and the Duesenberg started off down the drive with its characteristic exhaust noise: a deep syncopated rumble from the twin chromed tailpipes. Astrée turned once to raise her hand in a kind of distracted 'Bye' sign to me. As they disappeared down the street I saw them kissing, framed in the small rear window of the car.

And so I was left to my own devices in the big house for a few days. Astrée telephoned once; it was three o'clock in the morning and they had just got back to the hotel from the Hungry I in North Beach. Over the phone I could hear Dirk murmuring as he nuzzled her neck from behind. That was the last I heard from them. The trip evidently went more or less as planned. Coming back along Highway 1, they had reached the scenic stretch on the coast just south of Big Sur when a van driven by a long-haired youth under the influence of some hallucinogen or other crossed the center line and crashed straight into the front grille which Dirk had gone to such pains to have replated. The wreckage burned fiercely, and the undertaker advised burying them both in the same grave, since the two sets of ashes were so mingled that it was almost impossible to separate them—I expect he meant it was too much trouble.

CHAPTER TWO

The bank, the trustees, and the attorneys took care of everything. To my surprise Astrée and Dirk had executed an elaborate will in my favor, too complicated for me to understand in all its details, in fact, setting up a trust that provided me with a generous monthly allowance and leaving the management of the estate to the trust department of the Sunset Bank. I had nothing much to do in those first few days except to think how to respond in some way to the profuse if somewhat conventional expressions of sympathy that I received from Astrée's and Dirk's many friends. Naturally I was afflicted with a certain amount of grief. I wasn't a monster, and I had been genuinely fond of

Astrée and Dirk. But I kept this pain to myself, as I had always done with my other expressions of feeling, and I confined myself to formulas of gratitude as conventional as the sympathy of the friends. I would sooner have taken off my clothes in front of those people than revealed my innermost feelings to them. At the funeral, since I had excellent hearing, I caught a distant murmur across the crowd, 'He always was a cold boy.' And perhaps I was; it seemed to me to be better to be cool about things than too hot. The hurt I felt over the loss of my parents was something like a thumb struck with a hammer, very painful for a while, interfering to an extent with one's proper functioning in the world, and impossible to conceal entirely from others. But I recovered. One always does, from a struck thumb. When I hurt myself as a child, Astrée would kiss it to make it well, then she would forget it and go on blithely about her own affairs. Neither she nor Dirk ever dwelt much on private misfortunes. As casual and even negligent as they had been in my upbringing, they gave me excellent training in this respect.

For a number of years I went on living alone in the big house in St. Albans Place. I had few friends and nothing to do in particular except to do what I wanted. It shouldn't be imagined that I was lonely or unhappy in any way. I enjoyed this solitary life intensely. My only enemy was boredom, and I found a thousand ingenious ways to combat this. Of course I had access to my grandfather's excellent library. Now and then I enrolled in a course at UCLA, in eighteenth-century French literature perhaps, or something more esoteric like the history of the Albigensian heresy, but for the most part I educated myself through private reading—like Proust and Virginia Woolf, or the Baron Corvo, that odd and elaborate impostor who was perhaps my favorite author in the panoply of eccentrics, recluses, and decadents I had collected for myself. I began exploring the top shelves of my grandfather's library, in the locked glass cabinets where years before I had found *Une semaine de bonté*. Here I discovered books that for a long time I thought nobody else knew about: Burton's *Anatomy of Melancholy*, Sir Thomas Browne's *Urn Burial*, Baudelaire's *Paradis artificiel*, and Raymond Roussel's *Locus Solus*. Roussel's elaborate and slightly mad world of the imagination, filled with its ingenious, complex, and totally useless mechanical contrivances, seemed to me a satisfactory analogue to the predicament of modern man—hypnotized by his elaborate technology until he spent his whole existence watching its wheels go around—in my case a seven-hundred-dollar turntable with its diamond needle, carving away in its groove like the torture machine of Kafka's tale 'In the Penal Colony.'

* * *

One of the first things I bought, after the fuss over my sudden orphaning had died away, was an excellent stereo system, the best that money could buy. It filled one whole end of the living room in its custom cabinets, and each piece of equipment was duplicated in the bedroom upstairs, so I could lie on the bed and control the whole thing with an array of electrical buttons at the bedside. As for music, I had no strong preferences, except for my dislike of the deafening electronic cacophonies of my own generation, so I started with what was in the house. There was a large glass case in the library downstairs full of old records. Most of them had been acquired by Dirk and Astrée—big-band swing from the Forties, musical comedy albums, old Cole Porter songs. But farther back in the cabinet, so covered with dust that it was clear nobody had touched them for years, I found a hundred or so old seventy-eights in faded paper covers. The collection included the French court musicians from Mouret and Philidor to Couperin, Lully, and Marin Marais; D'Andrieu and Loeillet; most of Telemann including the *Fantasien* for flute and orchestra; and scratchy arias from the operas of Galuppi and Paisiello. Evidently my grandfather had made a kind of professorial and erudite hobby of

18

this music that corresponded to the period of his academic specialty in the French pastoral. This was long before the contemporary fad for the baroque, and he must have gone to a good deal of effort to acquire these fragile old shellac records at a time when no one in particular could have been interested in them but himself, playing them, no doubt, on an old wind-up Victor phonograph that was still preserved, with a rug over it, in the attic in St. Albans Place.

In time I began to develop my own addiction to the music of this period, for reasons in myself that at first I didn't identify, or wasn't interested in analyzing. Like many people who live alone I was an insomniac, and often when I couldn't sleep I would spend half the night drinking—moderately, and staying carefully away from the thin edge of intoxication—and listening to these old records. With a little dry vermouth in my glass, sipping at it now and then, I could lose myself for hours in these highly symmetrical, highly intricate chamber pieces with their complex harmonies, their intricately interlaced fugal structures, the solemnly funereal, weirdly graceful stateliness of the slow movements. Their beauty and grace were quite obsolete; it was an elegance of court and drawing room, the music of a time when a tiny fraction of humanity enjoyed their exquisite and overrefined pleasures at the expense of the brute labor of the others. I preferred the past, almost any past, to

19

the present. There was no reason why you had to live in the present, I thought, especially if you had a little money. Partly through the accident of birth, partly through my own preference, I had arranged a life for myself in which I was surrounded by obsolete things, by anachronisms: old music, the old house with its stately and slightly spurious charm of a New England university town, old cars, the old books in the library. When I had to make an occasional foray into the flashy modern world of the 'L.A.' outside, to buy food or on some other errand, it was like stepping into the sunlight from a darkened theater—a sporadic and ephemeral expedition into the present, a harmless jag to the nerves. There is a story by Kafka called 'The Burrow' in which the narrator—an animal of an unidentified species—creeps out of his burrow now and then to contemplate its entrance from a distance and enjoy the mild sense of danger that this produces, knowing that security is immediately at hand whenever he wishes to return to it. This was exactly my impulse.

I was soon adding to the collection by buying records of my own, and in time I even became a fairly competent amateur musicologist in the period, just as I had become something of a scholar by reading the books in my grandfather's library. As I explored further into the subject I began to make a specialty of music played on authentic period instruments—the viola da gamba in place of the cello, the lute rather than the guitar, the recorder instead of the flute, or even odder old and unwieldy museum pieces like the krumhorn or the tromba marina. I would lie sometimes until daylight on the bed, listening to the thin and acerbic, slightly twangy tone of a Renaissance oboe, or a concerto played on an antique valveless horn—archaic, muffled, slightly brassy, like a hunting horn echoing in the depths of some medieval forest. Such records were hard to find, but I became an expert in searching them out, sometimes ordering custom pressings from specialty music houses in Europe, or rerecording my own cassettes from rare records in libraries. I corresponded with other rare-music collections in America and Europe, and I had a whole file cabinet full of notes and cross-references, rather badly organized, but which I hoped to make use of some time. Once, when I was taking a musicology course at USC, I even started to write a monograph on Pergolesi's string concerti and their possible sources in the works of Ricciotti, but I quit when I ran out of typewriter ribbon. I still have the manuscript, about thirteen pages, marked with the date when I abandoned it: June 14, 1976.

Still it was on accunt of this monograph, or at least of my efforts to write it, that I met Belinda, who in time became a good friend and perhaps even something more. I had been doing some

21

work on Pergolesi in the Doheny Library, and when I went for a coffee break in the student union I took my book with me and went on reading it while I sat at the long coffee-spotted wooden table. The atmosphere in the union was very informal. Everybody talked to everybody else. After a while I heard someone inquire, 'Why are you reading a book about Pergolesi?'

I looked up. She was a tall girl with sun-bleached California hair, blonde at the ends and darker down inside, and a tennis player's tan. Her clothes were casual, a cashmere sweater and a skirt. She looked much like any of the other students on the campus, except perhaps for her lipstick, which was a very pale pink, almost white, so that in contrast to her tanned face it gave her the slightly disorienting look of a photographic negative in which light and dark are reversed. That and her crisp and self-assured way of speaking, with a faint touch of irony.

'You know Pergolesi?'

'*La Serva Padrona*. The *Stabat Mater*.'

'Of course. Those are the ones that everybody knows. I'm interested in the concerti for string orchestra, which aren't as well known.'

She regarded me appraisingly for a moment, as though I were a picture she were contemplating in a museum.

'What about them?'

'I have a theory that they may owe something to an obscure Italian composer named Carlo

22

Ricciotti, about whom almost nothing is known except that he was Musikmeister in The Hague around 1740. Pergolesi's concerti are different from the rest of his work. The mode is no longer high baroque, it's preclassical. The whole harmonic development, and especially the way the accidentals are handled, very much resembles Ricciotti. It's even possible, in fact, that four of the six concerti are Ricciotti's work and not by Pergolesi at all.'

'Ricciotti was in The Hague in 1740. But Pergolesi lived to be only twenty-six, and died in 1736.'

Now it was my turn to give her a long thoughtful look. She was still the same, a tall girl with pale lipstick, a little more mature and self-assured than the ordinary coed.

'Yes. But no one knows Ricciotti's dates. He could have been working in northern Europe in the early 1730s, at the time when Pergolesi was supposedly composing his concerti. In any case the attribution of the concerti to Ricciotti has to be made on stylistic and harmonic grounds rather than biographical evidence, because there is no biographical evidence.'

This lecture of mine seemed to amuse her more than anything else.

'Who in the world are you, anyhow?' She added, 'If you were anybody I would have heard of you.'

'Why should you have heard of me?'

23

'Because I know everybody who works in early music in L.A.'

'I keep pretty much to myself.'

⋆　　⋆　　⋆

It was a double misunderstanding; we each took the other for a student—which was an easy mistake to make, since we met in the student union and I looked a good deal younger than my age—whereas in fact I was a rich dilettante, and she was a professonal musicologist who just happened to be on campus to do some work in the library. She was a programmer for the classical FM station KUSC, which had its studios near the campus, and she had her own weekly program of early music called *Quires and Consorts*. In fact I had occasionally listened to this program at home, although it was some time before I connected the voice that came out of the speakers with the Belinda I met in the union.

After we got over our initial amusement at this *malentendu* we became friends and frequently went out together—to concerts and ballets, to dinner where we went Dutch and split the bill, or to old films. Out of boredom, more or less, I had developed an addiction to the primitive pictures that were put on by the classic films series at the County Art Museum or at UCLA. I liked them best when there was no

24

sound at all except for some scratchy music, or some inexpertly dubbed dialogue tacked on in a later epoch by hacks who scarcely cared whether they did a good job or not. Like my walks, the films for me were a kind of vulgar relaxation, a retreat from the excessive refinement of the world of books and baroque music which I inhabited in the house in St. Albans Place. I had my own private fantasies about them, which I didn't communicate to Belinda. For me, the world of the silent film was another world than our own—an artificial and synthetic world in which there existed another life parallel to our own and yet different—a world where other physical laws operated so that impossible athletic feats could be performed and devastating accidents happen without harm to the victim—where even the laws of psychology and character were different, where there was a freedom, an invulnerability, a kind of zany marionette behavior that made everything simpler and less complex than life in our real world of three dimensions. In spite of the stiffness of their movements and the rigid conventionality of their behavior, these black-and-white figures moving jerkily across the screen seemed to bear a charm that freed them from the limitations of the ordinary human condition. One envied, almost, their doll-like posturing, their kisses that produced soulful expressions but were followed only by fadeouts, the comedians in baggy pants who were run over by buses but only got up and dusted themselves off, the orphans who were certain to find in the end that they were the lost children of millionaires. There was no real suffering in this world, no boredom, and no mortality. When people were shot they only fell down, dramatically and with pathos, as they had been taught to do by directors with the aesthetic sensibility of second-hand pants dealers. If they were young they were always young, and if they were old they were always old. And if they were young they were beautiful—as I was myself. In the projection hall I almost forgot my three-dimensional existence and lost myself in this play of jerky cardboard figures on the screen.

I can't think that Belinda really cared much for these primitive works of art, but she came along, probably more amused at me than she was at the pictures. Sometimes after a concert or a movie I would bring her back to the house in St. Albans Place. She was impressed with the house, and with my general way of life, no doubt, but always with the touch of irony with which she regarded most things. We would have a drink or two and we would kiss sometimes, lightly, as friends. Nothing more. I don't know what she wanted of me. Perhaps a more intimate physical relation—if so she never spoke of it or made any sign, even though it was she who had made the first overtures in asking me from across the table in the union, with her distant little smile, 'Why are you reading a book about Pergolesi?'

As for me, I knew very well why it was that I felt no desire for Belinda, at least no overt sexual desire. Partly it was her general tone of an emancipated young woman, her self-assurance and aggressiveness in a conversation, her tenacity in adhering to a point when she knew she was right, her private air of amusement at my own little quirks. But above all it was her status as a professional musicologist, one who made her living from her profession. While I was confident enough of my own expertise in this field not to feel any sense of disadvantage, it nevertheless prevented me from feeling toward Belinda as I would have to feel toward her if I were to desire her sexually. There was no emotional jealousy—it was a purely physical matter. It was simply that I felt myself incapable of going to bed with a person who knew more about music than I did. If we did, I felt, she should have to be the one who was on top. So nothing happened, beyond our friendly kisses.

Meanwhile, unknown to Belinda, I was experimenting in a light-hearted way with other forms of carnal amusement—some a little dangerous, enough to lend them spice. I became a frequenter of those spcialized places of encounter that are provided in Los Angeles, as they are in other large cities, for ephemeral adventures with persons of one sex or another, discreet bars with names like Foxey's and Just for Tonight. The people I met in such places, on the whole, were impressed with the house in St. Albans Place when I brought them there, and unlike Belinda they didn't smile at my eccentricities. They also did what I wanted them to do, and not what they wanted. Some of them I didn't even have to pay. It was enough for them to have brushed up briefly against a fantasy that was beyond their imagination, a refinement of decadence that afterward must have seemed to them something encountered only fleetingly in a dream. When I grew tired of this game I turned to sidewalk hookers, expensive call girls, and even the boys in tank tops and tight jeans who hung out late at night along Santa Monica Boulevard. I discovered, somewhat to my satisfaction, that I was polymorphous-perverse enough to be capable of almost any sexual bizarrerie to be found in this complex and cynical city where practically everything, from a joint of grass to a cold-blooded murder, could be bought for a price. I was incapable, it seemed, of only one sexual variation, that of going to bed with Belinda. My friendship with her continued on for a number of years, more or less in the same vein, or according to the same rules. I don't think she had any other suitors. In my private thoughts I jokingly referred to her as my fiancée—she herself always told people we were 'just friends.'

Except for Belinda, and my music and books, I had few other interests. I went out to dinner once in a while, sometimes with Belinda and sometimes alone. Sometimes I tinkered a little with Dirk's classic cars—or the two that were left, the Invicta and the Hudson—although for some reason I never found as much satisfaction in polishing them as he had. When I wanted to go somewhere too far to walk I usually drove the big Hudson phaeton, saving the more fragile Invicta for some special adventure, perhaps, that lay ahead in the future. I drank a little but I didn't make a hobby of it. I almost never went to bars except to singles bars, where I didn't drink at all, in order to maintain the advantage of clarity over my adversaries. I had never been attracted to drugs, although I could have afforded any that I wanted. The real world, so called—the world I found palpably around me in my waking hours—had always seemed so evanescent and ephemeral that I was never quite sure whether its objects were going to be there when I reached out to touch them; and I was reluctant to bring any further unreality into my consciousness by introducing chemicals into my body that would additionally weaken this tenuous web that connected me with reality.

One evening—it was a Tuesday, I remember, since Belinda had her program that night—I had gone out to dinner alone at an Italian restaurant

29

on Melrose Avenue. I came home about nine, took off my necktie and coat and hung them in the closet (I was careful about my clothes, and I dressed rather formally), and fixed myself a drink. I switched on the FM and set it to 92.5. After the station break there was a pause and then I heard her low-keyed and confident voice. 'Good evening. This is Belinda Blaine, your host for *Quires and Consorts*, KUSC's weekly program of early music. This evening we shall hear as our featured work Jean-François d'Andrieu's *Premier livre de Clavecin*, a work which...'

Oddly enough I felt a little stir of desire, a thing that had never happened when Belinda was actually present. By the telephone was a business card: 'Ace Escort Service. 50 foxy girls. Dial day or night 555–6712.' I picked up the card and looked at it for a moment, and then I put it down. Instead I took off the rest of my clothes and went into the bathroom to look at myself in the mirror. The measured tinkle of the harpsichord came through the open door from the other room. I stood for some time looking at the image in the mirror—the thin and skeptical, slightly immature face with a shock of dark hair over the forehead, the pale complexion, the slender body with perhaps a touch of the feminine in the softness of the contours and the fragility of the shoulders and elbows, the perfect and flowerlike organ visible in the patch of hair

30

at the bottom of the abdomen. It struck me for the first time that my body was a kind of amalgam or union of the bodies of Astrée and Dirk, both of whom had been very attractive people. I was pleased and satisfied by what I saw in the mirror. My doubts vanished. I forgot about it then and finished my drink, listened to the rest of Belinda's program, and went to bed. I always slept the same way, in Christian Dior satin pajamas, alternating a blue pair with a maroon week by week, crouched in a kind of fetal position on one side of the large double bed in which my grandparents and my parents had slept, leaving space at the side for another person. I slept well and woke up content with myself and as serene as an angel.

The next day I called a glass shop on Western Avenue and had them come and install mirrors over the whole bedroom—a large one on each of the three walls facing the bed, and another huge one, eight feet by four, on the ceiling directly over the bed. I waited impatiently until they were gone. Then I stripped everything off the bed except the bottom sheet, took off my clothes, lay down on the bed, and took my pleasure with myself, while I turned successively to watch the images in the four mirrors. The experiment was a considerable success; not only was I excited by my own beauty but I felt there was no one else in the world who was worthy of it, no one who deserved this body but myself. Gradually this practice became a habit, and I continued in it with no sense of guilt or no feeling that I required anything else of myself or anyone else. I was self-sufficient. My parents' friends at the funeral had been wrong to say that I was a cold boy. When I caught sight of myself in the mirrors, especially the large one overhead, I was filled with a hot and powerful desire that demanded to be satisfied immediately. But one one ever knew about this but myself.

CHAPTER THREE

Looking out one day through the leaded panes of the living-room window, I saw a curious figure examining the house from the sidewalk. He was a very old man, I could see that even from a distance. Although it was a mild spring day, he wore a shabby overcoat which he left open with the tails flapping behind him. He was hatless and bald on top, with uncut white hair that hung in a fringe around his head. The notion struck me immediately that he was not an American. He stood there for some time looking at the house reflectively with his lips pursed, as though he were thinking of buying it. He walked away down the sidewalk, looked at another house a few doors down, and then came back. Finally he came up and knocked on the door.

At either side of the door there was a narrow frosted window with decorations cut in the glass, but I could see only a blurry shadow through this. I opened.

'I want to rent your room,' he said in a reedy voice. He seemed to have a slight middle-European accent, although I wasn't able to identify the language.

I could see now that the coat was a genuinely odd garment. The material was a kind of imitation suede, light gray in color, with a soft furry surface that was worn smooth in places. It was cut like a trench coat with pockets all over it, except that there weren't any straps. There were stains on it here and there and the tails were frayed from wear.

'What are you talking about? What room?'

'Any room. It doesn't matter. I want to rent a room in your house.'

I was amused more than anything else. 'But why this house?'

'It suits my needs. The location and also the design. There are not so many houses like this.'

He twitched his nose and looked cautiously around as if to see whether anyone was overhearing our conversation. His ears were oversized, and he also had large, rather protruding eyes, which flickered constantly and never quite met my glance. I saw now that he had a cleft lip which had evidently been repaired by surgery; a fine scar braided like a shoelace ran down the center of it. It left him with a slight lisp, and it was perhaps this that I had taken for an accent. His complexion had a gray cast to it as though he weren't very well. Still he was very energetic, or at least nervous. He had a way of jumping at me every time he spoke, with an abrupt little spasm that almost lifted him off the ground.

'Who are you anyhow? How did you get in here? This is supposed to be a private street.'

'Why shouldn't I come in here?' he said with some indignation. 'It's a free country. This is America. It isn't Germany after all.'

'Well, come in,' I told him, suppressing my smile.

He entered and I shut the door. He had the musty smell about him of somebody you might meet in a free soup kitchen, or some dingy place of business like an unsuccessful pawnshop. I saw now that he was even older than he had looked from the sidewalk. The wrinkles of his face gave the impression that they had dirt in them, although this was perhaps only a feature of his complexion. He was very fragile; he seemed hardly more than a wraith inside the voluminous overcoat.

'Won't you take off your coat?'

'No. I would expect to be treated with a little more courtesy. After all I am not nobody.' He proffered a card. He had evidently been carrying it around in his pocket for years; it was so wrinkled and creased that it resembled a soiled rectangle of cloth more than a piece of cardboard. On it I made out the words 'Julius Nesselrode.'

I handed it back to him. 'I'm afraid I've never heard of you.'

'You've heard of me,' he insisted querulously. 'Everybody in pictures knows who I am. I have been a director and a producer and at one time I was a studio executive. Which room is it that you wish to rent me?'

'This isn't a rooming house.'

'No. It's a fine old mansion, designed by Kohlman and built in 1921.'

I reflected. My life was rather boring. Nesselrode was original. At one time or another I had, in fact, thought of taking in a roomer, perhaps a college student, just to have someone to talk to. It would be amusing perhaps. It was possible that he was a dangerous madman—I didn't believe for a moment that he was a film producer or ever had been—but even that would be entertaining; at the worst there might be a nasty little episode or two before I had them come and take him away. 'I'm afraid it won't be cheap,' I told him with a perfectly straight face. 'Fifty dollars a week.'

'I got money,' he said, still crossly.

I decided to put him in a spare room on the second floor, which as it happened was one of several that had been my bedroom when I was a child. Even with the three of us living in it the house had been too big, and I often moved from room to room as the whim struck me. There were many times, I am sure, when Astrée and Dirk didn't even know which room was mine. The one I put him in faced toward the rear rather than toward the street. It gave out onto a rather charming vista of old trees in an emerald lawn, stretching away to a glimpse of an artificial lake. I possibly had the idea in the back of my mind that if I put him in a front room he might exhibit himself indecently at the window, or commit some other tactlessness. I tried to get along with my neighbors and with the St. Albans Place Owners Association as well as I could. Another advantage of the room was that it was at the opposite end of the house from my own. At the top of the stairs there was a broad corridor, with my own master bedroom on the left. This corridor continued through the house and then branched to the left, leaving place for a small room beyond it at the rear. There were several rooms between his and mine, and we wouldn't disturb each other. It was true that he had to pass directly by my door to go down the corridor, but I had the impression he would do this discreetly. In fact I never heard him go past the bedroom door in all the time he lived in the house.

The room was furnished, after a fashion. There was the narrow single bed I had slept in as a child, a dresser, a threadbare armchair, and an old European armoire with carvings on the doors. In one corner was an object of furniture typical of the Twenties: a tall narrow wickerwork table, no larger than a dinnerplate, with legs like tiny fawns' hooves resting on the polished rugless floor. 'Maybe it's cold up here in the winter,' said Nesselrode dubiously.

'I'll put in an electric heater.'

'Sometimes I write things.'

'I'm sure there's a desk.' There was an eighteenth-century French escritoire that had belonged to my grandfather around somewhere. Perhaps in the attic. I would look around for it.

'I haven't got the fifty dollars right now,' he told me. 'I am expecting a remittance.'

Oh, fine, I thought. It was not ten minutes since he had crossly told me, 'I got money.' But I was still secretly enjoying the whole business. It was the first thing that had broken the monotony of my existence for several years.

★ ★ ★

The name Nesselrode seemed to me spurious and at the same time faintly comic, probably because I associated it with a certain flavor of ice cream rather than with human beings. But when I looked it up in the *Britannica* in my grandfather's library I found that it was in fact an authentic name, whether or not my roomer had any legitimate right to it. A Count Nesselrode had been Russian ambassador to Lisbon in the eighteenth century, and his son, Karl Robert, was an eminent international statesman who took an important part in the Congress of Vienna in 1815. Karl Robert died in 1862. After that there were no more Nesselrodes, at least not eminent enough to appear in the *Britannica* or in the biographical dictionary which I also consulted. The family, as far as I could make out, were Westphalians and not Russians, although there was also a minor Austrian branch. My roomer's accent, insofar as it was not due to a cleft lip, seemed to me more Austrian than anything else. Perhaps he was an authentic Nesselrode. At least it was likely that he was a genuine Austrian. As for Julius, it seemed a plausible name for such a person and I accepted it.

To verify his claim that he had been a director and screen producer the *Britannica* was no help, and it was necessary to pay a visit to the USC library. I soon found what I was looking for in a book on films of the pre-1914 era. Julius Nesselrode was listed as one of several European émigrés who were active in the picture business in the pioneer days. Apparently he had been only a producer, because he wasn't mentioned in the discussion of early directors and no films were attributed to him. In another book the index led me to a single brief reference. 'Hans Reiter, who was said to be the inventor of both the camera dolly and the closeup, was one of several directors brought to the U.S. in this period by Julius Nesselrode.' That was all I could find. I was left with my riddle only half solved. There was no question that there had been a real Julius Nesselrode who had been a producer in the silent film days, but the dates didn't work out very well. The man who had taken a room in my house could not have been old enough to be the same person who was making pictures as early as 1910. No birthdate was given in the sources I found, but even assuming that he was as young as twenty at that time, which seemed unlikely, he would have had to be ninety in 1980. My roomer was an old man all right, but he seemed too spry and energetic for an age so phenomenal, even though his energy manifested itself mainly in querulousness. I decided that he was probably an impostor and had found out about Nesselrode in the same way I had, by running across his name in some book on silent films. Whether he had assumed the name for some fraudulent purpose or had merely deluded himself into believing he was the original

Nesselrode was impossible to say. Probably the latter. He had nothing to gain by passing himself off as somebody he wasn't, except perhaps a free room.

If he was a conscious impostor, however, he was a crafty and assiduous one. He never forgot his role and he never made a mistake, as you might expect from someone who was getting on in years and suffered occasionally from a faulty memory. We crossed paths occasionally in the morning—he had 'kitchen privileges,' as they are called, although he never seemed to avail himself of them except to make himself a pot of tea—and he would occasionally mumble something about his alleged career as a producer. 'I knew them all,' he told me once in the kitchen, not seeming to address me particularly and looking off in the other direction. Then, at intervals of ten seconds or so, he muttered the names of various well-known celebrities of the silent film era, sniffing after each name, as though to defy me to say that he hadn't known them.

'And X? And Y? And Z?' I went on, baiting him with other well-known names.

'I know them all,' he said, looking away from me into the cupboard for something or other, perhaps the tea.

It was only after a moment that I noticed he had slipped into the present tense. It was the first evidence that he was genuinely deluded.

40

Then he turned around and stared at me directly—a thing he almost never did—even though he kept his head turned a little so that his eyes fixed on me only from the diagonal.

'I could get you into pictures,' he said.

The line was so banal that I almost laughed outright. The thought passed through my mind that he was perhaps a homosexual. There had been other times when he had looked at me in this appraising way, as though he were examining my personal qualities and licking his lips a little over them.

'You're a good-looking boy.'

I played along with him. It was an amusing game.

'I don't particularly want to be in pictures.'

'You're the type,' he insisted. 'I got plenty of people into pictures. It's not hard. You just do what the director tells you. They tell you everything to do.'

I began to see now into his mind, enmeshed as it was in a confused skein of time that was not that of the real world. An interesting and malicious idea occurred to me. Cunningly I phrased my next remark.

'I don't think my voice is right. It's too high.'

He rose to the bait. 'You don't talk. There's no sound in pictures. You just do what the director tells.'

I was right. He was a madman and he lived entirely in the past. It was for this, probably,

41

that he had fixed on the idea of renting a room in the old house in St. Albans Place.

★   ★   ★

Aside from tea—which he made out of my tea bags without asking for them—I couldn't see that Nesselrode ate very much. It was not clear to me just how he nourished himself. Perhaps he lived on old dreams, or the blood he sucked out of the ghosts that populated his memory. This, however, would have implied that he was the real Julius Nesselrode, and I was not convinced of that yet. According to our agreement he wasn't supposed to do any cooking in his room. Occasionally I would catch a glimpse of him floating up the stairs with a cabbage, or a bunch of carrots, which he carried loose in his hand and not in a paper bag, so that perhaps he plucked them out of somebody's vegetable garden. He carried the teapot upstairs too—it was the only one I had and from then on I had to make my own tea in a saucepan—and once, as he went past the living room toward the stairway, I caught a glimpse of something in his hand that looked like a can of V-8 juice. Evidently he had a can-opener in there.

The first indication I had that his eating habits might be anything like normal, or that he might be conducting any more elaborate culinary operations in his room, was when I

42

discovered that the toaster was missing from the kitchen. This was no ordinary toaster. It had belonged, probably, to my grandfather; at least it had been in the house from the time of my earliest recollections. No question of automatic devices or of the toast popping up. This toaster, of a nickel-plated finish that was tarnished like a valuable antique, was wedged-shaped in contour and narrow at the top, with four small black legs to hold it up. On either side was a door that opened downward, with holes for ventilation. You opened the doors, put in one or two slices of bread, and turned on the switch in the cord that led to the wall. A glow could be seen from inside, through the curlicue holes in the doors. The only way to tell when the toast was done on one side was by guess, or by examination. This was why Astrée and Dirk had burned the toast so often. They decided to kiss, or have an argument over the breakfast table, and forgot to open the doors. When these doors were opened—there was a small black knob on each one so that you didn't burn your hands—the half-toasted bread slid out and in doing so turned itself over, so that when the door was closed again the untoasted side was presented to the glowing wires inside. This, of course, was only if the toasted side was done to your satisfaction. If it was overdone, you scraped it with a knife—I can still remember this scratchy rhythmic sound, as irritating as a finger on a

43

blackboard. If it was underdone, you simply repeated the process of opening and shutting the door, and the slice turned itself over a second time so that the partly toasted side could be finished to the proper golden brown. On the top of this device, in ornate embossed letters, was the inscription 'Omega Homemaker.' How old this appliance was I don't know, but I can only testify that mine was still working in 1980, and made excellent toast if you paid attention and didn't let it burn.

I searched over the kitchen for the toaster and couldn't find it. Usually I simply left it on the kitchen counter, or on the table in the breakfast room adjoining. Nesselrode had perhaps put it away in the wrong place; I went through the cupboards, moved around the spices and the carton of salt on the shelf over the stove, and even made a desultory examination of the broom closet. Perhaps, I thought, Nesselrode had taken it too upstairs, where he was gradually assembling an impromptu kitchen in violation of our agreement.

There were no keys to any of the bedroom doors; they had all disappeared years ago and none of the bedrooms could be locked. It was the middle of the morning and Nesselrode was out of the house, as it happened. He frequently disappeared on mysterious expeditions of his own and sometimes stayed away overnight. I went upstairs and searched in a cursory fashion

44

through his room. There was not very much furniture in it, and the toaster was a large object which would be hard to hide. I satisfied myself in five minutes that it wasn't there. The empty V-8 cans were in the wastebasket, along with some carrot tops and a few old cabbage leaves, which gave off an abominable smell. Except for that, the room was much as it had been when I had occupied it as a child.

I did discover one odd thing, however. In going through the dresser, which had four drawers, I found that two of them were empty. A third contained what little clothing Nesselrode owned that he did not actually carry around on his body—four socks, all unmatched, a spare hernia supporter, a threadbare paisley cummerbund, and three pairs of underwear complete with urine stains. The fourth drawer was full almost to the top with scraps of paper. Several of them were slips with the address of the house in St. Albans Place scrawled on them. Evidently he did have difficulty with his memory and was afraid, perhaps, that he might forget where he lived. The rest of the drawer was filled with pictures of women crudely cut out of magazines and Sears Roebuck catalogs. By preference he selected figures in their underwear. There were several hundred of these paper dolls in the drawer. I didn't examine them all, but the dozen or so I looked at were all mutilated in one way or another. Some had daggers, drawn with a fountain pen and dripping blue blood, protruding from their breasts. Others had their heads cut off, with more inky blood running down their necks. Most of them had been slashed with a razor blade across the breasts, the middle of the body, or lower down; sometimes the face. Without exception the genitals had all been attacked in a special way, evidently as the last step in the process—by being jabbed with a fountain pen, leaving a ragged hole with traces of ink around it. I smiled, shutting the drawer. I could hardly object, considering my own rather odd sexual proclivities.

★   ★   ★

The most logical explanation, I thought, was that he had pawned the toaster. He still hadn't paid me even the first month's rent, even though he had lived in the house now for several months. Surely they couldn't have given him much for the toaster, unless it was old enough to have become a valuable object of nostalgia for some collector. Still it didn't cost much to buy a can of V-8 juice now and then, and you could live on a modest budget if you didn't pay your rent. Perhaps he was a shoplifter; he had the shifty and beady alertness of a person who would be adept at stealing small objects, and there were certainly enough pockets in his odd overcoat to hold many cans of V-8 juice. I thought of asking him downstairs to dinner now and then, or even taking him out to the Italian restaurant on Melrose. But I decided against it. Neither did I ever take up with him the matter of the missing toaster.

I thought no more about it until the next object turned up missing. This was more serious, since the object was more valuable and I had a certain personal attachment to it. It was the camel saddle that had stood at the side of the fireplace in the living room for as long as I could remember. It was an odd object, looking not very much like the saddles used for horses, and consisting of a framework of oiled wood with a leather seat suspended in it. The leather was dark and stained. Evidently it was a souvenir my grandfather had brought back from his travels; on the leather at one side was embossed 'Cairo 1928' in a curly script, with an enormous decorative C as big as a man's hand. It had a good smell: old seasoned wood, oiled leather, and some other spicy and exotic odor like an Algerian souk. You could use it for many things. I sat in it when I was a child, Astrée sometimes lay on the floor and used it for a pillow when she was reading, and in the winter we stacked the kindling in it for the fireplace.

The camel saddle was gone. There was no question of its being in Nesselrode's room; it was not the kind of thing that you would

47

absentmindedly take away and forget to bring back, like a toaster. Nesselrode had done something with it. I was sure that nobody had broken into the house, and besides what thief would take a camel saddle and leave the sterling silver, the Sisleys by the fireplace, and my several thousand dollars' worth of stereo equipment?

'Have you seen my camel saddle?' I demanded of Nesselrode the next time I saw him.

'A what?'

'Camel saddle.'

'I didn't know you went riding. A fine sport.'

Perhaps he hadn't caught the word camel, or perhaps it was his idea of a joke.

I seized him by the lapel and prevented him from going upstairs. I even shook him a little. I was still amused with him, but I was a little annoyed too.

'Mr. Nesselrode. There was a camel saddle sitting there by the fireplace, the last time I looked. It's been there for fifty years. It had a wooden framework and a leather seat and it said Cairo on it. Now did you take it or not?'

He disengaged his lapel from my fingers, gently and with dignity. 'Young man, you should treat me with more respect. I am not nobody. I am Nesselrode after all. I could get you into pictures.'

'Yes, I know. I'm the type. What did you do

48

with the camel saddle?'

'It is probably on a camel somewhere. What else is there to do with a camel saddle?'

'If you give me the ticket I'll go and redeem it. I don't care about the money.'

'So Nesselrode is a thief now.'

'Listen, Mr. Nesselrode. Would you like to come downstairs and have dinner with me tonight?'

'No. I don't eat. Nothing.'

★   ★   ★

And then finally there was the table. This was a heavy and cumbersome piece of furniture that my grandfather had shipped out from Cambridge when he retired from Harvard. It was round and at least eight feet in diameter, built of solid oak. It was supported by a massive column in the middle, which split up into four legs with ball-and-claw feet. It had never been moved from its position in the dining room in all the years I had lived in the house; I doubted that four men could have lifted it. Yet it was gone. Nesselrode, I conjectured in a way not very convincing even to myself, had hired movers and had them carry the thing away to an antique dealer, or to some fantastic pawnshop that accepted oaken tables with ball-and-claw feet. I hadn't been out of the house for several days except to duck out briefly for groceries or to go to the library. I was left with two alternatives: that Nesselrode was a professional thief and had muscular accomplices, or that he was a sorcerer who could make things disappear.

I never saw the table again in this world. But I did catch a glimpse once of the saddle or one very much like it. It was a couple of weeks later and I had gone out to a program in the classic film series at UCLA. The feature was some flamboyant thing about a border war in the Khyber Pass: the British in pith helmets firing their Martini rifles from horseback, and the Afghan tribesmen, led by a bearded ruffian of a white man who wanted to be king, responding with their antiquated flintlocks. Puffs of smoke appeared silently at the muzzles of the guns. Then the screen went black and some white letters bobbed into view, as though floating in the darkened room.

'YOU'LL NEVER TAKE ME ALIVE.'

There was a cut to the bugler. He strained at his instrument in absolute silence, his cheeks working in and out. The screen went black again.

CHARGE!

Another cut to the bearded ruffian of a white man, on top of a camel that appeared to be stuffed, since it remained motionless while the grips rolled the canvas scenery behind it. He threw away his flintlock and drew a long curved saber. Just at that moment a British bullet struck him.

THE END OF A RENEGADE.

commented the white letters with detachment. Dropping the saber and clutching his breast, he slid slowly away from the camera. The round O of his mouth appeared in the middle of his beard. A spurt of blood sprang out of the tunic under his fingers, and then he fell off the camel completely. The last thing to go over was his leg in a ragged puttee. As it disappeared from view it clearly revealed a large embossed C on the leather underneath. The rest of the inscription was too small to read at a distance, at least for someone who didn't know what it said.

I went on sitting through the rest of the picture. It was almost the end anyhow. I was in a curious emotional state. I was not excited exactly; I was quite calm. With a dispassionate clarity I examined the two alternatives. It was possible that the saddle had been used in the film and then afterward bought by my grandfather on his trip around the world. But this explanation didn't really convince me. The film had obviously been shot in a studio and not in Egypt, and it was unlikely that the saddle had

51

been brought to Hollywood for the film and then somehow found its way back into a tourist bazaar in Cairo. Besides the dates didn't work out. I checked the program. The film had been made in 1915. The inscription on my saddle had read 'Cairo 1928.'

The second explanation was that it wasn't the same saddle. As the image on the screen gradually faded from my memory I became less certain on this point. After all in the picture I had made out only the large C on the saddle; perhaps the date that was too small to read had been 1915 or even earlier. It was quite possible that there were two such camel saddles in the world; by all odds, in fact, there were probably hundreds. But neither of these theories, it occurred to me, explained what Nesselrode had done with the saddle only a month before. I was sure now that the saddle I had seen in the film was my own.

★　　★　　★

Yet I never mentioned the saddle to him again, just as I had made no mention of the disappearance of the toaster. Instead I decided to build my strategy around the oaken table, which was unwieldy and unique enough so that its disappearance couldn't be put down to chance or turned off as a joke. I decided to confront him directly on this point—not so much to get the table back, since this was probably impossible, but mostly to amuse myself, and also to confirm my growing suspicion about what had happened to the table.

Through some sort of delicacy, although I had ransacked Nesselrode's room when he was away, I never went there when he was occupying it—perhaps I was afraid I would find him jabbing a pen into paper dolls. Instead I managed to cut him off one morning just as he was leaving, crossing the hallway in his shabby overcoat and assuming, as soon as he caught sight of me, his pasty and unconvincing smile.

'Mr. Nesselrode.'

'Well, what is it? I can't talk all day. I have business.'

'I want my table back.'

He muttered in an undertone, 'Table?' Rather than responding to my demand, he seemed to be asking himself if he had ever heard of a table. He didn't seem to think that he had. Without meeting my eyes, he looked furtively past me at the front door, as though hoping that I would step aside and let him go out of it.

'It sat right there.' I pointed through the arched opening into the dining room. 'It is very large. You couldn't miss it. It isn't there any more.'

'I don't remember it,' he said vaguely.

'Please don't pretend ignorance. We are both too intelligent to play games.'

53

This bald flattery was exactly the right tactic. After another regretful glance at the front door, he twitched his nose and turned directly to me. He pursed his lips. He examined me with his lucid protruding eyes and then looked away again.

'Well then, let us talk about it. Perhaps my business is not so important.'

'There's no need to talk about it. I want it back.'

'That is not so easy.'

I examined him. His manner was still furtive rather than uneasy. He gave the impression that there was something he could tell me if he wished, but he hadn't yet decided whether to do so or not. After a moment I said firmly, 'I know where it is, and so do you.'

There was a silence. Then he said, with another darting and diagonal glance at me, 'I've already said that I could get you into pictures.'

'Let's go then,' I said shortly.

We left the house together. I took nothing; I didn't even lock the front door.

CHAPTER FOUR

He waited patiently while I unlocked the rusty chain on the pedestrian gate opening out onto Olympic. It must have been this gate that he himself went in and out by—unless he made himself invisible in some way and came in past the guard's kiosk on Wilshire, which seemed unlikely—but he gave no sign that he had ever seen the gate before, let alone that he possessed a key to it. Once out on the sidewalk he set off briskly, in a kind of uneven lope, and I had to exert myself to keep up with him. It was somewhat extraordinary. I wouldn't have expected a man of his age to be so energetic. His two legs one after the other sprang out from the skirts of the unbuttoned coat, like the limbs of a mechanical doll, propelling him along the sidewalk at a pace of perhaps four miles an hour. He said nothing. He hardly seemed to notice that I was walking beside him. Another odd thing was that in some way he seemed to adjust his pace to the traffic lights that he could see coming up toward him as he passed the cross streets, so that we never had to stop for a red light and always crossed on the green, while at the same time I had no impression that he was slowing down his pace at any time for this purpose. On the contrary he seemed to accelerate his speed from block to block until my legs began to ache. This, evidently, was what he did with himself in those mysterious periods when he was gone from the house. I had sensed from the beginning that there was something queer about him that I had not yet identified, in addition to all his other queernesses, and now I knew what it was. He was a pedestrian in Los Angeles, a city where such animals were as rare as auks or Siberian cranes.

At Fairfax he turned left without warning, leaving me striding along in a straight line and then veering around abruptly, like a character in an old comedy, to catch up with him. 'I am surprised that a young man like you is not more athletic,' he mumbled as though to himself. 'You should work out with dumb-bars.'

'Do you work out with dumb-bars?'

He didn't answer. Perhaps he hadn't heard, or hadn't really been talking to me. Continuing on down Fairfax, he turned right on Pico. Then, after only a few blocks, he turned left once more on La Cienega. This far south it was not the fashionable part of La Cienega, the restaurant row above Wilshire, but a rather tawdry neighborhood that had been a suburban shopping district back in the Twenties and had now fallen into decadence, like so many things in this part of the city—a little enclave of squalor with Beverly Hills on one side of it and Culver City on the other. We passed a vacuum cleaner shop, a shabby motel, an auto-body shop run by Chicanos who played transistor radios full blast as they worked, a vacant lot, and a camp used-clothing store called The Second Time Around. A little farther on, just beyond Pickford, we came to the Alhambra Theater.

56

This place was more or less familiar to me. I had even gone to movies there, in a brief period several years before when it had shown classics. After that it had declined to the level of old Godzilla films and Mexican movies with titles like *La Otra Mujer* and *Pasiones de Sangre*. Finally it had gone out of business completely and was now boarded up and covered with dust. It was an old stucco building in fake Spanish style, with the eaves at the side covered with red tiles—even though the rear roof beyond was only tar paper—and a curved stucco archway leading to the ticket window. A couple of yellowed movie posters still remained in the frames with their broken glass, and the walls were covered with the usual graffiti found on all abandoned buildings.

There didn't seem to be any way to get in at the front. The doors beyond the ticket office had sheets of plywood nailed over them. While I was looking at this I found that Nesselrode had disappeared. I followed around to the side of the building on the alley and found that in some way he had opened the employees' door and disappeared in through it; perhaps he had a key. I followed in after him. The inside of the building was as dusty as the outside; evidently no one had used it for some time. But to my surprise I saw there was an illuminated light bulb hanging from the ceiling overhead on a long and rather frayed wire. It was a tiny old-fashioned bulb with a yellow filament glowing in it, and it cast the light that a candle might into the gloomy and shadowy spaces of the theater. At first, coming in from the dazzle of the sun outside, I could see almost nothing. There was a musty, mousy closed-space odor in the inside of the place. But as my eyes adjusted to the gloom I saw that the interior of the theater was almost intact, if rather dirty. The seats were still in place, gray with dust, and there were even a few candy-wrappers and cigarette packages strewn around on the floor from the last performance, which had probably been several years before. In keeping with the spurious Spanish decor there were heavy beams overhead with brown paint slapped on them, and faded red-velvet hangings along the walls. At the front, on the stage, the curtain was open and the screen was visible, grayish in the dim light. To the rear, where the block-shaped projection booth intruded into the otherwise perfectly rectangular interior, there were two small windows like eyes, so dusty I could see nothing through them, although I had the impression that a light of some kind might be on in the projection booth too.

Nesselrode snuffled. He reached into the pockets of his coat as though searching for something and then took his hands out again. He gave no sign that he was aware I was with him. He looked not at me but at the screen.

'Why have we come here?'

'This is a good theater. It shows the best pictures. I could name you a dozen.'

The present tense again. It gave me a slightly creepy sensation, as though I too were being drawn into this hallucination of his distorted and shaky old man's memory.

'It did once. Now there's nothing here.'

'You have to go through to get there. It's necessary.'

He said nothing more in explanation of this rather cryptic remark. From the outside the sounds of the city were still faintly audible: the swish of passing traffic, a tinny radio running somewhere, a child yelling, a distant police siren. Yet everything was muffled and deadened; it was as though only the inside of the theater was real and the outside sounds had been created synthetically by some electrical device. They were like the unconvincing sounds of animals, screeching apes and squawking macaws, that are played on a loudspeaker while you are going through a badly organized Jungle Trip in an amusement park. Perhaps, I thought, they *were* artificial and came from somewhere behind the screen rather than through the walls from outside.

Nesselrode still did nothing; he seemed not so much indecisive as deliberate and patient, like a man who was shortly to do something difficult that he was still planning out—a brilliant play at billiards, or a feat of acrobatics. Then he took my hand.

This was so unexpected that I scarcely had time to resist. It was a dry fleshless hand, feeling in my own like little more than some dry bones enclosed in leathery skin. It gripped me not tightly but firmly, in the way that a lover holds the hand of another. My original suspicions about him, when he had first told me, 'I can get you into pictures,' were revived. But if he was a fairy he was a very old fairy, and his predilections no longer took any physical form. He had taken my hand only to lead me to the front of the theater and up the worn and rickety steps to the stage. Why he didn't simply tell me to follow him I didn't, at that time, understand.

There was a forestage in front of the screen about five or six feet wide, curving gently as it extended out into the darkened theater. In front of us was the screen, much larger and higher than it had seemed from the back of the theater. I looked at it with some curiosity. It still seemed more gray than white, perhaps because of the dim illumination. I had imagined that such screens were made of canvas or some other heavy material coated with a white iridescent chemical substance, probably because I was thinking of the collapsible amateur screens used for home movies. But the large rectangle with rounded corners standing vertically before us was not white; it gave the impression that it was

60

a light gray in color, slightly translucent, and made of something that gave it a faint glassy sheen; it resembled unexposed but developed photographic film. Through it I thought I could catch a glimpse of shapes on the stage behind—a stepladder, perhaps, and a couple of crates piled carelessly one on top of the other.

Perhaps it was not really the projection screen at all but only some kind of plastic drop or dust screen that was used to separate the stage from the rest of the theater. Nesselrode, still holding my hand and glancing at me sideways with his bulging and faintly glittering eyes, advanced a step or two forward. I followed him. Then we went on and passed through the Screen.

The sensation was difficult to describe. It was as though we had slipped through a film that clung lightly to our shoulders and legs and then sprang free with a slight elasticity, tremoring like disturbed water after we had passed through it and then gradually resuming its smooth and unfeatured surface. The substance gave the impression that it was faintly cool, also that it had an odor like old celluloid or collodion, an aroma that clung to us for some time after we had passed through it. I turned to look back at this odd integument which seemed so solid and yet which we had passed through so easily, but Nesselrode led me on by the hand. We stopped in the middle of the stage. The outlines I had glimpsed through the Screen were clearly visible now: a stepladder as I had thought, some piled-up crates, a tool box, a stack of lumber turned gray with age and covered with dust like everything else in the theater.

All these objects were in various shades of gray or black. The color seemed to have disappeared from everything. Perhaps this effect was connected in some way with the gray light that filtered through the Screen from the dimly lighted theater behind us. Everything had a flat, slightly unreal look. It was preternaturally quiet. I had the sensation too as though my body were lighter than usual, invulnerable, capable of unusual motions or previously impossible acrobatic feats. I held up my hand and looked at it. It was as pale and papery as Nesselrode's face.

I became aware that Nesselrode was no longer holding my hand, although I hadn't noticed the moment when he released it. He was exactly as before; the odd light on the stage only enhanced his grimy grayness and the impression of fragility, of unreality, that he gave even under ordinary conditions in normal light. He turned and gave me a long serious glance, frowning slightly. Then he sniffed, twitched his nose, and went off without a word to the rear of the stage and down some steps that were almost invisible in the semidarkness. I followed him.

These steps—which I descended solely out of faith, since I could see almost nothing—went down to some kind of storeroom or corridor at the rear of the theater. Beyond this I could see a rectangular outline of light around a door, like a line of white fire drawn with a pen. He went up to this door, fumbled with another key—this time I could hear the scratchy grate of a lock turning—and opened it. A glare of overpowering blank-white sunlight poured into my face.

It was a moment before my eyes adjusted to this. The air was lucid and glassy and seemed to shimmer slightly. The bright sunlight that filled it seemed to come from every direction, and no sun could be located. Everything was strongly outlined, with sharp edges and almost painfully bright surfaces. We were standing in a vacant lot behind the theater. But there hadn't been a vacant lot before, I remembered; there was an alley and then the backs of the houses on the next street. Nesselrode stood patiently while I oriented myself and took measure of my surroundings. I was still in the city where I had been born, the only city I had ever known. But it was transformed.

The boulevard, which I could see around the corner of the theater, had shrunk to a narrow two-lane street. The air over it was cluttered with telephone and electrical wires on wooden poles. The secondhand clothing store was still there, with a sign saying, 'Mona's Knits and Fine Imports.' I recognized other landmarks, but everything seemed smaller and the buildings were raw and new. The Alhambra Theatre looked as though it had been put up yesterday. The fresh stucco glared in the sunlight, and the fake tiles along the eaves gleamed between the strips of white mortar. We walked around to the front. The ticket office was closed, of course, at this time of day, but the posters in their glass frames announced a picture with Vanessa Nesser and Roland Lightfoot.

'An excellent theater,' muttered Nesselrode, looking not at the theater but off down the street. 'All the best pictures are shown here.'

The very air was transformed. The yellowish haze characteristic of the city I had known was gone; in its place was a glassy and absolutely transparent atmosphere as clear as the finest gin. I could see all the way to the Santa Monica Hills and even the distant Sierra Madres above Pasadena, with Mount Wilson bulging up in the middle of them. We started down the sidewalk, continuing in the direction we had come a half an hour or so before, toward Culver City. For a few blocks there were food markets with bright enameled signs, furniture stores, and shops and restaurants in odd architectures, one of them the shape of a Dutch windmill. Once this shopping district was behind us the city itself seemed only half built. The streets were paved and curbs laid, and there were even concrete streetlamps installed, but sometimes for several blocks there were no houses, only vacant lots with weeds sprouting waist-high. On one lot there was a huge sign the size of a billboard that blared, 'Land Opportunity! Buy Now for Investment! Last Half Acres on West Side $50.' A little farther along somebody had built a house. It was in the same fake-Spanish architecture as the Alhambra Theater, with tiles along the eaves and a tiny stucco archway at the side. A small palm about two feet high had been planted in the front yard. It was surrounded on all sides by vacant lots.

*　　*　　*

I had some fair idea where we were, although everything was transformed and slightly disorienting—simpler, more clearly outlined, lacking in detail, crude and raw. There were no colors; everything was in black and white. From the hills to the south I knew we were not far from Culver City. We crossed a few more streets and then turned right on what I recognized as Washington Boulevard. It was a broad and pretentious affair, even though it seemed only half finished. There were two lanes of asphalt, and in the middle were some streetcar tracks with a trolley wire suspended over them on a line of black poles. Beyond the pavement on the other side was a stretch of dirt, then a wooden fence, then the open fields. A black Ford flivver came along toward us on the other side of the street, shimmering in the glare. I turned to look at it. It went by with a steady clatter from its innards and disappeared in the distance, the spare tire at the back gradually shrinking until the whole thing dwindled into a bobbing dot on the asphalt, warped and distorted by the heat.

'You haven't seen a car before?' asked Nesselrode with heavy sarcasm. 'Come on. We haven't got all day. I got business.'

I turned to follow him and we went on. Ahead to the left, in the near distance, was a chain-link fence, and inside it was a lot containing what appeared to be a number of hastily erected galvanized-iron buildings, with an occasional smaller stucco one with a tiled roof.

It was only about another ten minutes' walk. We crossed the boulevard on the diagonal, since there was almost no traffic. I had fallen a little behind, and Nesselrode turned around impatiently with a motion of his hand. We entered through the open gate just as an elegant Packard limousine swept out, piloted by a chauffeur in uniform, with a young woman in a silk print dress and a picture hat in the rear. There was a guard at the gate, but he was half asleep with his chair propped against the wall and paid no attention to us. I followed Nesselrode up the concrete main street of the lot. The sun bothered me. It wasn't the heat; in fact now that I analyzed my sensations I realized that there was no physical sensation of heat, only this white and transparent glare that seemed to penetrate everything, even my own body, leaving no room for any private shadow or secret inside. I crossed over to the side of the street and followed along in the shade of a building. Nesselrode turned around to see what I was doing, made a curious grimace of contempt, a twitch of the nose as if to say, 'What's the matter with you young people any more, can't stand a little sun,' and went on.

In any case we were soon out of the sun. He continued on down the street in his jerky way, glancing back now and then to see if I was following, and presently turned into one of the large barnlike galvanized-iron buildings. I followed him. Inside there was a vast emptiness, like a train station or a deserted warehouse. In various corners of this space, odd and incomplete little simulacra of the outside world had been flimsily constructed with canvas, boards, and papier-mâché—a railroad coach with the side missing and the seats gaping like teeth, a part of a theater including the balcony and a corner of the stage, and a big-city tenement flat with its rooms separated by cardboard partitions. There was nobody immediately in sight, but at the far end of the building there were lights and activity. I could hear voices in a low subdued tone. Standing out sharply at the rather dimly lit end of the building were a half-dozen or so rectangles that glowed with a white light almost as intense as the sun outside. These, as we came closer, proved to be reflector screens on wheels, turned at various angles to catch the white glare of the klieg lights overhead. In the middle of the lighted area a bearded man in a stovepipe hat was standing on a platform decorated with bunting. Beside him sat another man in a chair, looking at his own notes for a speech. Arranged in chairs before them were a dozen or so men in frock coats and a pair of women in white skirts down to their ankles. Outside the circle of light, behind the camera and the reflector screens, were a number of other figures that I could make out only dimly. Supervising everything was an energetic man with a bull neck, wearing a white shirt, riding breeches, and puttees, and carrying a rattan crop which he slapped impatiently now and then against his leg. His hat might have been suitable for an African safari; it was a canvas affair with a broad brim turned down all around and a zebra-striped band.

'Reiter, a brilliant man, a genius,' said Nesselrode.

Reiter seemed to know Nesselrode well and

only grunted to show recognition. He paid no attention to me.

'Are you ready, Sid?' he yelled to the cameraman. He paced back and forth and slapped the rattan crop against his puttee.

'I'm reloading.'

'Well, hurry up. We're paying scale to all these people standing around scratching their asses.'

'A genius,' Nesselrode repeated. 'He invented putting the camera on wheels. Now everybody does it. Reiter also invented the closeup.'

I saw that in fact the camera was mounted on a rigid tripod like a frame for a teepee, fitted at the bottom with three large rubber-tired caster wheels.

'Can the chatter. Quiet on the set, everybody,' yelled Reiter, still pacing restlessly back and forth like a tiger in a cage. He went back and looked into the viewfinder of the camera. 'Fine. Fine. Don't touch the lights.' He sprang back to the set and began prowling around the edges of it, swinging his rattan crop as he went. He never spoke except at the top of his voice. 'Ready, everybody?' he yelled. 'Camera! Action!'

The cameraman, with his cap turned around backward, applied his own eye to the viewfinder. The camera began running with a light clucking sound. The man in the stovepipe hat raised his right arm and stretched it to the miniature crowd.

'But, in a larger sense,' he said.

Reiter ran around to the other side of the set. 'Crowd!' he barked.

The cameraman pushed his machine around to point at the crowd, who were listening intently.

'Lincoln!' yelled Reiter.

The camera swung back to the bearded man.

'We cannot dedicate,' he rumbled in a ceremonious baritone. He lowered his right arm and stretched out the left.

'We cannot consecrate.' He lowered the left arm and raised the right again.

'We cannot hallow.' With a grave look, he lowered both arms and turned the hands toward the crowd with palms outward, as if to show he had nothing in them.

'This ground.' He raised both hands and placed them on his breast.

I hardly paid attention to the rest of the speech. The single camera swung constantly from the crowd to the speaker. I was more interested in the agility with which Reiter, a heavy and muscular bull-necked man, ran constantly back and forth around the edges of the set as he shouted and barked at the actors, careful to stay out of the circle of light at the center which was sacrosanct to the camera. His eyeglasses, with lenses so thick that through them his eyes appeared like two milky

70

underwater creatures, now and then caught a gleam of light from the reflector screens. With one hand he slapped the rattan riding crop against his leg, and with the other he scratched nervously at his throat through the neck of the open shirt.

'Lincoln!' he yelled.

The speaker was just concluding. He was making his most histrionic gesture of all, a broad spreading of the arms that seemed to encompass not only the listening crowd but all truth, wisdom, and idealism.

'. . . Shall. Not. Perish. From the earth,' he enunciated with emphasis on each of the phrases which he separated carefully one from the other.

'Crowd!'

On this signal the crowd raised their own arms and began waving them wildly.

'Hurrah.'

'Hurrah.'

'Hurrah.'

Reiter turned from them and sprang away to the other side of the set. 'Lincoln!' he yelled.

The camera swung back to the speaker. But he was silent now, standing with hands clasped and head slightly lowered as though in meditation. He turned to one side. The man sitting in the chair stood up and they shook hands.

'Cut. Good. Print that,' yelled Reiter.

He took his hat off, produced a handkerchief

71

from his pocket, and wiped his head with it. He was almost bald and his head was closely shaved. His skull, rather than round, was formed entirely of intersecting planes and seemed to be polished; it reflected light like the finest marble. He put his hat back on and then took off his eyeglasses and polished them too, but not with the same handkerchief; he had another one for this purpose.

'A two-reeler,' said Nesselrode. 'Would you believe, only twenty minutes of picture and it takes a week to shoot.'

★   ★   ★

The bearded man mopped his brow. The makeup girl came up and repaired the damage to his cosmetics, filling in his wrinkles with a little brush. The grips began dragging everything— klieg lights, generators, reflector screens, and Reiter's canvas chair in which he never sat— over to the next set. This consisted of two walls of some room or other in the White House. There were lace curtains on the windows of the flimsy walls, which were propped up on the outside with two-by-fours. For furniture there was a chair, an oaken table, and an American flag hanging on the wall. The bearded man, in the same costume except that he had taken off his hat, stood talking to a plump lady whose monobust filled the front of her ample linen blouse.

Reiter examined the shot through the viewfinder. Then he sprang down and began pacing around like a cat again. 'Lights. Camera. Action,' he yelled.

The bearded man stood with his knuckles resting on the large round oaken table with its ball-and-claw legs. 'Mary,' he said, 'my mind is made up. I am going to Ford's Theatre tonight whatever the danger. I must show myself to the people.'

'Cut!' yelled Reiter. The lights went out and the clucking of the camera stopped. 'Morton, what is wrong with you? Is your face paralyzed by some disease or what? You say everything exactly the same. Make your face different each time you say something.'

'Different how?'

'Oh, my God.' Reiter slapped his breeches irritatedly with the crop. 'Do I have to tell you every little thing? Mind is made up. Resolution. Whatever the danger. Contempt for danger. Show myself to the people. Courage.'

The bearded man adjusted his string necktie, took a breath, and rested his knuckles on the table again. The plump lady began wringing her hands in anxiety even before he began speaking.

'Lights. Camera. Action.'

The bearded man pressed his lips together, raised his head, and gazed resolutely at his wife.

'Mary, my mind is made up.'

He frowned darkly and clenched his fingers, both those of the hand resting on the table and the other that hung at his side.

'I am going to Ford's Theatre tonight whatever the danger.'

He straightened his body to its full height, removed the frown from his face, and gazed into the distance with a stern and courageous look of determination.

'I must show myself to the people.'

'Cut. Good. Print that,' yelled Reiter.

'Reiter, a genius,' repeated Nesselrode.

The klieg lights went out. The grips began dragging everything over to yet another set. Reiter followed them, switching his crop, and Nesselrode and I came along after. This set had two parts to it. Below was a little corner of a theater stage, and above it and to one side was a balcony with a box at the rear. The extras, still in their Gettysburg Address costumes, took their places in the balcony. The camera ground away at several shots of these people staring at something in front of and below them, at the end of each shot clapping mechanically like dolls. Responding to Reiter's shouts, the crowd smiled and then unsmiled at certain points. In the box, the bearded man and the lady with the monobosom gazed unsmilingly down at the stage, she anxious, he resolute and calm.

'Cut!' yelled Reiter.

He turned to me, seeming to notice me for the

first time.

'A good-looking boy.'

'He's the type to be in pictures,' said Nesselrode, staring at me with one of his sideways twitches. 'Already I told him so.'

'Has he ever worked?'

'No, but a natural. A genius. He could go far.'

It struck me that Nesselrode used the word genius rather loosely. Still I couldn't help feeling flattered.

Reiter no longer slapped his breeches with his crop. His manner became natural, almost amiable. He was a human being after all.

'Why don't you try it?' he asked me in a friendly tone. 'It's easy. Just for a lark.'

'It's like I told you,' said Nesselrode. 'You don't have to know something. Just do what the director says.'

The costume people appeared. I allowed them to clap a frock coat on me and fasten a bow tie with an elastic clip around my neck. The black trousers I had on would do, but they pushed me down into a chair and put riding boots on my feet. I stepped up onto the tiny fragment of stage and an old-fashioned horse pistol was thrust into my hand. I fired away at the bearded man on the balcony, who fell from his chair with both hands on his chest. 'Sic semper tyrannis!' I cried spontaneously, catching my spur in the flag and breaking my leg.

75

They helped me up. 'Not bad for a beginner,' said Reiter. The bearded man in the balcony got up and dusted off the seat of his breeches. The lady with the monobust had been waiting all through this scene to belch. She now did so politely, holding her hand before her mouth.

'You see, Morton,' Reiter told the bearded man, 'this boy knows how to act. As he fired, he screwed his face up into a grimace of resolution.'

'It wasn't that,' I said. 'I was afraid of the noise of the gun going off.'

'It doesn't make any noise,' said Reiter.

It was true; it didn't make any noise. I hadn't noticed.

CHAPTER FIVE

Everybody dispersed. The grips wandered off together to a low platform a short distance away, sat down on it, and lighted cigarettes. A gang of carpenters appeared and began prying apart the Ford's Theatre set with crowbars and throwing the pieces onto a pile at one side. Everybody else had disappeared. There was no sign of Nesselrode and Reiter. I couldn't imagine where everyone had gone off to so suddenly; it was as though they had evaporated by magic. The only one left was the scriptgirl, a crisp young woman with bobbed hair and a tailored suit. She was

76

sitting in a canvas chair flipping the pages of the script and crossing things out.

'Excuse me. Where . . .'

Without looking up she pointed toward a door at the other side of the studio. She went back to crossing things out in her script.

I pushed open the door and went out into the blinding sunlight. Directly opposite, across a yard of dirt thinly sprinkled with gravel, was a long stucco building with a sign reading 'Commissary' over the door. I went in, more to get out of the sunlight than anything else.

The large room inside seemed only half finished. There was no ceiling and the bare beams showed overhead. Along the middle were long wooden tables with benches, something like those at a summer camp for children. At one side was a bar where you could get coffee, doughnuts, and desiccated sandwiches made of white bread curled up at the corners. The place was filled with people and everyone was smoking and chattering.

I got a cup of coffee for myself and wandered around looking for a place to sit down. Every bench seemed occupied and a number of people were standing. Most of the people in the room were in costume; I caught sight of Lincoln in his stovepipe hat, Mary Todd Lincoln with her monobust, and a figure or two from the Lincoln picture extras. Others from other pictures were dressed as Austrian diplomats in white uniforms or Indian chiefs with feather headdresses.

After a while I began to notice that the people in the room were not distributed evenly. They seemed to cluster about certain foci of interest. As I studied this phenomenon I saw that they had gathered around stars or important directors, as though drawn by a kind of magnetism, or in the way bees are attracted to the scent of flowers. This was why so many people were standing; they had gathered behind other seated people in order to be as close as possible to some person of importance. Reiter was the center of one of these groups, and so was Charles Morton, the bearded man who had played Lincoln. Another group had gathered around a handsome young man with a clipped mustache, and I recognized him as Roland Lightfoot, whose photograph I had seen in the playbill at the Alhambra Theater.

I moved around through these groups trying to find an empty place at a table where I could sit down with my cup of coffee. Then I stopped: seated at a table nearby with a crowd of people around her was the most strikingly beautiful woman I had ever seen. She had a clear porcelain-pale complexion, with dark eyes and dark eyelashes. Her face was a perfect oval, the features delicate, the mouth small but mobile and expressive. Her dark hair, bobbed short in the fashionable boyish style, accentuated the almost shocking whiteness of her face, like the shadow of a blackbird on snow. Even more than all this it was something about her poise or her manner that caught my attention. She seemed conscious of the admiration she attracted and held her chin up in an imperious and theatrical, slightly affected way, and yet she had the air of being constantly amused by everything. As I stared at her she caught my eye and our glances were locked for a moment. She smiled briefly, then she looked away.

I made my way down the room through the crowd, the coffee still in my hand. By some incredible luck there was a place free on the bench across from her. I manipulated my legs over the bench with care not to spill the coffee. She watched me as I did this, still with her air as though she were amused at something, perhaps at me.

I saw now that she was sitting with another actor, a lean man somewhat smaller than ordinary size with the look of an acrobat about him. He was dressed like a vaudeville English lord, in a cutaway coat, striped trousers, and a collapsible silk hat. His face too was white, but in his case it looked as though it had been painted with white paint. His smile was an acidic rictus that seemed permanently frozen on his face. The monocle in his eye was only an empty metal ring; there was no glass in it.

He went on examining me with his slightly insane smile, and I found this unsettling. I turned back to the girl with the dark eyes. At closer range I saw that she was perhaps not as young as she had seemed at first; her face was smooth and perfect but without gloss, like expensive bond paper. I didn't know what to say. After a moment it was she who spoke, with a quick friendly lifting of the corners of her mouth.

'How did it go?'

'All right.'

I stared at her. Everything about her was fragile, symmetrical, and perfect. Her pale complexion seemed to radiate a faint coolness. Against this the darkness of the eyes and the lock of hair over the brow, the expressiveness of the small mouth, offered a mélange of artificial and yet disturbing beauty that struck with the kind of power one sometimes feels in the presence of a work of art, a perfect alabaster fragment perhaps from the antique world. For the first time I noticed what she was wearing: a simple white frock, almost childish, and a ribbon in her hair. Her glance was clear and candid; there was something childlike about it too, in spite of the nuance of irony that lingered always just below the surface of her expression. I took a sip of coffee and set it down. I tried to collect my wits to think of something to say.

'I don't believe I know who you are.'

'Of course you do. I'm Moira Silver. And this is...'

She turned with a theatrical gesture of introduction to the man at her side. He was carrying an umbrella in his hands clasped behind his back, and without changing his expression he manipulated this so that the silk hat tipped up in the back and then came down again.

'Lord Muldoon, at your service.'

I ignored him and turned back to the girl. 'Have you been in pictures long?' I managed to articulate.

'Oh, for a long time,' she said.

'They haven't been making pictures for such a long time.'

'Yes, but you see, here everything happens so quickly that we have a different concept of time.' She smiled again, seemingly pleased that she was able to answer my question so adroitly. After a moment she said, 'But you haven't told us your name.'

'Alys.'

She and Lord Muldoon exchanged a look at this. They both remained perfectly grave, although the sardonic rictus remained fixed on his face. Perhaps it was only makeup, the painted smile of a clown.

I still felt cold and hot at the same time. I wondered if I was blushing. Since there were no mirrors, I raised my hand for some totally irrational reason and looked at it instead. It was as white as the other faces around me. She

81

watched with calm curiosity as I did all this.

'Smoke?' inquired Lord Muldoon with his skull-like grin.

He drew two long thin cigars from the inner pocket of his coat and offered me one. The other he put in his mouth. I looked around but there were no matches on the table. Lord Muldoon was feeling around in his pockets, first the left and then the right. He came out with—nothing, just his hand. Holding it out in the air before him, he scratched his thumb against two fingers. Nothing happened. He looked at the hand with a frown. He made a slight adjustment to an imaginary screw of some kind, using the fingernail of the other hand as a screwdriver. This time, when he scratched the two fingers again, a pale, steady flame leaped out and stood on the upright thumb. He offered this to light my cigar. I puffed until I got it going. He lit his own. Then, instead of blowing out the flame, he simply folded up the lighter—that is to say, he put his thumb back inside the two fingers and the flame disappeared.

Moira laughed, a little tinkle like a running brook. Then, after a pause, she looked at me again in her candid and friendly way, seeming to study me. The little smile was still there, but her manner was grave.

'Has anyone shown you around?'

'Shown me around?'

She came around the table and took my hand.

I got up.

'Ta ta,' said Lord Muldoon indifferently.

Moira led me out through another door at the side of the commissary, one I hadn't noticed before.

*　　*　　*

We went down a path that led off toward some sets erected on the bare and dusty ground in the distance. From the rear you couldn't tell what the sets were, but when we passed through a gap between two of the flimsy board-and-canvas structures we came out into a western cowboy town, complete with saloon, boardinghouse, hitching posts, and a broad main street suitable for shootouts. The set looked a little shabby and the torn canvas was hanging down on the front of the boardinghouse; it hadn't been used for some time. The next set was more pleasant; Moira led me along a sidewalk through what appeared to be a modest suburban neighborhood with rose-covered bungalows, picket fences, and so on.

'A nice place to marry and settle down,' I suggested.

'Yes. And then, we could go on our honeymoon.'

We passed through another set of flats and came out into a little corner of Venice, with palazzi, a cupola or two of St. Mark's basilica with the fake marble walls propped up with two-by-fours, and a pair of gondolas in a canal of greenish water about fifty feet long. A pleasant coolness came up from the stretch of water, even though it was stagnant. A few old telephone poles with decorative wooden tops were driven into the mud at odd angles. We skirted along the edge of the canal, passed through the ornate papier-mâché portal of a palazzo, and found ourselves on a sylvan path leading through a grove of shady sycamores. There was a white fence along one side of the path. In the distance there were buildings, a shingled roof and a fragment of white clapboard wall with a window. I could hear the plash of running water.

Moira still held my hand, in a way that was friendly but utterly without intimate significance, as one child holds the hand of another. We came out through the trees into a grassy pasture. Beyond it was a small and neatly painted New England farmhouse, and a little farther along a mill over a brook, with the mill wheel slowly turning. There were buttercups here and there in the grass, and bees buzzed lazily. Over the tops of the trees I could catch a glimpse of the corrugated-iron studios in the distance.

Here someone had been shooting a picnic scene. In the meadow by the millrace there was a white cloth laid out with a wicker picnic basket on it. Some napkins, paper cups, a thermos bottle, and other flotsam from the lunch were scattered around, and there was a ukulele lying near them on the grass.

We sat down together on the grass, Moira smiling in her significant and slightly mysterious way.

I told her, 'We seem to be living our life backwards. This is where we meet and fall in love.'

'Oh, it doesn't matter in which order you shoot things. They fix it all in the cutting room.'

She was still playful; it was all a game. I picked up the ukulele and tuned it. 'My dog has fleas.' I set it down again. For some time we lay propped on our elbows without speaking, in the fragrant meadow filled with the murmur of bees. A distance of perhaps four feet separated us. I made no attempt to move toward her. The pull of desire I had felt in the commissary was still there, but now that I was alone with her I found myself curiously paralyzed. My limbs were light, but it seemed precisely for this reason that I was unable to move them. It was as though they were made out of air and lacked substance. What I desired so strongly was immediately before me, so near that I could have reached out and touched it. But an awe of its perfection, a holy dread of the forbidden sanctities under the white frock, held me back. From my wide reading in literature I recognized the sensation, even though I had never experienced it before: I had fallen in love.

We went on lying on our sides in the grass, without moving and without saying anything. I examined her fixedly, and she looked back at me with her self-contained little expression of amusement. After a while I became aware of a light humming from somewhere, as though it were coming from the air above and behind us. At first I attributed it to the bees, but it was a different kind of sound, a mechanical whir as of some well-oiled and silent machine constantly running. I realized now that this sound had been in the air for some time, perhaps from the moment when I had first passed through the Screen in the abandoned theater with Nesselrode. I was fully aware of it only at times like this when other things were quiet. And along with the sound came an odd sensation, the kind of intuition you have when someone is looking at you from behind. I turned around. There was nothing.

When I turned back to Moira I knew from her expression that she too was aware of this odd sound, and even that she knew what it was. 'Oh, that's just the eternal Eye,' she said languidly. 'That watches over us at all times. To be sure we don't do something naughty.'

'And if we do?'

But she offered no satisfactory answer to this; she only shrugged. It was as though it were something that you didn't speak about, or that was considered so trivial that it was not worth mentioning. I tried to ignore it and put it out of my mind. I centered my attention on her face again. It was not, I confirmed now upon closer examination and in the open sunlight, the face of an extremely young woman. I judged her to be about my own age, that is, thirty. The childlike gestures, the naive and sensitive smile, the crisp white frock, were exterior trivia, hardly more than makeup. They were her professional trappings, the tools of her trade. Under them was a mature woman, a body charged with sexual promise and rich in its mystery and complexity, even though it was childlike in its form. Yet in the trivial play of our game in the grass I could only address this outward semblance of Moira; I could only pretend too that she was the child she pretended to be.

Plucking a long stem of grass, I stretched it out and playfully tickled her face with it. She wrinkled up her nose and laughed a silvery little tinkle. She snatched the blade of grass from me and began chewing it, holding the other end, as though to contribute her part to the rustic quality of our game. I reached out for the ukulele and began strumming it. Then I offered a sample of my singing voice, a sort of countertenor with a thin schoolboyish tremor to it.

'Down by the Old Mill Stream,
Where I first met you . . .'

She threw away the blade of grass. Her smile disappeared; she became oddly grave. She watched me expectantly and curiously out of her dark eyes, her head tilted a little to one side.

'With your eyes so blue,
Dressed in gingham too.'

The smile reappeared. She looked down at her white frock and smoothed out the skirt, with a casual and yet sensuous gesture that unconsciously drew attention to the feminine curves of her body. 'It's linen.'
I went on.

'And it was there I knew . . .'

She waited silently, with an expectant expression, to see what it was that I knew.

'That you loved me true . . .'

Here she became grave and lowered her eyes, as though embarrassed or flustered. This gave the impression that she was looking down at her own body in the white dress, which of course caused my attention to be drawn to it too. There was a faint flush in her cheeks perhaps.

'You were sixteen...'

Here a ghost of a smile appeared, and she shook her head gravely.

'My village queen...'

Pleased, she looked down at the white dress again and smoothed out the skirt.

I concluded, stretching out the words and lowering my voice almost to a whisper.

'Down by the Old...
Mill...
Stream.'

There was a silence. Then she turned away, as though gazing at something in the distance, and said blithely, 'You're a quick study. How did you learn all this? Surely you didn't improvise it.' When she caught my eye again she couldn't suppress a playful little laugh.

'Moira.'

She remained motionless in the same posture, half reclining, propped on her elbow in the meadow. I threw away the ukulele. Then I pushed myself up and leaned forward toward her, slowly, as slowly as the hand of a clock, awkwardly bent over my stiffened arms in the grass. The arms passed the point of verticality and went on a little beyond it. I felt that the forward part of my body was precariously supported and might collapse. I was still unable to reach her face; it floated tantalizingly a few inches from me. The ridiculousness of my posture, threatening at any moment to topple me forward in the grass, was overwhelmed in the intensity of my desire to kiss her. We both remained fixed for an instant that seemed an eternity, my arm quivering. Then, after a hesitation, she too bent forward a little and her face moved through the air toward me. For an instant I felt the cool separateness of her lips, pressing lightly against mine. Then the sensation was gone.

Perhaps my eyes had been closed; I opened them and saw her on her feet, slipping rapidly away with a glance over her shoulder. I scrambled up, stumbling, and set off in pursuit of her. The very intensity of my desire, which seemed to turn my limbs into a hot liquid, prevented me from moving with the necessary agility. Wavering a little and groping with my hands, I moved through the glaring sunlight after her. Somewhere behind my back I was aware of the faint whirring of the Eye. I tried to recall whether she had smiled as she had glanced over her shoulder. It seemed to me that, if I could establish this fact clearly, then I would know my fate and the future of my love for her, one way or the other, would be revealed. But I had no memory of it, and besides she was always smiling in her faintly ambiguous way. The white dress disappeared around the corner of the mill house. In some way I found myself on the wrong side of the mill stream, which was six feet or more wide and too broad to jump.

*   *   *

When I turned I found Nesselrode behind me, wearing his shabby gray overcoat as usual, his fringe of straggly white hair glowing in the sunshine.

He said crossly, 'Ah, at last I am finding you. What are you doing, anyhow? This is not permitted. Moira is supposed to be working.'

'I imagine she is. At least she isn't here, is she?'

He said nothing to this. We were both irritated with each other—I because he had interrupted my idyll, although this was irrational because it had been interrupted anyhow by Moira's getting up and running away, and he probably because he suspected what I was up to. His shifty eyes took in the ukulele in the grass. Then he turned abruptly with a gesture to me. We went off together down the path through the sycamores, he leading the way and I following. I had no idea where to look for Moira anyhow. She might be anywhere. Instead of entering the commissary as I expected, or the studio where they had been shooting the Lincoln picture, he went straight on down the main street of the lot and out the gate onto the boulevard.

'Where are we going?'

He muttered into the air, 'You've been naughty. Okay, so maybe you don't want to be in pictures.'

'Mr. Nesselrode . . .'

He made no reply. Once again he seemed to have forgotten that I was with him; he went on in his rapid pace down the sidewalk without turning his head to see if I was behind. I went on after him with great reluctance. I had an urge to turn around, to flee from him and go back to the lot in search of Moira; I was certain I would find her sooner or later. Yet in another part of my mind I felt I had to follow Nesselrode; he was my only guide over the landscape of this black-and-white Dante's Inferno and if I lost him there was no telling what might happen to me. The air about me, thin and artificial, seemed charged with a vague menace, and even my own body felt insubstantial. Without his help I might wander around forever through these weedy vacant lots until I expired from exhaustion, or simply dissolved into thin air. Besides I had the impression that, in spite of his pretense of ignoring me, he would immediately turn and catch me in his dry and bony hand if I tried to

92

escape. In this way, without exchanging a single word, we came in a half an hour or so back to the Alhambra Theater.

We entered as we had come out, through the stage door at the rear. Nesselrode closed the door, and we were in almost total darkness except for the rim of sunlight around the door behind us. We groped our way along the corridor and up the stairs to the stage. Here there was a little more light from the grayish shape of the Screen at the other end. The piled-up crates, the heap of lumber, and the stepladder were exactly as they had been, coated in a light film of dust. Without being told I took Nesselrode's hand. Or, to be precise, our little ballet—one in which we each pretended to ignore the other—was more complicated than that. I was standing two feet or so behind him and to the side, and I stretched out my hand tentatively in his direction. And he, without turning around, facing away from me so what he couldn't possibly see what I was doing, felt back in the gloom with his own bony fingers until they met my own, as accurately as though they were guided by some kind of sixth sense. It was the way lovers reach for each other in the dark, I thought, each knowing where the other's hand is, or the way a mother can feel for her child and instinctively touch it without looking around.

Attached by our hands in this way, and elaborately ignoring each other, we passed back through the Screen in the same way that we had come through it, I wasn't sure when—perhaps the day before, or perhaps only a few hours. The theater of course was deserted. Nesselrode fumbled with the employees' door at the side, and finally it opened with a scraping noise. To my surprise when we came out into the city again it was twilight. After the blankness of the black-and-white world I had left behind, the intense, glowing, almost incandescent color of everything struck me like a blow. People's faces were orange, the storefronts blared tangerine and bright yellow, even the asphalt of the pavement seemed purple rather than black. As night fell the neon signs of the shops were coming on one by one, glowing and wriggling worms that hurt the eyes with their glare. The headlights of passing cars bored yellow holes into the air.

He set out to cross the boulevard in the middle of the block, ignoring the hurtling traffic.

'Watch out for the cars,' I warned him.

'Let them try to hit me. I am more agile than they think,' he said.

CHAPTER SIX

I have said that I was the sole heir of my parents and inherited their fortune totally. This was not entirely true, or at least it was an oversimplification of the matter. My possession of the estate was limited by certain conditions that Astrée and Dirk (more probably Dirk; Astreé couldn't have cared a pin what I did with the money) had seen fit to attach to the will in the form of a trust agreement. This arrangement was understandable given that I was only eighteen when they had the will drawn up shortly before their deaths, but as far as I could tell it was still in effect now that I was thirty, and was apparently to go on into perpetuity as far as I knew; no one had ever explained it to me very well. In fact I had never even seen a copy of the will, as far as I could remember, but the funds under the trust agreement were managed by the West Los Angeles branch of the Sunset Bank. The bank took care of most of my financial affairs, investing the capital as they saw fit, paying the taxes and insurance on the St. Albans Place house, preparing my income tax returns, and transferring to my checking account each month a sum far too large for me to spend, even if my tastes had not been as austere and restrained as they were.

It was shortly after I came back from my first expedition behind the Screen that I received a personal communication from a person who—as I assumed at first—was a representative of the bank, or at least connected in some way with this trust arrangement. The telephone rang, I picked it up, and a voice said in a barking tone, 'Ziff!'

Since I had never heard this vocable before, I was silent for perhaps two seconds, uncertain whether to reply 'Who?' or 'What?' I finally decided on 'Who?'

'Eldon Ziff. We have to talk a little about your life, Alys.'

'My life?'

'Yes. There are some problems that have arisen in connection with some of its ramifications.'

The voice was a vibrant masculine baritone, an energetic and confident voice, and yet there was a note of seriousness in it, a kind of mortician solemnity, that suggested that the problems were real and grave and needed to be talked about. I was caught totally unprepared (I had been lingering over a late breakfast, including toast made by holding it over the burner of the stove on a fork) and could only repeat in an idiotic way the key word of each statement.

'Ramifications?'

'Yes. This is a word referring to branches,

96

like those of a tree. As a person grows older his life develops ramifications. That is, with increasing sophistication and experience, new interests and new concerns grow up which lead him in new directions, and these in turn branch off into subinterests and subconcerns, just as a tree grows branches. Some of these proliferating branches are sound and some are rotten.'

'I don't see what business this is of yours.'

'Now then, come come, Alys. You know very well that you are not entirely free to conduct your life along lines which, to say the least, are rather bizarre, and might if they were divulged incur the moral disapprobation of persons who—'

'Let's not talk about that on the telephone.'

'Just as you prefer, Alys. Let's have lunch together then.'

'Why don't we meet in your office? Or you could come here,' I countered, feeling more assertive and defending myself as I began to recover my wits a little.

'Well you see, Alys, it's a highly personal matter and I didn't think you'd care to discuss it in the office with a lot of people around. I thought you'd prefer a more intimate ambience.'

'You don't have a private office?'

'How about the Bistro in Beverly Hills?'

It was all rushing on too fast for me. I felt swept away by the energetic baritone voice that answered no questions, countered every objection by ignoring it, and seemed to drive straight at the goal it had decided on in advance.

'All right.'

'Do you know where it is?'

'Yes.'

'Let's say today.'

'What's the hurry?'

'Are you sure you know the place? It's 246 North Cañon Drive. That's Two Four Six, just north of Wilshire. The word Cañon has a kind of bendy thing on top of the n. It's called a tilde.'

'Yes.'

'Be there at one. I'll phone for a table.'

He hung up. It occurred to me only then—in fact only ten minutes or so after the call—that at no point in the conversation had he said he was acting in behalf of the Sunset Bank or had anything to do with that institution. The phrase 'might if they were divulged,' in fact, suggested that he might be a quite ordinary blackmailer.

★ ★ ★

By the time I had bathed and dressed it was already after twelve. The next decision was which of the two cars to take. My life, I was beginning to see, was sometimes complicated by these nostalgic hobbies. The Invicta, a 1925 tourer with a handmade body, was a beautiful

98

machine but somewhat temperamental. Ziff's invitation was so peremptory that in the back of my mind I was a little afraid of being late. Besides the delicate coachwork might be damaged in traffic. I decided on the Hudson, which was enormous and unwieldy to handle but could buffalo its way past ordinary cars, being a good two feet higher than they were, and was rugged enough to withstand any slings and buffets that Los Angeles traffic could hand it. I backed it out down the winding gravel driveway with skill, since I had done it many times. I often took the Hudson when I went with Belinda to concerts and films. It was a double-cowl phaeton with a second windshield for the back seat, and sometimes she liked to ride back there alone as though she were the Queen of Sheba, gazing out aloofly at pedestrians and owners of mere Cadillacs. Belinda had a well-developed sense of humor, which I would have appreciated more if it had not sometimes extended to me and my own personal habits.

Guiding this behemoth down the street and past the guard in his kiosk, I turned out onto Wilshire and headed west. It was not very far and perhaps I had allowed too much time. When I went to Beverly Hills—usually to buy records, but sometimes to go to lunch at the Brown Derby or the Bistro—I always parked at the Beverly Wilshire Hotel, pretending successfully that I was a guest. This had several advantages. You entered the broad drive behind the hotel where there was a glass canopy overhead to provide shelter from the rain and sun, and a carpet to step out onto. There you stopped your car, a valet took charge of it, and when you came back he delivered it to you swiftly, deftly, and courteously. It was kept somewhere under cover (I never knew exactly where it was that the valet took it) so that when you got into it again it was cool and free from dust. From the carpet under the canopy you stepped directly into the cool opulence of the hotel, where you could browse around in the various shops off the lobby in case you were early for your appointment. The only disadvantage was that it was very expensive, so that it often cost me as much to park my car as it did for my lunch. This of course was a matter of absolute indifference to me. The valets knew the Hudson and drove it away without showing either any alarm at its ferociously clashing gears or any amusement at my eccentricities. I came there often enough that they remembered me, and they knew that I tipped them well.

As I had expected, I got to Beverly Hills a little early. Leaving the Hudson for the valets to take care of, I went into the lobby and spent twenty minutes or so browsing through the books in Brentano's, which had an entrance door inside the hotel. At exactly three minutes to one I went back into the lobby and out the door onto Wilshire.

I crossed Wilshire on the traffic light, went two blocks down to Cañon, and up the street toward the restaurant. It was only about a half a block. When I was perhaps three doors from the restaurant I became aware that someone on the opposite side of the street had stepped out onto the pavement and was crossing it diagonally toward me. He was a lean but muscular individual a little taller than average, walking with a kind of pounce. He was wearing a safari jacket over a shirt open at the neck, knitted silver stretch pants, and suede loafers. His face was tanned and his hair was expensively styled, coming down to the collar in the rear and cut in a Dutch-boy fringe over the forehead. I, of course, wore my usual conservative coat and tie.

Our two courses intersected. I inspected him and he closed in briskly without meeting my glance, as though he had known me for a long time. Threading his way adroitly between two parked cars, he came up onto the sidewalk with a bound. Without introducing himself he said, 'You're just on time, Alys. Good boy.'

I was used to his patronizing manners from the phone conversation and paid no attention to them now. We went in. In the polished and reflecting gloom inside the door it was difficult to see anything until your eyes adjusted. He pronounced the single syllable 'Ziff!' in the same barking way he had over the phone.

The captain, with the menus folded under his arm, bowed slightly and with dignity. 'Mr. Ziff. A table for two.' With another bow he led us away through the tables set with white linen and silver to an alcove at the bottom of the room.

The tables in this part of the restaurant were arranged in a long row and fitted tightly together, so that a waiter had to pull ours out in order for me to get in behind it. Then the table was replaced, effectively sealing me in. Ziff sat down in the chair opposite me and reached down to adjust his trousers around his crotch. Then he stared at me intently.

The captain was middle-aged, bald, and rotund. He seemed to be Italian. He showed no disposition to surrender the menus to us yet.

'What would you like to drink, gentlemen?'

Ziff ordered a double Chivas Regal and water. I considered. 'Something very light.'

'A Shirley Temple?' the captain suggested with polite sarcasm.

'No, that's too light.' I paused. 'A dry vermouth, on the rocks, with a twist. A Cinzano,' I added, wishing to be decisive.

'Dry Cinzano rocks and a twist.' The captain departed. Ziff and I were left to go on with our inspection of each other. At close range, and now that my eyes had adjusted to the dimly lit room, I saw that he wore a heavy but absolutely plain gold ring on the forefinger of each hand. On the third finger of his left hand he also had some kind of class ring. Around his neck, in the opening of his loosely woven net shirt, was a fine gold chain with a small golden Z hanging from it. An aroma of expensive cologne sifted across the table from him.

The interior of the Bistro was done in fake French décor, with painted decorations on the pillar glasses. The woodwork was dark polished mahogany, and the upholstery on the banquette where I was sitting was a black synthetic leather. The chairs were old-fashioned cane-bottoms with bentwood backs. Across the table Ziff teetered back and forth on his chair, in even rhythm, while he watched me thoughtfully. Our drinks came. Ziff brought his chair to the level, drained off half his Scotch, and set the glass down. Then he got down to business.

'You see, Alys, the thing is, you've been living as though you were a totally free and independent individual. But nobody is totally free and independent.'

'Not in the absolute sense, I suppose.'

'That's what we're talking about, Alys. The absolute sense.'

'Let's be more specific. What exactly is it about my behavior that bothers you?'

'It doesn't bother me.'

'That you want to talk to me about.'

'We can't be more specific at this point, Alys. We're talking about the absolute. The absolute is the opposite of the specific.'

'All right,' I hazarded. 'What is it absolutely about my behavior that bothers you?'

'It doesn't bother me. It's that you're too free and independent, as I've said.'

'You don't believe in free will?'

'In the metaphysical sense, yes. In the social sense, no individual can engage in total freedom of choice in an organized society. He's limited by the specific mores of the society in which he finds himself.' While he talked he reached out and began rearranging the objects on the table in a mechanical way, as though he wasn't aware of what he was doing. He moved the saltshaker an inch or two, adjusted the candle lamp in the center of the table, and shifted the ashtray slightly. 'In the psychological sense,' he went on, 'the individual is unable to engage in free choice because his every act is conditioned by his inner psychic processes, which are not accessible to his will. Is there something wrong with your drink?'

I sipped a little of my Cinzano. 'But these things are true of everybody.'

'Yes, but in your case I've obtained professional opinion, and according to the psychiatrist I consulted these bizarre forms of behavior you've fallen into are all in your mind. *All in your mind*, Alys,' he repeated, staring at me with particular significance with these words.

I had no idea what he was talking about,

except that evidently he or somebody else had been following my life more closely than I had realized. I decided to be amused. 'You mean that I've been—under surveillance?'

He reached down behind the table to make an adjustment again. Evidently the silver trousers were a little too tight. 'I have my responsibilities, and you have yours. I'll take care of my responsibilities. It's yours we're talking about now.'

'I agree that your responsibilities are your business. But it seems to me that mine are my business.'

It was characteristic of our relation that Ziff called me by my first name, whereas I called him nothing in particular at all—if I had called him anything I would probably have called him Mr. Ziff. The reason was perhaps that for him, in his legal and professional capacity, I was forever a child—the child of my parents—the heir. Just as you say *tu* to little children and dogs in French, so Ziff called me Alys.

'Look, Alys,' he said, lowering his voice a note or two. 'I know everything about you. Everything.' He rearranged a few more things on the table between us, putting the saltshaker back where it had been in the first place. 'I won't go into my methods. They don't concern you. Just let me remind you that, according to the terms of the trust agreement embodied in your parents' will, you are required to conduct an orderly life and not engage in acts of moral turpitude.'

I didn't know whether he was referring to my engaging in onanism with mirrors, or taking in a roomer in violation of the rules of the St. Albans Place Homeowners Association. I glanced around the room. The tables were very close together and anything that was said in the room could be clearly heard by the other patrons. I remembered Ziff's rather curious remarks that if we met in his office too many people would overhear us, and I might prefer to meet in some place more 'intimate.' The Bistro was intimate all right. Whenever I moved my elbow it touched that of the film-producer type who was sitting at the next table with a blond young woman.

I lowered my own voice a little. 'So, although . . .'

The menus finally came. I ordered a quiche, and Ziff a filet mignon with pommes parmentières. 'And a Chambertin '78,' he added. 'A Clos Saint-Jacques if you've got it, but be sure it's a '78.' It was the right wine for a steak but not for a quiche, but I didn't say so. The captain took the order and the waiter brought the wine immediately. Most of the waiters were young Chicanos; they were handsome, elegant, and dexterous. Ziff ignored them and never spoke to them; he dealt only with the captain.

'So,' I went on in my lowered voice, 'although you claimed we were discussing the absolute, you do have some specific objections to my conduct.'

In the middle of sampling the wine he stopped and stared at me. I was smiling lightly, since I still had difficulty taking the whole business seriously. However it was a little difficult to smile while Ziff's eyes were fixed on you. They gave the impression, somehow, of a pair of telescopic rifle sights with cross hairs. Although he didn't hold the eyes still long enough for me to tell for sure, it was even possible that there were tiny crosses in the pupils, as in the eyes of a cat.

He considered my question. After what seemed to me a good deal of thought he said, 'No, I don't.'

His steak came, and my quiche. He cut a precise cube of the steak, put it in his mouth, and chewed it methodically. When it was thoroughly masticated and swallowed he set down the knife and fork, one on either side of the plate.

'What we have to discuss are the absolute value systems of life, Alys, and the nature of reality. Now listen carefully. This is important.'

'All right.'

It was not so important, however, that it prevented him from cutting another cube of steak, putting it in his mouth, and chewing it in

107

his methodical way. When he was finished with this he resumed.

'You're interested in art, Alys.'

I thought for a moment before I responded. 'What do you mean by art?'

'I mean the construction of beautiful and interesting, but useless artifacts.'

I didn't contest this, although it seemed like a rather curious definition. 'Is there anything wrong,' I asked him, 'in being interested in art?'

Now he thought for a moment. 'No,' he responded after a while. 'Art has made a significant contribution to our civilization. I myself have a great but limited respect for its values. Many people are attracted to art and it is easy to see why. *Ars longa, vita brevis*. Art is eternal, and in art we are immortal. But.' He slowed down and stared at me even more significantly as he said what followed. 'But. Art is artificial, art is not real. Life is temporal. In life we are mortal. But life is real.'

He picked up the knife and fork again, started to cut another piece of steak, and then set them down again to see if I was paying attention to what he was saying.

'Is everyone in your profession so profound?'

'I studied philosophy at UCLA before I went to law school,' he said.

'One can perhaps enjoy both.'

'Both?'

'Art *and* life. Why should they be mutually

exclusive?'

'When I was talking with you on the telephone I took up the subject of ramifications, a term you were apparently not familiar with.' He shifted the candle lamp again, and even reached across the table to move my own plate a little to one side and line up my knife and fork. This compulsion of his to rearrange things on the table gave the impression that a part of him, a part of which he was not entirely in control, was playing some sort of elaborate rapid game like chess, using the table setting as counters, at the same time he was conducting his conversation with me. 'As each life proceeds,' he went on, 'it divides into branches like a tree. In time it develops so many ramifications that the individual is unable to follow them all. He has to decide, Alys'—and here he stopped and fixed me with an unusually meaningful glance— 'whether he wants to follow one branch or the other. It's like a kid,' he said, 'climbing a tree. You can follow one branch or another, but not both. Some branches are sound and some are rotten.'

'You said that on the phone.'

'Yes, and now I'm saying it again. I'm telling you to come down off that branch, Alys.'

'You're good on metaphors too. Did you study poetry at UCLA?'

'You're damned right I did.'

There was a silence. I smiled a little. Then I

said, 'I haven't asked very many questions, you may have noticed. There are a good many I could have asked. But now there's one in particular I'd like to put to you, if you don't mind.'

'Certainly, Alys.'

'Just who in the hell do you think you are?'

This caused him to adjust the silver trousers again. It was perhaps just an unconscious tic. 'Why,' he said, 'I'm nobody of any particular importance. Since you don't have parents of your own, I'm just a friendly figure to hover around and be sure you don't get into any trouble. In loco parentis, you know.'

'It was an odd family, but I don't think they were crazy.'

'You know more Latin than that, Alys.'

'You know a lot about me, don't you?'

'I already told you. I know everything. I have nothing to do night and day, Alys,' he said without a discernible trace of irony, 'but follow you around the world to be sure you don't get into trouble.'

The thought struck me that possibly he wasn't a bank officer at all but an obscure relative of some kind. I tried to remember whether I had ever heard of a cousin Eldon. There had been scores of people around the house when I was a child, some of them rather bizarre, and I had never got them all straight in my mind. Perhaps he was some sort of uncle of

110

mine who had been appointed executor by the court. Or perhaps, as he himself implied, he was only my guardian angel and had been appointed by God Almighty.

We had finished our lunch, he told the captain. (He didn't ask me.) The check came almost immediately. Evidently Ziff had other places to go and had trained the Bistro to fit the pace of his life. When the captain came with the saucer with the check in it he set it correctly in the middle of the table, perhaps an inch closer to Ziff than to me. Ziff, reaching out to the center of the table, rearranged the salt and pepper and also the candle lamp, and, as though he were doing it only absentmindedly, he also displaced the saucer with the check on it so that it was closer to me than to him. This seemed fair enough to me. It was a good lunch and I had also enjoyed the conversation. He had a genuine gift for rhetoric, of a rather sinuous sort. I took out my billfold and set two twenties and a ten on the saucer. The bill was a little over forty dollars, and with the tip it was about right. The waiter pulled the table out into the aisle to set me free. I was still interested in Ziff's discourse on art and reality; or at least I wanted to cat-and-mouse him a little more about it.

'Did you say that in art we are immortal?'

'It's not worth it, Alys.'

That was all I could get out of him. When we were back out on the street he did his converging act in reverse: I set out down the sidewalk toward Wilshire on the shady side of the street, and he veered away and crossed Cañon on the diagonal, turning now and then to look at me, as though he wanted to be sure I was going back to my car and not engaging in some act of moral turpitude. I lost sight of him shortly before I got to the corner of Wilshire.

CHAPTER SEVEN

For several days after that I didn't know what to do with myself. My usual activities—playing records, reading books, tinkering with one of the cars—didn't seem to distract me very much. I loafed around the house, drinking a little more than I usually did, picking up a book and setting it down, listening when I was in another part of the house for the telephone, although I didn't know very clearly who it was that I expected would be calling me. I didn't see much of Nesselrode in that time. He seemed to have his own affairs to attend to and was seldom in the house. I didn't prowl around in his room any more either. At least one more object in the house turned up missing—an elaborately chased paper knife with Arabic inscriptions on the handle—but I didn't regard it as very important. I opened the bills and other mail with a steak knife borrowed from the kitchen.

The disappearance of the paper knife, however, reminded me of something, and I found myself rummaging around in the programs for the silent film series at UCLA and at the County Museum, not only the current programs but old ones going back a year or more. Some of them had stills from the pictures, but I didn't find what I was looking for. The more I looked the more restless and curious I became. Finally I went back to the USC library. The two books I had consulted before were mainly about production and had very few references to actors. There were a number of other books on early films, some technical, some simply memoirs of stars, directors, and producers. I found nothing in them either. I began to wonder whether Moira Silver, Lord Muldoon, and the Charles Morton who played Lincoln had really existed or were only something I had dreamed, or some kind of Magic Theater evoked by that devious and slightly menacing sorcerer Nesselrode.

I consulted the reference librarian, a thin young man with an anxious sideways glance who looked something like Kafka. He didn't seem to find my questions odd, although he didn't say specifically whether he himself had ever heard of any of the people I was talking about. 'Your best chance of finding something would be in old fan magazines,' he told me, still looking to one side as though he were afraid his supervisor would find him revealing all this to me. 'As a university library we don't acquisition popular periodicals.' (This piece of jargon reassured me; he was human after all.) 'Why don't you try the L.A. Public downtown.'

★   ★   ★

In the Public Library at Fifth and Hope, an interesting building in the shape of a Babylonian ziggurat, I quickly found what I wanted. There wasn't room in the periodicals section for all the old popular magazines, and they were relegated to a storeroom in the basement. Everything was covered with dust and the lighting was poor. There was no index, no catalog, and no particular system to the way the materials were stored. Everything was stacked haphazardly on metal shelves, and in many cases the carelessly piled magazines had slid down and were scattered over the floor. When I did find the old movie magazines, however, they were all more or less in the same place, in a kind of cave or niche at the end of the storeroom. The nearest light was about twenty feet away. I turned it on and began looking through the stacks of old magazines, some of them yellowed and brittle with age.

There were copies of *Photoplay*, *Screen World*,

and *Hollywoodland* going back to the Twenties. Before 1918, evidently, there were no fan magazines, although there was one called *Movie World* which turned out to contain mainly information for theater operators and projectionists. I spent about two hours going through magazines without finding what I was looking for. In all that time no one else came into the basement, although I did hear a scuttling noise now and then, perhaps a mouse working its way under the shelves in the dark.

Then, after I had moved several stacks around to get at the magazines in the back, I found one I hadn't noticed before. It was called *Picture Land*, although in later issues the title seemed to have been changed to *Pictureland*. The stack was in no particular chronological order at all; neither was the collection complete. The issues seemed to range from the period just after the war to around 1928, when the magazine apparently went out of business. It was the period I was looking for.

I couldn't read them very well in the half-darkness, so I carried them an armful at a time to a place out under the hanging light bulb. There I squatted down on the floor, surrounded by the mounting heap of magazines. It was about a half an hour later that I first found something in the February 1920 issue of *Picture Land*. In a double-page photo layout entitled 'Stars at Work & Play' there was a picture in the lower right-hand corner captioned, 'Young starlet Moira Silver, seen here lunching with producer Julius Nesselrode. Their names are romantically linked.'

Moira, smiling up from the table in the glare of the primitive flash powder of the time, was exactly as I remembered her: the porcelain-pale face, the dark eyes, the fine and sensitive mouth, the expression of ingenuous and slightly mischievous childishness. Nesselrode seemed to be in his early thirties, but I could have easily recognized him even without the caption. He already had his jumpy rabbit look, yet he was oddly handsome in his beady and alert, slightly bug-eyed way. I knew now whom he reminded me of; he looked like Heinrich Himmler. He had a thin mustache and he was staring straight at the photographer without a trace of a smile, the magnesium flash reflected in two tiny white points in his eyes. He was wearing an impossible sports jacket a little too large for him, with checks as large as a horse blanket's.

But it was the image of Moira that transfixed me. In spite of the synthetic quality of her childishness, in spite of the oversimplified, almost diagrammatic quality of her beauty with its too-perfect complexion and its conventional dark eyes, it was a curiously stirring face. I found I was unable to turn the page. Sitting there on the dusty floor under the light bulb, I felt a cool perspiration breaking out on every part of my body. The more I stared at the photo the more mysterious and elusive it seemed. It was only a rectangle of paper perhaps two inches by three. The edges of the page where the light had seeped into it were yellowed and slightly brittle. But the picture itself was set far enough inside the page that it had escaped this corruption of time; it was still blank-white, glossy, and lithe, with a slight slickness to the surface. *Picture Land* was printed on better paper than the average fan magazine. I focused my gaze on the face, on the dark eyes that gazed out from under their lids with a coy and perverse innocence.

Moira.

Moira.

Gradually the cold layer of moisture under my clothing evaporated, leaving me slightly feverish and dry-mouthed. I decided not to get up and go upstairs to the water fountain. I set the February 1920 issue carefully aside where I could find it again, wiped the dust from my hands onto my trousers, and went on looking through the stacks of magazines piled on the floor around me. In another hour I had turned up a dozen or so photographs of Moira. I found a curious pattern. In the earlier photos, from 1920 to June or July of 1923, she was usually with Nesselrode and usually in cafés or night clubs in Hollywood. As far as I could see she had not made any pictures in this period, although she was usually identified as a 'starlet.' Then, after 1923, the photos were all publicity shots and stills from her films: *The Coquette, Pirate of the Dunes, Save My Child, The White Telephone*. Perhaps after 1923 she had been too busy working to go out to night clubs with Nesselrode. Yet it seemed curious that precisely at the moment she had begun to succeed in pictures and had been cast in leading roles, she had disappeared from the Hollywood social scene and was no longer photographed in public. A notion occurred to me that, after 1923, some vaguely sinister power of Nesselrode had somehow impeded her freedom of movement. Perhaps from 1920 to 1923, while their names were 'romantically linked,' he had only courted her, so to speak. Then, after she fell to him (I could only think of it in those terms), she was his possession, in some way I could only guess at, and was no longer free to appear in public. This notion left me feeling slightly cold again, although I couldn't have said why. I dismissed it from my mind, or tried to.

One photo in particular, in the period after 1923, caught my attention so that I stopped and stared at it for a long time. It was a still from a picture called *Pirate of the Dunes*. Moira seemed to be inside some sort of tent or room hung with rugs and shawls. Since it was a medium closeup all that could be seen of her clothing was an ordinary white blouse, with the top button

118

unbuttoned. Her hair was slightly disarranged. With her lips parted and her head lowered a little, she was staring at the camera with a curious expression of fear in which, unmistakably, an element of the sensuous was mingled. Whatever it was that stared at her from the camera eye, she seemed to fear it and desire it at the same time. The fragile tendons of her throat stood out clearly, outlined in tiny shadows. Her lips seemed about to pronounce a word. I had the impression that if I concentrated on the photo and surrendered myself to my deeper impulses, to my subconscious, I might guess what this word was; and in this word would be revealed the whole secret of this enigma in which I had—in some way and hardly knowing when I had begun—entangled myself.

I carefully sorted out all the magazines that had pictures of Moira in them and turned down the corners of the pages so I could find them again. Then I arranged them in a neat pile and, carefully lifting up the stack of magazines at the end of the shelf, put my collection on the bottom and the others on top of it. The only way you could tell the ones I had selected from the others is that they were more neatly stacked.

When I got home I was still in a state of feverish excitement. I fixed myself some dinner, started to eat it and found I had no appetite, and went upstairs to listen to some music. For a quarter of an hour or so I lay on the bed listening to Pachelbel's *Canon,* a soothing piece of baroque music said to be used to calm mental patients in hospitals. But even this failed to induce the nepenthe-like euphoria that it usually did. I switched the music off and went to stare out the window into the darkness. There was no question, I realized, that my behavior in the past few days had been a little peculiar. I had always seemed a little queer to others, but now I was beginning to seem queer to myself. I decided that perhaps I had better interrogate myself a little about it and see if I could find out what I was up to.

To begin with, I asked myself in what I hoped was a detached and objective tone of self-analysis, why was I so fascinated with Moira? To this, I could only reply that she seemed in some way to correspond to some latent image in my memory, a gauzy other-self which had always been there and had only been brought to the surface by the photograph. Moira was inside me. Ah, but wasn't it perhaps only a case of a light Oedipus complex, the most common and banal imprint in the modern male consciousness according to the delegation from Vienna? Possibly, I conceded. We form our reveries of women from the women we have known, and the woman we know best is our mother. And yet, in the plain point of fact, I hadn't really known Astrée very well. It was impossible to be intimate with her. She went through the gestures of intimacy but everything was a game. She was artificial, ephemeral, elusive—you could no more possess her than you could possess a paper doll. Just like Moira, I told myself.

Well, all this was morbid. I decided not to monkey around with my subconscious any more. If you started turning over old rubbish there was no telling what you might find.

*   *   *

The next day I went back again to the L.A. Public. But by this time I knew I had found all the pictures of Moira in the storeroom, and I had come for a different purpose. I was armed. I squatted down on the floor again, in the slightly wavering light of the bulb hanging from the ceiling, and pulled out my stack of magazines. The particular issue I was looking for was easy to find: in addition to turning down the page with Moira's picture on it I had also turned down the corner of the cover. The date was September 1925. It fell open in my hands to the still from *Pirate of the Dunes*.

My emotions as I stared at the page were curious and not really describable. I felt an intense desire, but it was an abstract one. It was only paper after all that pulled at my emotions, as intensely and keenly as I felt the sensation.

121

There was no question that I had fallen in love, but it was like falling in love with someone in a book—which one sometimes does, as a child. The thought occurred to me that there are all sorts of things, in this existence of ours, that bar us from the women we desire. There are the barriers of chastity, of matrimonial bonds, of social class or a difference in race. But the most curious and elusive of these barriers is that of time. We may fall in love with Cleopatra (as I did at the age of ten, reading Shakespeare alone in my grandfather's library) or with Eleanor d'Aquitaine, perhaps, in a painting in a museum. But these women are forbidden to us by the gulf of mortality that separates us from them—a dark valley, bottomless and impassable, that no one has ever gone into and come out of again—it is, precisely, that bourn from which no traveler returns. This was the gulf that separated me from Moira. Yet, I thought, seeking to control my excitement, I knew the path into that valley.

Reaching into my coat pocket, I removed the small packet I had prepared when I left the house—a razor blade wrapped in several layers of waxed paper and secured with a rubber band. I looked around me. The storeroom was, of course, deserted, and in the silence I could have heard the footsteps of anyone approaching. It took me several minutes to cut out the picture, because of a problem I had not anticipated in advance. I found in myself a strong desire not to cut out the yellowed and slightly brittle margin that extended a half-inch in from the edge of the page. Neither did I want simply to sever the whole corner of the magazine and then cut off the yellowed edge by laying the picture on the floor. I wanted to remove *only* the picture itself, in its pristine form on slick white paper, leaving the rectangular hole of the same size intact in the magazine. This took a little doing, because the picture, being at the lower right-hand corner of the page, was enclosed on two sides by the brittle yellowed edge, and it took a delicate hand to cut out the picture without breaking the margin around it. My heart rose in my throat a little as I made the right-angle cut at the corner of the page, but I managed it perfectly. I held in my hand my heart's desire, something I wanted more than I had ever wanted anything in my life—Moira's white face with the dark eyes staring at me, eloquent with the unknown and unspoken word that hung on her lips.

This picture was a little larger than the others in the magazine, perhaps three inches by five. I preferred not to fold it. I slipped it with care into the pocket of my coat, along with the razor blade wrapped up in waxed paper again and secured with its rubber band. I reminded myself to be careful not to thrust my hand carelessly into the pocket of the coat, or even into my trousers pocket, which might wrinkle the coat and thus the paper with the photograph on it.

My next task was to get out of the library undetected with my prize. Taken objectively, this was not really so difficult. No one searched you as you left the library, and people cut things by the hundreds out of magazines, books, and even encyclopedias, to judge by the number of holes you found in pages. But it was the first crime I had ever committed, as minor as it was. If I was nervous about it, it was simply because the object in my pocket had a value for me that it couldn't possibly have for any librarian, as neurotic as members of this profession are about the mutilation of the materials under their care. With a Dostoevskian Pale-Criminal smile I was unable entirely to suppress, I went up the stairs, down the corridor and past the periodicals room, and out the exit on Hope Street, where there was a guard at the turnstile to check the materials you carried with you. I had nothing in my hands and he hardly gave me a glance. The rectangle of paper in my pocket burning against my hip, I made my way down Hope Street and turned left on Sixth toward the Biltmore, where I had parked the car.

*   *   *

Once safely home in the privacy of my bedroom, I slipped the scrap of paper carefully from my pocket. It was intact and unwrinkled. I looked around for a place to put it. Except for the bed, the most important piece of furniture in the room was an old-fashioned sideboard with a silver-framed mirror at its back and a number of drawers with intaglio silver handles. Of course there were mirrors on all the walls of the room, as well as on the ceiling, but the mirror over the sideboard was the only one with a frame around it. I attempted to wedge the photograph under the edge of the frame, but the paper edge, slightly furred by the razor blade, bent and threatened to wrinkle. I saw this wasn't going to work.

My eyes came back to the sideboard, which I used as a dresser. On it was a small silver frame with a photo of Astrée in it. The frame more or less matched the fittings on the sideboard; the silver edge, about a half-inch wide, was elaborately chased and the carved parts filled in with black. If you turned it over, a triangle of the cardboard back was cut away and folded out to serve as a stand. This business was held into the frame only with a pair of thin brass clips. I bent these away and removed the cardboard back and the photograph. It showed Astrée in a picture hat, at the wheel of the Duesenberg, turning sideways toward the camera with a blithe smile as though she were just leaving on a trip and saying 'Bye' in her offhand way.

I was about to drop it in the wastebasket.

After a moment I changed my mind and put it away in the top right-hand drawer of the sideboard, which also contained a collection of various other objects such as mismatched socks, empty deodorant containers, keys to unknown locks, a tube of Vaseline, a ribbon or two, and a partly used pack of condoms. Then I forgot it and as far as I can remember I never opened that drawer again.

The frame had a black mat in it which was designed to hold a three-by-five-inch photograph. The picture from the magazine was a little larger than that, but by shifting it around under the mat I was able to arrange it so that nothing important was obscured. I fastened the picture to the back of the mat with Scotch tape. Then I reassembled the whole business again: the frame, the mat with the photo, and the cardboard back.

I bent out the stand at the rear and set the frame on the sideboard. Immediately I was struck with the perfection of what I had done. If I had searched over every shop in the city I could never have found a frame so exactly suited to this picture. Not only did the sizes of the picture and frame match almost perfectly, but the aesthetics of the ensemble were faultless. The old-fashioned silver frame gave the impression that it was from the same period as the picture, and it probably was. The paint in the depressions of the silver was faded and had lost its gloss. Then came the black mat, also flat and without gloss. The picture itself, in the style of the time, was printed in slightly excessive contrast; the blacks were a little blacker than in real life and the whites a little whiter. In the center was Moira's moon-white face with its dark eyes staring directly at me, even when I moved a little to one side of the picture or the other. The paper was not quite flat and had a slight gloss to it, so that a faint sheen appeared here and there as the light struck it. A shadow played over Moira's brow, just above the right eye. I couldn't tell whether it was something in the original photograph or an artifact of the way I had inserted the picture in the frame.

CHAPTER EIGHT

The photograph remained there in the silver frame, multiplied and reflected in the various mirrors that lined the walls of the bedroom, and I gazed at it idly as I dressed every morning standing before the sideboard. My old life went on much as before; nothing had changed at least in its external details. And yet I wasn't the same as before, even if I might pretend outwardly that nothing had happened. There was a curious distracted or hypnotized quality to my state of mind, as though I were sleepwalking my way through my life.

Then about a week after my second visit to the L.A. Public I remembered something. The idea struck me like a flash and I closed the book I was reading and sat bolt upright in the chair. A few days before, I remembered, the monthly program for the various cultural events at the County Museum had come in the mail. Because I was distracted by other things at the time I hadn't opened it. In fact, it was some time now before I could find it. After some searching I found it on the mantelpiece, in a pile of advertising circulars and other unopened mail.

I slit the envelope open and pulled out the brochure. When I had read about halfway down the page I came to the film listings, and as I grasped what I was reading my nerves gave a little jump. I glanced at the calendar. The films were always on the second Friday of the month. It was tonight.

After a little thought I called up Belinda and asked her if she would like to go to the movies. I knew she was free on Friday evenings and we had gone to films in this series before. She said 'All right' in her usual matter-of-fact way, cheerfully but also without enthusiasm.

I drove to pick her up in the Hudson phaeton. She had a small studio apartment on Budlong not far from the USC campus. By long custom I didn't go in to get her at the door; I just tapped on the horn. She came out and got in the car without a word, in a slim jersey skirt, a sleeveless sweater, and some ceramic costume jewelry, with flat sandals that left her ankles bare. She never wore hose. Her blond hair was loose and she pushed it back carelessly with her hands. She was tanned, blithe, and slightly ironic as usual. We didn't talk very much in the drive out to the Museum. Once she said, 'Been working in the library?'

She meant the Doheny at USC. I said, 'In the L.A. Public, downtown.'

'You should get more fresh air. You're looking rather pale.'

'Pale?'

'Pale and hectic. You have an Edvard Munch look. As though pursued by demons.'

I didn't comment on this image. 'How do you get *your* tan?' I asked her.

'There's a reflector booth in the health club I belong to. I spend a couple of hours a week in it.'

'I thought you used to play tennis.'

'I did,' she said, 'but in the reflector booth you can get tanned all over.'

I didn't take up this gambit, if that was what it was. We arrived at Wilshire and Fairfax and I put the car in the May Company parking structure. We walked out through the store and across the street to the Museum.

She caught me covertly examining her, and she saw that I was looking at her tan. 'If you

129

don't believe me,' she said, 'I'm prepared to prove it.' She smiled. I was struck with something odd and slightly artificial about her. Then I realized it was her pale pink lipstick, almost white, which stood out strikingly against her tan. Her blond hair too was lighter than her skin. It was as though she were a photographic negative of a dark-haired woman with dark lipstick. For some reason I found this repulsive and at the same time attractive.

We went into the lecture hall and found some seats. I took the folded program out of my pocket and studied it again. By now I knew it almost by heart. There were some comedy shorts and then a pair of two-reelers, *The Coquette* with Moira Silver and *The Great Emancipator* starring Charles Morton and directed by Hans Reiter. It seemed that this second film was supposed to be socially significant. 'THE GREAT EMANCIPATOR. *1924*. The first picture in which the young and adolescent Hollywood deliberately came to grips with political issues, even if only at a rudimentary level. Lincoln is shown not only as a myth figure and folk hero, but as a political thinker of a certain profundity, struggling with the problems of freedom and responsibility and of the human condition. This early Reiter film marks a step forward in the political development of the director who is later to become a prominent anti-Fascist, and then to be banned from the screen in the Fifties as one of the controversial Hollywood Ten.'

It didn't have much to say about *The Coquette*. '1925. Hans Reiter, Director. John Condon, the Bogart of the Silent Era, demonstrates his skill at sinister and blasé eroticism. This two-reeler set in Paris is Moira Silver's first starring vehicle. Bryan Gilbert and Mary Frances are seen in supporting roles.' I handed the program to Belinda. She glanced over it for a moment and then stuck it into the space between our two seats.

The lights went down and the comic shorts came on. Some firemen in oversized helmets dashed around at terrific velocity trying to extinguish a burning barn. They pulled out a hose from the fire truck, stuck it into a duck pond, and then started up their pump. Along with the water, ducks, geese, smaller waterbirds, and finally a large and indignant white swan came flying out of the nozzle and hurtled toward the flames. The farmer, a yokel in Dutch chin-whiskers, took off his straw hat and stamped on it in rage. In the other short some boys chased a flapping chicken which suddenly swelled until it was four feet tall. They dashed back across the screen in the other direction, the chicken now chasing the boys. They ran through a henhouse where men were at work plucking chicken corpses. When they emerged from this the boys were covered with feathers and the chicken was nude, still in hot pursuit.

Belinda laughed. I pulled out the program and tried to study it again as well as I could in the semidarkness. It didn't tell me any more than it had before. Moira's name was mentioned only once, and then only in passing. When I looked up Belinda was still laughing and the boys, feathers streaming from them, had fled into a bank where a bunch of comic cops were chasing some inept robbers around and around in circles, leaping over counters and vaulting over the benumbed employees. The robbers dropped unbelievable amounts of money from their open suitcases as they ran. The boys shot out the other door of the bank, now covered with ten-dollar bills instead of feathers.

'THE END.' Some dots, streaks, and black frames with numbers ran through the projector, and the lights came on again. Belinda took a breath to recover from her laughing spasms. Everyone else had been laughing too. The hall was only about half full but the comedy shorts had produced a great air of camaraderie. People looked at each other and grinned.

Next came *The Coquette*. When the familiar face floated onto the screen I felt a kind of cool slow shock, a vibration of the nerves. There were not very many close-ups, and Moira was seen only in full-length views, with an occasional medium shot so that she was visible from the waist up. The photography was crude, with hardly any shading or nuance; she resembled a plaster statue with dark expressive eyes. She spent most of her time turned away from the camera talking to the other characters and then listening as they replied. There were many captions. Only now and then did she direct her drooping, faintly mysterious glance toward the camera. Each time she did so I felt a trickle of icewater running through my limbs. I scarcely noticed the other characters, and anyhow the plot was so rudimentary that it was hardly worth following. Moira, as Renée Renaudet, a French girl no better than she should be, was engaged to marry a businessman, Bryan Gilbert. The caption explained,

BUT SHE HAS NOT TOLD HIM OF
HER SULLIED PAST.

The past turned up in the form of John Condon, his hair slicked greasily down onto his head, who was described as a 'theatrical manager' but was obviously a pimp. He threatened to reveal Moira's secret to her rich fiancé unless she returned to her former trade (the theater of course). She pouted, vacillated, and stared at him languorously from under her dark lids.

HELPLESS, HE TOO BEGINS TO FALL
UNDER HER CHARM.

133

Finally she made a deal with him. She led him into a cheap hotel. The screen went black again.

A HALF AN HOUR LATER.

They came out, Moira now a free woman, although there was a mask of shame visible on her face like a faint spiderweb. The ending, I thought, was neatly done. Of course it was Condon's picture and not Moira's. Instead of following her back to the obligatory clinch with her intended, the camera stayed with Condon as he glanced around once at her departing figure, shrugged, and idled on down the boulevard, a cigarette dangling carelessly from his lips. Sure enough, on the next street corner he found another 'actress' to manage. This one had a dark Mediterranean face and a sullen manner, so the audience didn't mind if she was 'sullied.' She and Condon went off together, and he pointed down the street at a client for her to proposition. Iris out. THE END.

The lights went on again.

'I do love that old corn,' said Belinda.

I said nothing. I felt cold and odd, a little light-headed.

'And now, it seems,' she said, 'we have social significance.'

The hall darkened again and the titles for *The*

Great Emancipator came on. Charles Morton, in rustic garb and without his beard, was seen splitting rails. Still young but in a clean white shirt, he addressed a political gathering in Illinois. He ran for President. He was inaugurated and paced about in a melancholy way in a White House made of canvas flats. He spoke in gentle terms to his wife Mary Todd Lincoln about her unfortunate tendency to insanity. 'Mary, you must...' The two of them disappeared for a few seconds while the white letters trembled on the black screen.

'MARY, YOU MUST GET A GRIP ON YOURSELF.'

They reappeared, as Morton silently mouthed 'yourself.' She got a grip on herself, the War began, and Blue and Gray soldiers charged up and down hills, spiking cannons and falling dead. This grieved Lincoln, or Morton, so that long wrinkles full of shadows appeared in his cheeks. He had his beard by this time, and almost as we watched white hairs appeared in it on account of the War.

'MARY, MEN ARE DYING AND
I MUST ACCEPT THE RESPONSIBILITY.'

Evidently this was what the program meant by calling him 'a political thinker of a certain profundity.' The plot of a silent film, I reflected, could somehow make even the life of Lincoln seem implausible. Mary hardly paid attention to him because she was about to go crazy again. This only added to his concerns and the wrinkles grew deeper. The makeup girl was busy with her black grease brush.

A shot of some graves on a grassy hillside. Back to Morton again. He had his stovepipe hat on now and was standing on a platform draped with bunting. He raised his hands in various histrionic gestures.

'BUT, IN A LARGER SENSE.'

The camera cut to the crowd, who were listening intently, and then back to Morton.

'WE CANNOT DEDICATE.'

He lowered his right arm and stretched out the left. He disappeared from the screen again while the white letters, bobbing slightly, remained for somewhat longer than was necessary to read them.

'WE CANNOT CONSECRATE.'

Another shot of the crowd. A man standing in the front row uncrossed his arms and crossed them the other way.

136

His wrinkles seemed to deepen. He turned toward the crowd and spread out his arms.

'THIS GROUND.'

The short crude takes and the wobbling captions on the black screen continued in alternation, one after the other. Morton had his stovepipe hat off now and was talking to his wife, who seemed not so much demented as bewitched. She stared into the camera wide-eyed and pale, as though she could see into the future.

'MARY, MY MIND IS MADE UP.'

I began to feel odd again. There was a kind of cold empty place inside me, as though one of my viscera were missing.

'I AM GOING TO FORD'S THEATRE TONIGHT
NO MATTER WHAT THE DANGER.'

Mrs. Lincoln raised her hands in remonstration, begging him to stay in the safety of the canvas White House. But his expression firmed and his brow deepened in thought.

'I MUST SHOW MYSELF TO THE PEOPLE.'

137

The camera, still fixed on Lincoln's face, did a fade. It wasn't an iris-out or a blur-out. I wasn't quite sure how it was done. The figure on the screen slowly evaporated in a ghostly way, as though it were made of sugar and dissolving into water. A few uncut frames flicked by, scarred with dashes and white spots, and then there was another caption.

THAT NIGHT, AT THE THEATER.

I closed my eyes. I could hear programs rustling, people shifting in their seats, a whisper or two, and a faint mechanical murmur that was perhaps the projector running in the closed booth to the rear. I could feel Belinda's bare arm touching my own. I opened my eyes again. Lincoln and Mary were gravely watching the play, he all hung over with philosophical resignation, she twitching with anxiety.

BOOTH, THE DISAFFECTED ACTOR AND
CONFEDERATE SYMPATHIZER

I shut my eyes again. When I opened them a few seconds later the caption had changed.

. . . STEALS UNNOTICED INTO THE THEATER.

A figure appeared on the screen, horse pistol

in hand, glancing over his shoulder to be sure no one was following. I caught a glimpse of a thin handsome face frozen into a grimace of determination, a kind of a wince. It was visible only for an instant. The vacuum inside me widened until I felt I was only an empty space. All at once I was in the grip of an uncontrollable terror. I stood up, seizing Belinda's arm.

'What is it?'

Without answering I pulled her after me. We crossed the row of seats to the aisle, stepping on everyone's feet and raising a murmur of protests. People stared at me, either because I was acting strangely or because they too had recognized me on the screen, I wasn't sure which. I didn't look back at the screen. Releasing Belinda's arm, I hurried up the slightly inclined carpet to the rear of the hall and out into the lobby. She followed me.

She was only mildly exasperated. 'For heaven's sake. What's the matter?'

'Nothing.'

'You started up like Macbeth at the sight of Banquo's ghost.'

'That's what I saw.'

'I don't know what you're talking about. Don't you feel well?'

'Didn't you see it?'

'I saw a rather bad picture about Lincoln.'

I didn't say anything to this.

'Was it because you thought it was such a bad

picture?'

'No.' After a moment I said, 'It was just that I thought I saw . . . somebody I knew.'

'In the audience?'

'On the screen.'

'Charles Morton has been dead for thirty years.'

'Yes.'

After that we didn't talk very much. I asked her, 'Have you ever had that dream where you go to a funeral and approach the casket and look in, and the corpse is you?' She said, 'It's in every psychology book.' We walked around the corner and into the side entrance of the parking structure, since the May Company was closed by this time. Belinda still seemed to be more amused than puzzled. She was used to my eccentricities by this time, although this—she evidently felt—was one of the more bizarre ones. I allowed her to think whatever she wanted. We got into the car and I drove it rather violently out onto the street.

After a block or two on Wilshire, seeking about for some kind of conventional phrase to articulate, I said in a rather strangled tone, 'Where do you want to go now?'

'It's still only eleven. We could go to a late movie.'

Seeing that her attempts at humor didn't amuse me, she inquired after a moment, 'What did *you* have in mind?'

'Would you like to come back to St. Albans Place?'

'I'd be enchanted.'

'For a drink,' I said savagely

*   *   *

She often came back to the house with me, of course, after we had been out in the evening to a concert or a film. Our behavior was always quite correct—a drink or two, perhaps a kiss or a light embrace—all playful and committing neither of us to anything. But this night was different, and we both knew it. I handed her a Bacardi on the rocks and she sipped it, regarding me gravely over the rim of the glass. I set my own glass down and began pacing around slowly in the big living room.

'It seems you have something on your mind,' she said.

She was a nice person, really. She wanted to help. But I wasn't sure I could explain it to her. The sight of my own face on the screen had disoriented me so badly that I wasn't sure any longer who or where I was. The word *estrangement* came to me and hung fixed in my thoughts. Everything seemed strange to me, as though I had never seen it before: the house, Belinda, my own body, even my own thoughts. There were two explanations, it seemed to me, for what had happened—for what was happening. One was that the world behind the Screen really existed and I had really been there, and that a little rift through to this world had been broken when I caught a glimpse of my own face in the Lincoln film. The other was that the general oddness of my life and the strain I had been through recently had induced a mild nervous disorder—that I had simply fallen in love with a picture in an old fan magazine, and my visit behind the Screen and my encounter with Moira had been only a harmless hallucination, or a waking dream, rather than something that had really happened. According to Ziff, some psychiatrist had said that it was all in my mind. In this case, I would have to pretend that I had not seen my own face appearing in the Lincoln film, that I had simply mistaken some other person for myself, and also that my recollection of having previously acted the part before the camera was somehow a false memory that had formed in my mind *after* I had seen the Lincoln film at the Museum. Whichever it was, that glimpse of the uncanny in the flat black-and-white world of the screen had frightened me to the point where I felt that my only chance of recovering reality, of recovering my sanity, was to take shelter in Belinda's arms, the only warm and living flesh immediately available, in an embrace that would reassure me of the existence of the daily and mortal world. I switched on the stereo and dropped a record onto the turntable: the 'Dance of the Seven Veils' from *Salome*.

She began to laugh. 'Where on earth did you find that?'

'In a sale bin at the drugstore. It's very sensuous, don't you think? Let's go up to the bedroom.'

'All right,' she said, 'as long as we can hear this beautiful music from there.'

We went up the stairs with our drinks, taking the record with us. She looked around curiously. She had never been in the bedroom before. 'Why all the mirrors?'

'It gives me something to look at.'

'Now you can look at me.'

It was true. Everywhere I looked I could see the two of us: she calm and amused, I distracted, nervous, and jerky. I felt desire though—an adequate amount, in my estimation, although it was marginal. I was desperately anxious for the thing to come off, feeling that it was my only chance to retain my grasp on the solid world that I felt fading and slipping away from me by the moment, like Lincoln dissolving on the screen. I turned to her and took her in my arms and we engaged in a long cinematographic clinch. I could feel her neat hard breasts against my chest, and I raised my hand with the idea of caressing one of them. Then I changed my mind and decided to wait until later, although I had the impression that she drew the upper part of her body away slightly in order to permit this gesture in case I attempted it. We separated and I took another sip of my drink, which I had set down on the antique sideboard.

Behind me—as I could see in the series of mirrors on the walls of the room—she began lazily pulling off her clothes. I too began undressing. In the mirrors I could see not only myself, multiplied a dozen or more times, but her own image from every possible direction, front, back, and sides. The costume jewelry came off, then the jersey skirt and sweater. She kicked off the flat-heeled sandals. Even through her slip I could see she didn't wear a bra, and in any case I had felt this clearly when I embraced her. The slip came off, leaving her clad in a tiny fragment of bikini underwear. She was right; the reflector booth tanned her all over. I tried not to look as the triangle of nylon came off, since my degree of desire was already adequate, but this was difficult with so many mirrors in the room.

I was still facing toward the sideboard, unbuttoning the last button on my shirt. At that precise point my eye caught the picture in the silver frame on the sideboard. I stopped what I was doing as though frozen; it was as though the projector had jammed and left me fixed in that single frame, motionless and paralyzed. For a long time I stood that way without moving a

144

muscle and without taking my eyes from the picture. My thoughts were utterly vacant except for the image of that paper-pale face with its dark eyes and its thin and sensitive mouth. After a long time, numbly, as though I were awakening from a sleep, I began rebuttoning the shirt again.

★   ★   ★

Belinda didn't say much on the way back to her apartment. There was an odd little set about her mouth I had never noticed before. Yet she still seemed, in most ways, her usual blithe self. It was after midnight and there was almost no traffic. The big Hudson went down Vermont Avenue through a mainly black district of small shops and apartment houses. She was sitting on the far side of the front seat leaning against the door. After a while she said distantly, 'Could you stop at a drugstore? I need to buy a vibrator.'

I glanced at her sharply. 'There aren't any open at this time of night.'

She only smiled. When I stopped in front of her apartment on Budlong she got out, said, 'Bye,' and disappeared into the darkness of the doorway. I made a U-turn and started back, enveloped in my private thoughts and driving so slowly that on Vermont a police car pulled up and examined me for a few seconds before accelerating away ahead of me down the avenue. The lights of the city floated by, dreamily. I could hardly hear the whisper of the tires on the pavement. Perhaps, I thought, I had gone a little deaf. It was no doubt a functional condition that would disappear after the effects of the evening wore off.

I eased the Hudson into the garage and carefully shut the door. The lights were still on downstairs and I left them on. As I remember, I didn't even bother to lock the front door. I went up to the bedroom and began unbuttoning my shirt again before the sideboard, going through exactly the same motions that I had a half an hour before. The picture frame was still in the same position on the polished ebony surface before me. When I was half undressed I stopped and stood there for a long time, staring at the face in the picture. After a while a very faint murmur, a whisper as though of a voice singing absentmindedly in an undertone with pauses between the phrases, seemed to come out of the past, out of the walls perhaps or out of the photograph I had thrust away into the drawer.

> 'Ain't misbehavin' . . .
> I'm savin' my-self
> For you . . .'

CHAPTER NINE

I had to talk to Nesselrode. But for some reason he was ignoring me now. I hadn't encountered him face to face for some time, and I caught only occasional glimpses of him in the house. I knew he was still there, because sometimes at night I would hear the stairway creaking as he went up to bed, and now and then in the morning, alerted by the sound of the front door closing, I would look out the window and see him hurrying away down the sidewalk in the direction of the rusted gate on Olympic. He generally went out in the daytime, some time between the middle of the morning and noon, and came back late at night. I left a note for him, and then another, thumb-tacked to the hat rack in the entry where he would see them when he came in. 'Mr. Nesselrode, I have to see you.' And: 'It's about the rent.' (He still had never paid me anything for the room.) And: 'Mr. Nesselrode, you cannot go on staying here under this arrangement. Please see me.'

These veiled references to the possibility of eviction, however, failed to move him, or perhaps he never saw the notes. I decided to lie in ambush for him. Now that the big oaken table was gone I had set up a card table in the dining room, and I sat there half the morning every day reading the newspaper and lingering over my coffee. With the door open I could clearly see through the living room to the stairway. He had no way to get out of the house without coming down the stairs. In spite of his extraordinary powers I didn't believe him capable of levitation, or even of going out the window and clambering down the outside of the house. He was an old man after all. It shouldn't be all that difficult to cut him off in some way and confront him.

A week passed and I hadn't managed to catch him. He always eluded me in some way or another, or perhaps he sensed that I was lurking for him and didn't go out. Then one morning, in the silence of the empty house, I heard the familiar sound of the stairway creaking. But he came down the stairs faster than I expected, and he was out the door and away down the sidewalk before I scarcely had time to get out of my chair.

I hurried out after him. To my surprise he turned left, toward the Wilshire entrance to the park with its guarded gate, rather than to the right toward Olympic. I could see him a block or so ahead, scuttling away down the sidewalk with his overcoat floating. When I got to the gate at Wilshire there was no sign of him and I couldn't tell which way he had turned.

I went back to the guard in his small kiosk. The usual daytime guard was a young man who seemed to be a part-time college student; I never found out precisely. He seemed to be intelligent, because he was usually working on calculus assignments, as well as I could tell, when he had nothing else to do. But he was afflicted with a bad stammer, which probably disqualified him for any other sort of job.

'Did you see an old man . . .'

He looked up with a pleasant expression from his paper covered with hieroglyphic calculations.

'The old man who came out just now. In the overcoat. Which way did he turn?'

'M-m-m-man. C-c-c-came. No.' He smiled.

*   *   *

It was that same afternoon, as I remember, that I received a telephone call from a person who didn't identify himself. When the phone rang the thought occurred to me for some reason that it was Nesselrode. There was no reason for him to call me, but nobody else ever called me in the daytime either, and if someone like Belinda called it was usually in the evening. I picked up the phone and a strange male voice said, 'Alys,' not at all in a questioning tone, simply pronouncing the word as a matter of fact.

'Yes.'

'I'm calling for Mr. Ziff. He says to tell you that ice cream is bad for you.'

'It is?'

'Especially the richer flavors.'

'Richer flavors?'

'Like Tutti Frutti. And Nesselrode.'

'Tell him to mind his own business. I'm not a child any more.'

He didn't contest the point. He simply hung up, having delivered his message. I wasn't sure that what I had told him was true. I might have been an adult in the legal sense, but I wasn't sure I was in the eyes of Ziff, or Nesselrode either, and I was beginning to have doubts about the matter myself. Such metaphysical questions aside, this telephone call annoyed me, and only fixed me in my resolve to run down Nesselrode somehow and—talk to him. 'Mr. Nesselrode,' I prepared my speech, 'I want to get back in pictures.' And 'Mr. Nesselrode, I'm not a child.' And: 'Mr. Nesselrode, you've been eluding me. That isn't fair, and you also stole my camel saddle and my oaken table and my toaster, and my Arabic paper knife.' Or, if I didn't say these things to him, I would say something or other.

The cat-and-mouse game went on. I suspected that Nesselrode was playing with me, although he had never shown any signs of a sense of humor. Perhaps he was merely sadistic. I remembered his cutting out and mutilating the paper dolls. The impulse to sadism was not so very different from comedy after all. They both involved disturbing the natural order and disorienting a person through treating him as an object rather than as a conscient being—for example when a comedian slips on a banana peel and is converted into nothing but a weight subject to the laws of physics. This would account for the extraordinary amount of violence in most silent comedies. People were always slapping each other or stepping on rakes that struck them violently in the back of the head. Comedy was the infliction of pain in a way not permanently damaging to the subject, and pleasing to the audience. Perhaps I could write a monograph on this subject, I thought, as soon as I got my other affairs straightened out.

Finally, a couple of days later (by this time I no longer drank coffee and read the newspaper; I sat in the chair with my hands on my knees, ready to leap), I managed to rush out of the house after him nimbly enough so that when I got to the sidewalk I was only a few yards behind him. I quickened my pace but so did he; it was astonishing and slightly uncanny to observe the speed he could accelerate to without breaking into a run. Neither did I run; I felt somehow that this would not be acceptable under the rules of our game. For me to run after him would be a kind of effrontery, a rudeness, which might well defeat my own purposes. I couldn't imagine myself saying what I wanted to say to him if I caught up to him on the run and grabbed his shoulder, panting.

I followed on after him walking as fast as I could, my legs moving in the gestures of that curiously artificial and absurd-looking sport, the walking race. It was very tiring, I found. I passed the guard in his kiosk. He mouthed, 'M-m-m-m...' and then gave up and smiled.

When I came out onto Wilshire I saw that Nesselrode had turned to the right in the downtown direction. He had gained a little on me while I was smiling at the guard and was a half a block away now, almost at the corner of Western. From all signs he hadn't noticed that I was behind him. I walking-raced on after him down Wilshire, across Western on the light, through MacArthur Park, over a sunken freeway with traffic streaming by in both directions, and into the downtown district. Wilshire ended at Grand, and Nesselrode crossed over to Sixth Street. At Broadway, only a little farther on, he turned right and then crossed to the opposite side.

Broadway was a kind of colorful and tawdry bazaar, thronging with pedestrians like an Algerian souk, decorated with flashy tin signs and pulsing neon lights, lined with cheap restaurants, pawnshops, cut-rate clothing stores, and fruit-juice stands. Nesselrode threaded his way through the crowd. A half a block down the street—after a glance behind him that failed, I was sure, to notice me—he disappeared into Clifton's Cafeteria.

I was familiar with this place. It had been there a long time; it dated from the epoch when Broadway was still the main thoroughfare of the city and the center of its shopping district. On the outside was a kind of Art Deco front with the name spelled out in neon letters. Inside it was a huge room decorated with plaster cliffs and boulders, with alpine terraces, running brooks, and waterfalls. There were two big redwood trunks with shaggy bark holding up the ceiling, and on one wall was a rustic shrine with a blue neon cross glowing over it. There was no sign of Nesselrode. I wasn't worried because I was sure he was in the place somewhere. I walked through to the rear, took a tray, and threaded my way through the steamy labyrinth of the serving counters.

I emerged after a few moments with a Salisbury steak, so called, and a mound of mashed potatoes the size of a hat. With a cup of coffee it came to a dollar eighty-six. I remembered my lunch with Ziff at the Bistro, which had cost fifty dollars. Of course that included the wine. But it struck me now for the first time that there was at least one resemblance between the two establishments. They were both fake. The Bistro was a fake French café, and Clifton's was a fake alpine landscape. Feeling pleased with myself for some reason at this discovery, I carried my tray off through the Alps.

It didn't take me long to find Nesselrode. He was sitting at a little table half hidden behind a pillar camouflaged to resemble a tree. He raised his head and caught my eye at the same moment. He showed no sign of surprise.

I put down my tray on the table and sat down. He twitched his nose at me. Then he examined what I had on my tray. He made a kind of grimace. 'How can you eat all that dead animal and starch?' he muttered. His own menu was austere: a plain lettuce salad with no dressing, a carton of yogurt, a pair of toasted rusks, and a large glass of what appeared to be vegetable juice.

I decided to take the offensive immediately, ignoring his comment on my own eating habits.

'I thought you told me you never ate.'

'I did?'

'I asked you to dinner once, and you said you never ate.'

He said evasively, 'I eat here. I meant I never eat at home.'

'At home?'

'At your house,' he said, shifting even more uncomfortably in his chair.

I elected not to bring up the cabbages and carrots I had seen him carrying up the stairs, or the empty V-8 cans in the wastebasket.

'Why not?'

'No reason. In place of home, I eat here.' A silence. He put several forkfuls of the lettuce

154

into his mouth, working his cheeks as he chewed. When he had swallowed he said, 'I don't eat much. An old man like me. A little keeps me alive.' Another attack on the lettuce, and more systematic mastication. He swallowed and said, 'When I was only a boy just from Austria, Clifton's gave me to eat for free.'

It was true that Clifton's, from the time of the Depression, had a policy that if you didn't have enough to pay for a meal, you could pay what you had. Of course Nesselrode wasn't 'a boy just from Austria' in 1929. Trying to get some information out of him was like unraveling a pair of copulating snakes. I went cheerfully chattering on. 'The prices are still reasonable. And the decorations are interesting.'

'Oh, ya.' He wasn't quite sure what I was up to.

'But that's not what I want to talk to you about.'

'No. You're like everybody else. You want to get into pictures.'

It seemed to me there was a light trace of sarcasm in his manner now, a thing I wouldn't have thought him capable of. I waited for him to go on, but he said nothing. Having disposed of the salad, he started on the yogurt, which he alternated with bites of rusk. His cheeks worked rhythmically.

'Mr. Nesselrode, all I want is another chance.'

He stopped and peered at me narrowly. He swallowed what he was chewing. Still holding the half-eaten rusk in his hand, he embarked into what was for him a rather long and philosophical speech.

'Many another young man has said that. But life is pitiless. It doesn't give to you another chance.' A pause. He seemed to evaluate me through his half-closed eyes, while at the same time behaving as though he preferred not to look at me directly, turning his glance to the side now and then or looking over the top of my head. He worked his mouth, then spoke again. 'Just sometimes it does,' he said equivocally.

This slight encouragement was enough. I pressed him.

'Where are you going after lunch, Mr. Nesselrode?'

'I have business,' he said evasively.

'Do you mind if I go with you?'

My heart was in my throat. I tried to appear as casual and offhand as I could. He narrowed one eye and focused on me again. 'The other time, you had a chance and you made an escapade.'

'Nothing happened. It was perfectly innocent.'

'When you are in pictures,' he advised, 'it is better not to have attachments to people.' As though afraid that I wouldn't follow this, he added, 'Especially those of one sex or the other.

156

I myself,' he said almost proudly, 'have no friends.'

'Not even Reiter?'

He stared in alarm around the crowded cafeteria and lowered his voice. 'What are you saying? Don't speak. Somebody might hear.'

'Let's go, shall we?'

'What's your hurry? So impatient. You young people.'

He drained his vegetable juice, in one long swallow in fact, as though he himself were in a hurry. He looked around for his paper napkin, found it on the floor, retrieved it, and wiped his mouth. 'You're all alike. You want to be a star already, when you don't even know how to make a face.'

I wasn't sure whether he was referring to acting technique or to the art of makeup. It didn't matter. We stood up. My own lunch was almost untouched.

'Aren't you going to eat all that dead animal and starch?'

'No, I'm not hungry.'

'Throwing away your money. Foolish. You young people. When I was a boy, just from Austria . . .'

We threaded our way down the alpine slope, crossed a brook on a little stone bridge, and left.

CHAPTER TEN

It was a long way from the downtown district out to Pico and La Cienega. But Nesselrode, with his mysterious pedestrianism, set out on foot down the sidewalk, although there were buses constantly going past us on both sides of the street. He immediately struck a pace so brisk that I had trouble keeping up with him. It was a warm day, and besides I was tired from chasing him all the way down Wilshire into town.

In spite of his rabbity way of bolting down the sidewalk, he too seemed a little less than his usual energetic self. He seemed to wheeze a little and suck the air as though he had difficulty getting it into his lungs. Once I saw him raise his arm and wipe furtively at his eye with the sleeve of his coat. If you exercised at all violently, this saffron-tinged air soon left your throat scratchy and your lungs began to get sore. I considered asking him to moderate his pace a little, but after all I was the one who had invited myself on this expedition and I could only try to keep up with him as best I could.

Once in a while we would be stopped by a traffic light and that would give us a moment's rest. But, as I had already noticed when I had gone walking with him on a previous occasion,

Nesselrode seemed to have an extraordinary luck with traffic lights. Again and again a red light would turn green just as we approached the intersection. Another instance, perhaps, of his sorcerer's powers. But he had been walking around the city for many years, after all, and probably he had mastered the rhythm of the lights so that he was able to quicken or slacken his pace to arrive at each corner just as the light turned green.

It was somewhere past Arlington, about halfway out to the West Side, that I first began to notice signs of a more serious fatigue in him. His face was greenish and he seemed to have even more difficulty in breathing. We were both perspiring. I noticed that the sweat on his upper lip ran down the scar at the center, which collected it like a tiny rain gutter. Once, out of the corner of my eye, I saw him wiping his eyes again with the sleeve of his coat. When he saw I was watching him he looked away.

'You young people any more,' he said. 'No stamina. A walk like this is nothing. When I was a strong young man your age . . .'

He didn't say what he had done. To judge from the photos in *Picture Land*, he had spent a good deal of his time in night clubs. A little farther on, a block or two west of Crenshaw, I became aware that he wasn't at my side any more, and when I turned around I saw him leaning against a lamp post a few yards behind,

159

clutching it with both hands. But he did so as though he were inspecting the lamp post for secret reasons of his own. Perhaps he was considering putting it in pictures. I didn't think this was very likely; it was a perfectly ordinary lamp post and it was solidly set in concrete. He examined it, twitched his nose at it one last time, and went on.

It was because I turned around to see why he was lingering at the lamp post, however, that I first noticed the car behind. It caught my attention because instead of moving in the stream of traffic it was creeping along at a walking pace with its wheels next to the curb, a half a block or so behind us. It was a perfectly ordinary car, a late-model Olds Cutlass of a nondescript gray-green color. Because it was afternoon now and we were walking west, the sun shone on the windshield with an opaque glare so that I couldn't tell anything about the occupants of the car, or even whether there was more than one of them. I stole a glance at Nesselrode. He never looked behind him and didn't seem to have noticed.

Abruptly, without saying anything to me, he came to a halt at a rickety health-food stand on a street corner. We stood for a few moments under the shade of a piece of garishly painted plywood that swung out to form an awning when the place opened. Nesselrode ordered a large glass of carrot juice, and I took apple juice, although I was very thirsty and would have preferred a glass of plain water.

The glasses were not very clean. Nesselrode put his down on the counter again and said, 'More carrot juice.' I glanced around. The gray-green Cutlass had stopped and was waiting across the intersection a few hundred yards away.

'Have another apple juice,' suggested Nesselrode.

'Thanks, no.'

'Try celery juice. Or celery and carrot, a mixture.'

I smiled and shook my head.

'Carrot juice,' he said, 'makes you see in the dark.'

'Is that so?'

He allowed me to pay for the juices. Then he wiped his mouth with his coat sleeve and set off down the street without a word. I followed at his side. The stop seemed to have refreshed him and he went back to striding along almost at his normal pace, although the sulfurous air still seemed to be bothering his eyes. I permitted myself another look around. Nesselrode was still exerting his sorcery over the traffic lights. We had crossed Fairfax on the green, but it had turned red just as the Cutlass approached the intersection. It was waiting there in the right-hand lane, its silvery windshield impenetrable to the eye. I noticed for the first time that there was a tiny antenna on top of the roof, not more than a foot long and as thin as a hair. I noticed it only because it caught the gleam of the sunlight for an instant.

★   ★   ★

We crossed La Cienega and then turned left on it, so that we were going down the right-hand side of the street. The Cutlass had to wait for the left-turn light and was quite a distance behind us by the time we reached Pico. Here we caught another green light; Nesselrode loped on across the pavement with his coattails flapping and I followed. The Alhambra was ahead on the right, only a short distance away. At this point I became aware of another car that was acting strangely. This one was somewhat more elegant and more conspicuous: a Pontiac Firebird coupé in violet with fiery gold pinstriping. It was coming toward us in the other direction. What it did that was unusual was that it swerved across the center line and pulled up at the curb on the wrong side of the street, directly in front of the theater.

We went on toward it. I looked around. The Cutlass had stopped a couple of blocks away, just after it had crossed Pico.

When we arrived in front of the Alhambra I hesitated and slowed a little. Nesselrode had still apparently not noticed either car. The door of the Firebird opened and Ziff got out. Since he had parked on the wrong side of the street he only had to open the door and step out onto the sidewalk. He stood there in front of the theater blocking our way. In place of his safari jacket and silver pants he now wore a sort of mauve leisure suit with a dark violet shirt, perhaps to match the car. I saw now that the car had what looked like enormous butterfly wings painted in gold on it, beginning at the front and expanding to their full size under the rear windows, done in elaborate filigrees by an expert pinstriper. Nesselrode stared at the car and then at Ziff, working his nose.

'Where do you think you're going, Alys?'

'Look here, Mr. Ziff. I don't know who you are exactly, but you have no right to interfere with my movements or even to pursue me around town in two cars like this. That's harassment.'

'Illegal,' put in Nesselrode. He seemed slightly alarmed by the incident but not at all surprised by it.

'You're making a mistake, Alys. It isn't real. The whole thing is bad. I explained this to you before.'

'Thanks for explaining it. I know what I'm doing. Now will you please stand aside?'

Instead he took hold of my lapel in a friendly, almost paternal way. 'I don't think you entirely understand the situation, Alys.'

I reached up to his hand and pulled it away. 'I'm just going to see a movie with my friend here Mr. Nesselrode, the famous producer.'

'Don't mention names,' Nesselrode muttered.

'He's a fake.'

Nesselrode looked furtively around. 'Perhaps someone could go for a policeman,' he suggested to the absolutely deserted sidewalk.

Ziff took hold of my shoulder this time. 'Alys, why don't we get in the car and drive around for a little bit. There are all kinds of things I want to explain to you.'

'Don't get in the car,' Nesselrode advised the lamp post at the edge of the sidewalk.

'So are you coming, Alys, or shall I say a word on my car phone to my friends down the street?' His Firebird, I now saw, had another little hairlike antenna on top of it exactly like the one on the Cutlass.

'What friends?' said Nesselrode, apparently seized with anxiety all at once. He looked down the street and seemed to catch sight of the Cutlass immediately. 'Gangsters. Capable of assault and battering even. Let's go.' He took hold of my arm.

Ziff's hand was on my shoulder, and he slipped it down and grasped the other arm. 'You see, Alys, I'm just acting in your own interest. I don't think you're necessarily aware of what you're getting into here. It's like a kid,' he said,

164

'climbing a tree. You're going up the wrong branch.'

I entered into this dialogue as in a nightmare. I knew it almost by heart by now. '*Ars longa, vita brevis.*'

'Art is long, Alys. But Art is artificial. Life is real.'

'Let go of my arm and we can discuss it like two civilized human beings. There's something to be said for Art after all.'

'What?'

'In Art we are not subject to time. As you yourself said, Art is immortal.'

The three of us were still standing on the sidewalk in the hot sun. 'Yes,' he said, assuming a reasonable classroom manner, 'but Art itself is not real. Our belief in the reality of Art, or more precisely what Coleridge describes as the willing suspension of disbelief, is in itself a form of mental illness.'

'Ah yes, your psychiatrist friend. But after all, he said it was all in my mind.'

'Everything is in your mind, Alys. I'm only in your mind.'

'As far as I'm concerned you can get out of it,' I gritted between my teeth. 'There are plenty of other things in there and I don't need you.'

He pulled from one side, Nesselrode from the other. Between them they might have pulled me apart, like the Cloven Viscount in Calvino's novel, except that neither one was pulling very

165

hard. There was a stylized, almost balletic quality to the whole thing. A black woman across the street, out walking with a little boy, had stopped to watch. Nesselrode might have shouted to her to call a policeman, but I knew he didn't really want a policeman. The policeman would only get involved in the discussion between Ziff and me on Life and Art and after a while he would lose his head. Besides I could not really swear to a police officer that Ziff was exerting force on me against my will.

They were both pulling hard enough, however, so that my shoulder joints were beginning to stretch a little. 'How about you, Mr. Nesselrode?' I inquired. 'Which do you think is more important. Life or Art?'

'The boy could be a star,' muttered Nesselrode between his teeth, again not to me or to Ziff particularly, just to the sidewalk at large.

'Where are the stars?' inquired Ziff, still pulling on his side. 'Do you see any around here? Are they walking the streets of Los Angeles today?'

'Don't speak,' Nesselrode advised me. 'Don't engage in talking with the man. He is a gangster. He is right now committing assault with personal damage.'

'He isn't, really,' I said, 'although his friends might. But he can't call his friends on his car phone until he lets go of my arm.'

Ziff let go of my arm and made a leap toward

166

his Firebird. He opened the door and began talking into a violet telephone. Nesselrode and I hurried around to the side of the theater and in through the ramshackle employees' door. Inside in the semidarkness he took my hand.

★   ★   ★

When we came out at the rear of the theater the stark contrast of black-and-white struck me again forcibly, even though this time I was prepared for it. We walked around through the vacant lot to the street. There we stood for a moment drinking in great quantities of the crisp and clear, absolutely transparent air. It felt like champagne to the lungs, refreshing and invigorating. I looked around me. To the south the Baldwin Hills stood out with exaggerated clarity, as though cut out of cardboard, and in the other direction the mountains seemed almost so close that you could reach out and touch them. Nesselrode still didn't look very well. I could see his chest going up and down spasmodically inside the unbuttoned overcoat, and his skin seemed grayer than usual.

'Are you all right?'

'Nah. You think the old man can't walk any more? Come on then.'

We set off together down the street in the direction of Culver City. My own way of walking, I noticed, was beginning to resemble his. We went along in a jerky and abrupt manner, yet somehow we made less progress than we had in our race out to the west side from downtown. When I looked down I could see my legs switching back and forth, but the sidewalk underneath seemed to go by only rather slowly. I made a great effort and for a time surged a little ahead of him. Then I had to stop for a moment and wait for him to catch up. 'What is it now, an Olympics hundred-yard dash?' he grumbled. 'We'll get there.' He was no longer wheezing but he seemed tired; his shoulders were going up and down in reciprocating fashion as though he could scarcely lift them.

Turning right on Washington, we came in due time to the lot with the chain-link fence around it. There had been some improvements, I noticed; a stucco office building had been erected in fake Spanish style, and workmen were just finishing a miniature sea suitable for naval battles, with a backdrop full of clouds behind it. As we passed they were filling it with a fire hose. Nesselrode led me directly down the main street of the lot toward the commissary, through the transparent white sunlight that seemed to penetrate through to my bones like X-rays. A few bushes had been planted around the commissary now, I noticed, although the rest of the lot was still only dirt scattered with gravel. Nesselrode pushed the door open and went in, and I followed him.

The place was almost deserted. Two cowboys, one with his boots off and his feet on the table, were smoking cigarettes at the far end. A couple of actresses were leaning on the counter talking to the counterman, a good-looking young man who, probably, had hoped to get into pictures but had never expected to end up behind the counter in the commissary. At a table near the middle Reiter was sitting with Charles Morton and Roland Lightfoot. Morton was dressed as a clergyman with his collar on backward, and Lightfoot was sportily clad in corduroy knickers, a tweed jacket, and an ascot.

Reiter looked up indifferently, as though Nesselrode had been gone only for an hour. 'Hello, Julius.'

'Don't speak,' said Nesselrode. 'I am tired completely out. It's terrible out there. The smog.'

Reiter smiled, wrinkling his forehead. 'Smog?' he repeated, puzzled.

'It's hot. A terrible day. Haze,' Nesselrode explained rather too quickly. He caught my eye and looked away again. He went on chattering to cover up his mistake. 'You should meet Lightfoot. A romantic lead, a genius,' he told me. Lightfoot extended his hand with a rather aloof smile. 'Business is good, no?' Nesselrode rattled on to Reiter. 'I see they are filling up the ocean.'

'We're just starting *Antony and Cleopatra* tomorrow. After that we'll use it for *America Ho*. Morton is playing Columbus.'

I said, 'Moira, I imagine, is going to do Cleopatra.'

Reiter stared at me curiously. 'Who?'

'No, no,' said Nesselrode nervously. 'Cleopatra is Vanessa Nesser. She must be an older woman, vamp. Moira is ingenue.'

'Ah, Moira Silver,' said Reiter. He seemed to understand things only when Nesselrode explained them to him.

'What *is* Moira doing just now?' I persisted.

'None of your business,' Nesselrode mumbled to himself. 'Already I have told him, don't have attachments to the actors. But he is young.'

'I'm thirty.'

'Young,' reiterated Nesselrode.

'You do comedy?' Reiter asked me abruptly.

'Comedy?'

'It isn't much. A second part in a Muldoon. We're shooting right now. But the guy we were using has a sore arm and can't fall down. It's a fall-down part.'

'Who's playing the feminine lead?'

'Moira Silver,' he said matter-of-factly, as though I hadn't mentioned the name myself only a moment before.

'All right.'

'All right?' said Nesselrode, alarmed. 'What

170

do you mean, all right?'

'I mean I'll do it.'

'Reiter, this is not a good idea.'

Reiter paid no attention to him. 'It's called *My Lord*. You're the fiancé. Muldoon comes along and gets the girl. We're starting to shoot again in a half an hour. You'd better go over the part with Moira and Muldoon.'

'Where are they?'

'Dressing rooms,' said Reiter shortly. He turned his back and went on with his conversations with Morton and Lightfoot.

I left hurriedly. I had no idea where the dressing rooms were, but I was afraid that if I lingered around asking any more questions Nesselrode would follow me, and that would spoil everything. As it turned out it wasn't very difficult finding the dressing rooms. There were only four kinds of building on the lot: the galvanized-iron shooting studios, the stucco office, the commissary, and a set of low wooden buildings with tar-paper roofs that looked like the barracks in a hastily erected army camp. All the rooms had outside doors and there were no connecting corridors. There were no names on the doors and I had no idea how to find Moira. After I had circulated up and down the dusty alleys between the buildings for a while I found a door open and put my head into it. An intense dark mournful-looking woman of perhaps forty, with heavy white makeup and black eyes, was

171

engaged in combing out her long black hair before the mirror.

'Moira Silver?'

Wordlessly, still evidently crushed under her melancholy, she indicated the building across the way with her comb. Searching in the direction indicated, I found another door slightly ajar and pushed my way in. Moira was sitting in a wooden chair at the other end of the small room, her hands in her lap and a faint smile on her face, doing nothing at all, as though she were waiting for me. She was wearing a gingham frock with lace at the collar, white ankle socks, and patent-leather shoes. The costume made her look about sixteen years old. Since she had her back to the mirror with its frame of light bulbs her face was in shadow and I could make out her expression only indistinctly.

'I knew you'd come.'

'I'm going to do a picture with you.'

'Ah yes. Barney fell off a haywagon and sprained his arm. It's a fall-down part.'

'That's what Reiter said. Can't we go somewhere?'

'We're shooting in a half an hour.'

'We could take a walk.'

'A walk? Where?'

'Perhaps—down by the Old Mill Stream.'

Turning to look directly at me with her little smile, she shook her head slowly back and forth.

'Why not?'

'Because you were naughty the last time.'

'Moira . . .'

'But in a half an hour you can be my fiancé.'

'Muldoon gets the girl.'

'Well, he's a star, don't you see, Alys. When *you're* a star *you* can get the girl.'

'I want you right now.'

'Greedy greedy.'

'It isn't that I desire you. I mean, I do desire you. But it's more than that. It's that . . .'

Her smile increased a little. 'What?'

' . . . that I love you,' I burst out, desperately and ridiculously.

'Oh, a lot of people do,' she said blithely. 'A different person loves me in every picture.'

'Moira . . .'

'You're a very dear boy.' She offered me a long languorous glance, indicating sincerity, then threw off this manner and stood up in a businesslike way. I approached her and she turned away, with slight coquetry. Without raising my hands from my sides I managed to brush my lips against her cheek as she turned her head. The cheek was cool and smooth, with a faintly clinging texture like silk. Immediately my desire increased to the point that I could scarcely control it. I imagined embracing her and feeling the hardness of her body under the simple gingham dress. In the silence I became conscious of a faint humming sound, above us and behind us, or perhaps simply coming from the air itself. Moira seemed aware of it too.

'We have to be on the set in twenty minutes,' she said, drawing away with what seemed to me a faint regret.

'I was supposed to go over the part with you and Muldoon.'

'There's nothing to it. You just fall down.'

THE FIRST PICTURE

Reiter was waiting on the set, slapping his crop impatiently against his riding breeches. He was wearing his safari hat with the zebra-stripe band and the brim turned down all around. It was an outdoor take, not far from the sylvan scene where I had walked with Moira before. 'Places!' he shouted impatiently. 'Everybody on set. Script! Where's the script-girl?'

'Here I am, Mr. Reiter.' She was standing behind the camera, carrying the heavy typescript in its black cover as usual.

'Where are we now?'

'Walk in the countryside. Fall into the brook.'

'Let's go. What's the matter with everybody? You're standing around dead on your feet. Reflectors on the lovers.'

The men pushed up the big reflector screens

174

and adjusted them. On me, I realized. As though I were awakening from a dream, or falling into one, I found myself standing in a little clearing in the grass next to Moira. The camera began buzzing only about ten feet from us. All at once I was aware, with a kind of cool chill, that I had passed a boundary into a deeper level in the flight from reality that Ziff had warned me so eloquently against. First, with Nesselrode holding me by the hand, I had escaped from the 'real' world (whatever that was) into the thin and flimsy black-and-white world behind the Screen. Now I left even that tenuous reality behind and passed through another invisible membrane, into a play of shadows that was totally conventional and fictive. And in parting company with reality, I had also parted company with my freedom. As the camera started rolling I found myself in a mechanical state in which I was not free to move, to speak, or even to reflect on my emotions except in the manner that was dictated by Reiter and the notebook with its black cover. And Moira too, standing at my elbow, seemed converted into a kind of marionette, a doll capable of exact simulacra of the expressions and gestures of flesh-and-blood beings. Our motions were jerky and the words put into our mouths by the black notebook were of the utmost inanity. We gazed at each other for a few seconds while the camera clucked. Shyly she took my hand.

We began walking down the path, while the reflector screens and the camera on a dolly rolled along after us at one side. The path was narrower than I remembered and Moira went straight down the center of it, so that I often found myself walking in grass up to my ankles or skirting around bushes and other small obstacles.

'Gaze at each other soulfully!' shouted Reiter.

I gazed at Moira soulfully, and she did the same, although there was always a certain nuance of irony under the surface no matter what emotion she was demonstrating. It was even more difficult to walk down the path, or beside the path, now that I was obliged to gaze soulfully at Moira instead of looking where I was going. I blundered into a blackberry patch and scratched myself badly before I was able to extricate myself and catch up again with Moira, who had continued blithely on her way still gazing at the empty spot in the air where I had been.

'Good, good!' shouted Reiter. 'Go on gazing soulfully! What's next?' he asked the script-girl.

'The tree branch.'

I fixed my eyes on Moira's face. It was not

176

difficult for me to simulate a soulful expression, because I was hypnotized by the desire I felt for the pale, childlike, and yet sensuous face with its dark expressive eyes. I went up and down unevenly as I trod in a ditch or rose up over a hillock. Then, still staring at her as though transfixed, I struck my head violently on the low overhanging branch of a tree.

'Good, good!'

I was almost knocked cold. I felt dizzy and almost fell. Pressing one hand over the rapidly growing lump on my brow, I hurried on after Moira, who continued at her normal pace and had not seemed to notice my accident.

'Keep looking into her eyes! Even for a second don't glance away!'

It was perhaps the shock of striking the tree branch that jolted me out of my trancelike state for a moment, and I found it was possible to think or even speak on two levels at once, pantomiming the actions in the script and at the same time making side remarks on the imbecility of it all to Moira.

'I think I've fractured my skull,' I told her under my breath.

Without altering her tender expression, she said, 'Isn't this where you wanted to come for a walk?'

'With you. Not with this crowd of clowns pushing cameras.'

She touched her finger to her lips, still

smiling. Ahead was the Old Mill Stream, and the pathway crossed it on a pretty curved bridge in rustic style. The bridge too, however, was narrow, no wider than the path. Moira, with her lovelorn glance fixed on me, went straight up the center of it. Although I was only two feet to her left I missed it completely and walked straight into the brook, clambering out on the other side soaked almost to the waist.

'Good! Good! Go take off your pants!'

I went over behind a clump of trees, and the camera on the dolly followed me to a point where I took off my pants and socks and wrung the water out of them, and also poured several cupfuls of water out of my shoes.

'Now get dressed again.'

I put my pants back on, pulled on the damp socks, and put on my shoes and tied them. The wet shoes and socks squishing a little, I walked back to the end of the bridge where Moira was now talking to Muldoon, who was in full kit with top hat and monocle and swinging his umbrella behind him in a dashing manner.

'THIS IS LORD MULDOON, HE HAS JUST
ARRIVED FROM LONDON, ENGLAND.'

Muldoon negligently extended his hand, and I found myself holding an empty white cotton glove. I didn't know what to do with it and looked around for a place to put it. Meanwhile

Muldoon had stopped swinging his umbrella and was bending over to kiss Moira's hand.

'IF I MAY TAKE THE LIBERTY.'

Moira put her fingers to her mouth to suppress a giggle. She looked at me questioningly, and I opened my mouth to say something. Muldoon offered her his arm, and the three of us strolled casually back toward the bridge again.

'Both gaze at her! One from each side!'

We both gazed at Moira, I still with my hopeless lover's moon-eyes and Muldoon with a careless and blasé confidence. When we came to the bridge Moira kept to the center as before, I of course walked into the brook again, and Muldoon sprang up with agility to balance on the rustic railing of the bridge. The umbrella unfurled as if by magic and he held it out at arm's length, miming a tightwire performer.

Her hands clasped in shy delight, Moira followed his every move. She had forgotten me now and was intent only on Muldoon and his capers. There was the obligatory near-fall; he tottered until it seemed that his center of gravity was far out in the air over empty space, balancing himself only with the quivering umbrella. He regained his equilibrium, poised himself primly on his toes, and did a ballet pirouette. His whole body turned suddenly feminine, while he grinned maliciously at this vein of perversity, of the androgynous, that lurked in his Protean form. Resuming his masculine guise, he tightwired on to the end of the railing, where he did a somersault in the air, managing somehow to turn a complete circle without entangling himself in the still-open umbrella. He landed on the ground as lightly as a bird, with his monocle still in place. He bowed. Moira clasped her hands again, and then, a thought striking her, looked around anxiously to see where I was. The camera panned around to show me wringing out my pants and socks again behind the tree.

'Good! Good! Print that!'

      ★   ★   ★

'Muldoon and the haywagon,' said the script-girl.

I was provided with dry clothes identical to those I had on, and Moira exchanged her gingham frock for a chaste and simple white dress like a nightgown, with a hem that came a little below her knees. This dress, which was translucent to the strong light of the reflectors and showed her form clearly, made me dizzy again with desire.

'Hurry up with that,' bawled Reiter. 'Are we ready? Reflectors on the lovers. Camera! Action!' He raised his crop and pointed it at me.

180

'Dear can't we find some place to be alone!'

'DEAR, CAN'T WE FIND SOME PLACE
TO BE ALONE?'

Moira made her chaste but mysterious smile—her specialty. Taking me by the hand, she led me away down another rustic path while the camera and reflector screens trundled along after us. Presently we came out by the rustic farmhouse a little beyond the Old Mill, and there we stopped while the camera focused on the farmyard.

The English lord, still impeccably clad in top hat and monocle, strolled onto the set and found an empty haywagon standing in front of the barn. He seized a rickety chair, twirled it once or twice, and then sailed up in a graceful somersault in midair, coming down on the bed of the wagon seated in the chair with one leg crossed over the other. He seemed to have no bones. He could bend any part of his body at will, all without losing a particle of his aristocratic dignity. He reached into his pocket for a cigar and lit it with his trick lighter-thumb. He puffed contentedly. He had not noticed the yokel with Dutch chin-whiskers who was holding the reins at the front of the wagon. An enormous load of hay appeared at the loft door overhead and slid down the chute, filling the wagon. Muldoon disappeared.

181

'Go! Go!' shouted Reiter. 'Take a hayride.'
He pushed us forward, jabbing me in the back
with his riding crop.

'OH LOOK, DEAR. WE CAN TAKE A HAYRIDE.'

We climbed into the wagon. Enthroned in the
soft and fragrant hay, we held hands and looked
at each other happily. Moira seemed to have
forgotten Muldoon. We were young and in love.
The yokel snapped his whip and the wagon
started off with a lurch. The camera, the
reflector screens, and the rest of the crew tailed
along after us. Wisps of smoke began appearing
in the hay around us.
'Don't notice! Pay no attention!' Reiter
shouted.
There was more smoke, coming mainly from
around me now. I stretched out my arm to
embrace Moira and was about to kiss her, then
withdrew the arm and reached down in alarm
through the hay to my trousers. I pulled out the
arm and shook it. The coat sleeve was
smoldering.

'FIRE!'

Moira smiled. Writhing, I tried to put out my
burning clothing. I leaped up, rolled about, and
did somersaults in the hay. Finally I fell out of
the wagon onto the back of my neck and dashed

182

off with alacrity toward the nearby brook. The camera followed me. My clothing was aflame and the seat of my pants entirely burned away. I leaped into the brook and disappeared except for one shoe and the top of my head.

When I clambered out, with water sloshing from me onto the dusty path, Moira with a pleased smile was allowing Muldoon to hand her down from the wagon. The yokel looked around in astonishment to find his hay on fire.

*   *   *

'He meets her parents,' said the script-girl.

Moira and I walked along the sidewalk through the suburban neighborhood with its rose-covered bungalows and picket fences.

> 'DEAR, MY MOTHER AND FATHER WOULD
> LIKE TO MEET YOU.'

We turned in at a gateway and entered the house. Moira's mother was arranging a geranium in the window. Her father, an irascible old gent, was sitting in a rocker with his glasses on the end of his nose, reading a newspaper. He put down the newspaper and glared at me over the tops of the glasses.

> 'SO, YOUNG MAN, YOU WISH TO MARRY
> MY DAUGHTER?'

183

I mumbled something. Meanwhile the mother had left off fiddling with the geranium in the window and was stretching up in an attempt to replace a light bulb in the chandelier hanging from the ceiling, high over her head.

'This is ridiculous,' I told Moira. 'Why should she be trying to change a light bulb when her daughter's fiancé is coming to call?'

Putting her head close to mine, she said something behind her hand. 'It's a fall-down part and ...'

'DON'T BE AFRAID OF FATHER. HIS
BARK IS WORSE THAN HIS BITE.'

' ... you have to fall down in every take.'

'Alys, go for the ladder,' yelled Reiter.

With a helpful eagerness I ran off the scene and came back with a stepladder, with which I first struck the doorway a heavy blow so that the whole flimsy set quivered. Then, turning around while holding the ladder horizontally under my arm, I managed to knock both Moira and her mother flat with it. They got up, smiling indulgently, and the mother handed me the light bulb. I erected the ladder and mounted it.

The action continued in its absolutely inane sequence. I stuck my finger into the empty socket and was electrocuted, leaping into the air and writhing like a caught fish but managing to come down onto the ladder again. The mother went off to the window for some unexplained purpose, perhaps to tend her geranium again.

'Rock, Alys!'

I began rocking back and forth on the ladder, attempting to screw the bulb into the upright fitting each time I shot past the chandelier. The camera left me and panned around to look past the mother and out the window. There on the sidewalk was of course Muldoon, swinging his umbrella and winking rakishly at the mother. The mother simpered.

'IT'S SOME ENGLISHMAN, DEAR.'

Moira nodded and moved her lips, no doubt explaining that she was already acquainted with Lord Muldoon. I rocked back and forth with greater and greater velocity on my ladder, still trying to screw in the bulb. The mother had gone to the door to let in Muldoon. Swaying to one side and another on the ladder, I finally passed the point of equilibrium and shot out the window. The light bulb, following its own trajectory, landed in the father's lap. He picked it up and glared at it as though he had never seen a light bulb before. I landed in the soft earth and was helped to my feet by a couple of grips. Inside, Muldoon was bowing with a little twirl of the umbrella, which charmed the mother.

185

'Take Eighteen. The construction site.'

'Alys, by this time you are beginning to look a little wan,' explained Reiter. 'All these fall-downs are taking their toll. However you are still hopeful.'

THE HOPEFUL SWAIN TRIES AGAIN.

Moira and I walked down the street of bungalows with their roses and picket fences. I smiled wanly. Moira was just as always, blithe, youthful, and insouciant.

'DEAR, LET'S GO SEE IF OUR APARTMENT
IS FINISHED YET.'

I shrugged and agreed. She took my arm and we hurried away down the sidewalk.

'OH, ALL RIGHT. AS LONG AS THAT
PLAGUEY ENGLISHMAN ISN'T THERE.'

We came to the construction site, where one wall was almost finished and a carpenter with a walrus mustache was hammering on the siding. He seemed to be the only one working on the building. Other parts of it were little more than a frail scaffolding of timbers.

186

I pulled a long rolled blueprint out of my pocket and unfurled it.

'THIS SHOULD BE OUR LIVING ROOM
RIGHT HERE.'

Moira stepped over a plank into the room beyond and assumed a coy, arch, and simpering expression.

'AND THIS WILL BE THE NURSERY.'

At this I smiled, broadly but rather uneasily, and adjusted my necktie. Muldoon appeared, of course, carrying a hammer and hypocritically pretending to hammer a nail into a wall at a place where no nail could possibly be needed. When he caught sight of Moira he dropped the nail and tossed the hammer over his shoulder. It sailed through the air and landed square on the head of the mustached carpenter. He clapped his hand onto his head and looked around irately to see where the hammer had come from.

Muldoon bent over to kiss Moira's hand, crowding so close to me that I was obliged to take a step backward. As a result of this I found myself in a small construction elevator, which immediately started upward. There followed a series of improbable physical concatenations involving the elevator, my own body, and the persons of Moira and Muldoon. A plank laid

187

over the top of the elevator shaft struck me on the head, Moira and Muldoon came up in the elevator which caused the same plank to vault into the air and come down on me again, and so on. Like the carpenter, I grimaced and felt the bump on my head. Moira put her hand over her mouth to repress a giggle. Muldoon looked around in a distinguished and reflective way, swinging his umbrella.

'I'M THINKING OF TAKING AN APARTMENT
HERE MYSELF, ON THE SECOND FLOOR.'

The camera panned to me, gnashing my teeth. The antics of the animated plank continued. I stepped on the loose end of the thing and fell down the elevator shaft, and Muldoon, who had been standing on the other end of it, soared up and landed on the roof above, which consisted only of a gridwork of unfinished boards. Crossing his ankles, he made a vaudeville performer's bow, to the applause of Moira.

Trying again, I stepped into the elevator and went up, striking my head as usual on the plank when I got to the top. The plank sailed up and landed on a roofbeam near where Muldoon was standing. He stepped onto it. The laws of physics operated in his favor as they always did, this time with magical ingenuity. Since he had stepped onto the short end, which was

188

counterbalanced by the weight of the long end dangling over empty space, he was lowered swiftly and yet gently to the floor below. The long end of the plank, of course, whipped around with violence and banged me on the head for what I hoped was the last time.

Stretching out his white glove politely, Muldoon invited Moira into the elevator. They descended, came out safely at the bottom, and walked away down the sidewalk. Moira looked back once at me. I was just coming to, opening my eyes and shaking my head dizzily. For an instant she gazed at me with an expression of concern. Then, with a rueful little sigh, she slipped her hand into Muldoon's elbow and went off blithely with him down the sidewalk. The mustached carpenter came up with the hammer and angrily accused me of having thrown it at him.

*　　*　　*

Reiter took off his hat and polished his head again. Then he put the hat back on. He looked a little tired. He slapped his leather boot with the riding crop. 'Where are we now?'

'Take Twenty-five. The Wedding.'

'Fine, fine. On set, everybody. Let's get moving, folks. Where's Moira?'

'AT LAST IT HAS ARRIVED, DEAR.
OUR WEDDING DAY.'

Moira's face was filled with bliss. And mirth. It was a churchyard scene. Everybody was in formal dress: the father, the mother, Moira in a bridal gown with veil, I in a cutaway coat and stand-up collar, and Muldoon who was to be Best Man. There didn't seem to be any bridesmaid; evidently casting couldn't spare anybody at the moment. Never mind; the five of us crossed the churchyard together, for some reason walking five abreast instead of going in Indian file. A pair of gravediggers were digging a grave. They stopped and leaned on their shovels to watch. I of course walked straight across the open grave and disappeared. I simply dropped out of sight. The gravediggers, entranced with Moira's beauty, hadn't noticed.

Inside the church Charles Morton was waiting, wearing his clerical costume with the dog collar. Closeup of some fingers playing an organ. All four of them stopped before Morton.

'WHICH ONE OF YOU IS THE BRIDEGROOM?'

They all looked around at each other. For the first time they noticed that I was missing. I was standing behind the camera next to Reiter, brushing clay off my clothing and attempting to straighten my right elbow which I had apparently dislocated in my fall into the grave.

190

There was a moment of indecision mingled with mild consternation. Then Muldoon offered himself with a graceful bow, crossing one ankle behind the other foot. He was still holding his umbrella, even though this was not customary at weddings, and he had failed to remove his top hat. Moira considered, looking first at her parents and then at Muldoon. She sighed. But after all! If that other fellow was always turning up missing and clumsily hitting himself with planks. Another moment of considering; then she smiled and took Muldoon's arm, still with a rueful expression around the eyes.

'Camera up! Roll up on the bride and groom!'

A medium closeup of Moira and Muldoon gazing into each other's eyes, she soulfully, he with a slightly mocking expression, glancing out of the corner of his eye at the camera. Moira, who seemed to have a tickle in her throat, made a little cough. Muldoon frowned at this breach of etiquette. Then, staring at her, he ad-libbed his own cough, an elegant English one. Moira coughed again, putting her hand to her mouth. Muldoon was seized with a series of coughs and clutched his chest. The minister looked alarmed.

'What's this? What's all this coughing? Cut! No, wait. Okay, let's let 'em roll.' Reiter by this time had a broad grin on his face.

The wedding turned into a Camille-like coughing contest in which Moira and Muldoon

191

competed in trying to die from consumption. She barked like a circus seal, he more deeply like a Saint Bernard. Between them they ran the whole gamut and range of catarrhal explosions. Moira clutched at her throat and rolled her eyes, her chest racked by spasms. Muldoon coughed violently in her face, then fell to the floor and writhed, his whole body shaken with violent paroxysms. He rolled to a spittoon which was for some reason provided in the church and coughed copiously into it.

Moira, not to be outdone, fell down too and began writhing, but there was only one spittoon and she had to cough into her handkerchief. Clearly he had the better of it, at least for the moment. Moira flung herself up over a pew, downstaging him and cutting him partly off from the camera. Her bosom heaved. Muldoon had no bosom to heave and she had drawn ahead of him. He reached into his pocket and came out with something: a ketchup bottle. Surreptitiously, his back to the camera, he unscrewed it and poured the contents down his chin and shirtfront. Then, concealing the empty bottle under his leg, he rolled over onto his back with his arms flung out. This put him closer to the camera and at a point where he was no longer blocked by Moira. Since it was impossible to conceal a ketchup bottle in a wedding dress, Moira couldn't match this. She attempted to increase the violence of her coughing, but she was already at the maximum. Muldoon coughed ketchup now; he had evidently managed to get some into his mouth.

By this time even the cameraman and the grips were laughing. The script-girl had dropped her book in an access of mirth and was down on her hands and knees picking it up. Reiter still wore his broad grin. Muldoon coughed again weakly. Then he gave a final jerk, stretched out all four limbs in different directions, and contracted them. Morton, bending over him, hurriedly administered the last rites.

'Cut! Great! Print that!'

Moira got up from the floor and dusted off her wedding dress. She stared rather crossly in Muldoon's direction. He with great fastidiousness was removing ketchup from his face with a handkerchief and didn't notice.

Reiter took off his African hat, got out his own handkerchief, and wiped the perspiration from his head. Then, putting the hat back on, he took out another handkerchief and polished his eyeglasses. This seemed to be his ritual whenever he finished a picture. With the thick lenses removed his eyes had a curious pale fishlike look; he blinked a little. He put the glasses back on.

'Well, it's in the can, I guess. However,' he reflected, 'I think we ought to do the construction site again. Alys didn't react right to the plank hitting him on the head. His reaction was always the same. He ought to look more and more pained every time the plank hits him. How many times does it hit him?' he asked the script-girl.

She consulted her book. 'Six.'

CHAPTER TWELVE

Moira was still in her wedding dress, although she had taken off the veil. We walked down the street of false-front bungalows and out into the square. I too had on my wedding clothes, with a good deal of clay on them from the grave. My elbow seemed to work all right now. It wasn't dislocated after all. Moira, like Reiter, seemed a little tired. It had been a long day's work. It was about five now, to judge from the white disk hanging in the absolutely clear sky to the west.

'Where can we go?'

'There's nowhere, really. It's all sets.'

We walked around behind one of the shopfronts and sat down, leaning against the back of the flat. Moira seemed amused to find herself sitting there on the grass in her wedding dress. She stretched out her legs and looked at her toes in their white shoes. The gown was a satin so white that it seemed iridescent. It was skillfully cut and fitted her perfectly. The bodice came up to her neck, but the dress was so tight that her bosom was clearly outlined in the flimsy material. Moira was a study in white. The gown was a glowing white, her face and hands a papery white without gloss and perfectly uniform in texture. Only her loose short hair, and her dark eyes like birds' wings, contrasted with this slightly uncanny albinism.

I was sitting cross-legged on the grass a few feet from her. I couldn't take my eyes from her. I had the premonition that if I went on staring at her carefully and intently in this way I might penetrate through to the secret of this enchantment she exerted on me. I had an irresistible urge to—I didn't know what. Perhaps just to be with her. To have her eyes meet mine. And yet merely sitting with her in this way left me unsatisfied and queer-feeling, floaty. It was as though something inside me, in my viscera or in my head, were missing, and there was an empty space there that only she could fill.

She went on contemplating her shoes for a while longer, then she turned to me with her usual girlish blitheness, only a hint of sensuality in the eyes with their half-lowered lashes.

'Do you have a cigarette?'

I went through my pockets and to my surprise found a rumpled pack of Chesterfields with three cigarettes still in it. Apparently it was part of the bridegroom costume as provided by the wardrobe department. There was even a box of small wooden matches. I offered her one and lit it, and then lit my own. She drew on the cigarette deeply and exhaled through her tightened lips, in the manner of a habitual smoker. The gesture contrasted oddly with her air of virginal girlishness. The combination was exciting; I felt a little stir of desire rise up in me again.

'Moira, I want to . . .'

'What?'

'Play a serious part with you.'

She drew on the cigarette again and set it down on the ground beside her.

'Aren't you satisfied? You're doing fine so far.'

'Fall-down parts are not what I had in mind.'

'But it doesn't hurt, does it?'

Reflecting back, I had to admit that it didn't hurt. Or did it? Perhaps it had hurt at the time and now I had forgotten it. I remembered reading an article about curare. It seemed that curare at one time was used as an anesthesia. When you gave it to people, they lay perfectly still and showed no signs of pain while you operated on them. But later it transpired that they were suffering the agonies of the damned, except that the curare paralyzed them so that they couldn't move so much as an eyelid to show that they were in pain. Perhaps this was the way it had been with the plank striking me on the head. Still, if I had forgotten it, the pain didn't exist, so to speak, and it didn't matter.

'I didn't mean that exactly. I meant that—I want to know you seriously.'

'We can't always have what we want ... here,' she said vaguely, not meeting my glance.

I said nothing for a moment, studying her face. Then I said, 'You're not happy?'

'We're not put into this world to be happy.'

'*This* world. Perhaps there are other worlds where one can be happy.'

'Yes. I used to be,' she said in a toneless voice, as though she were talking to herself. 'A long time ago. Would you believe it? There was a time when I was in love with Julie.'

It was moment or so before I realized she was speaking of Nesselrode.

'You used to go out with him in the evening.'

'Yes. I was his mistress,' she said quite simply. The old-fashioned term rang strangely, as though it were something in a book and not in a real conversation. 'It was fun. For a while. I didn't realize then ...'

'Did he love you too?'

'I don't know. He's not a very communicative person. It's impossible to know what he's thinking.'

'But at least he got you into pictures.'

'Not then. Later.'

'Moira.'

She looked up at me.

'How did he . . .'

We were both silent for a moment. It was as though a shadow had come over us, leaving a chill in the air. Then she said, 'Oh, that's all past now. It happened a very long time ago. Nothing can be done about it.' She stopped, and after a moment she went on in a flat, almost indifferent voice. She might have been talking about somebody else. 'I was just a kid from Bakersfield. My God, but I was young! Nobody has ever been that young. I knew nothing about the world, nothing about anything, except that I wanted to get into pictures. He told me he was a producer and he was; the others said he was too. Then all the clichés started happening. You know, the casting couch and all that. I didn't object. If that was the price you had to pay, it was little enough. Besides he was . . . You may find this a little difficult to believe. He was attractive in those days.'

All I said was, 'I've seen pictures of him.'

'Not attractive exactly, but desirable. Physically desirable. At first I didn't like his lip. When he kissed me I could feel the scar—ugh. But then . . . he taught me. He used to be able to make me come seven or eight times. You can imagine—a girl my age. I had no idea of such things. After a while I was addicted to it, as you might be addicted to opium.'

I began to feel a kind of chill creeping around on me under my clothing. I didn't know

198

whether I wanted her to go on or not. But I myself was addicted to her story. I had to know the rest of it.

'And . . . the pictures?'

'I kept on pestering him. I thought I could have both, you see. He would never answer me. He didn't argue. He still doesn't; it isn't his way. But he wouldn't take me to the studio and he wouldn't introduce me to studio people. The fan magazines called me a starlet, but that was just a euphemism for a mistress. Everybody knew that. When I reminded him of his promise—he had never promised me anything, but I kept on saying he had and after a while, perhaps, he believed it—he would only change the subject. Then one day he abruptly gave in. I think it was because . . . no, I shouldn't tell you that.'

I didn't know what it was but I didn't think I was going to like it. After a long moment I said, 'What?'

'He always had . . . a little trouble with women. Even with me. Even though he was skillful with women, he wasn't strongly masculine. And so one day he . . . we had a . . .'

'Fiasco.'

'Yes. I was still lying there, and he got up and went away to the closet and came back with a riding crop.'

'A riding crop?'

'Yes. It was a rattan thing, with a brass tip at

199

the end. I was quite afraid of it.'

'The same one that . . .'

'Yes. He held it up in the air over me and I screamed. I think that was what stopped him. He had a nice house in an expensive district and I think he was afraid that the neighbors would hear. But when he stood there holding the crop in the air I could see that . . .'

I helped her. 'The fiasco was over.'

'Yes. I put my clothes back on and neither of us said anything about it. But it was shortly after that—it was the next morning in fact—that he grabbed me by the arm and said, 'Okay, if that's what you want so much, I'll do it.' There was something about his eyes—they frightened me. But I had to obey; I could never stand up to him in anything. So he dragged me off to the . . .'

'The Alhambra.'

'Yes. He took me there in his car. He had a car with a chauffeur in those days.' I tried to imagine Nesselrode as a nonpedestrian, but without success. 'He had to pull me after him the last few inches,' she went on. 'I didn't like the look of the thing. But we went through it, and on the other side everything was black and white. And so,' she concluded, leaving out a good deal of the story and telling only the end, 'I became a star.'

She finished with her cigarette and crushed it out in the grass. She still had her curious stiff air of indifference, as though she were telling a story about somebody else.

'Did you ever try to . . .'

'Not at first, of course. I was excited by being in pictures and by all the fuss that everybody made over me. But then I began to notice some—odd things. Some things I didn't like. I asked him if I could quit. Or not quit exactly, just take a vacation for six months or a year. He wouldn't answer this either. I made a few silly attempts to run away. But I found out that it's as I told you. There's no place to go. And since then I've . . . gone on making pictures.'

'And all this happened . . .'

'I don't know. I lose track. Just a few years ago.'

'But . . . you got what you wanted, didn't you?'

'It wasn't what I expected. I wasn't happy making pictures. It was just work like everything else. I thought that I was young and good-looking and I could have anything I wanted. But the looks didn't do any good, because there was nobody to—go to bed with. You couldn't do that here. And it was impossible to escape to a place where you could.'

'I don't understand. Why . . . why can't we, just the two of us . . .'

'Because they own us. Once we're in pictures, we belong to them. And they don't want us to. They don't want us to have real lives.'

'But you're famous.'

She said quite simply, 'Movie stars are like racehorses. Everybody knows their name, but they have to obey the stable boy.'

She got up abruptly and smoothed out her gown. Then she tossed her head in a girlish gesture to shake the curls from her cheeks.

I got up too and dropped my cigarette into the grass. 'Moira...'

'Don't, Alys,' she said in a thin and unreal voice. 'It's ... what I want too,' she added awkwardly. 'But it's no use.'

I touched her elbow timidly with my left hand, then I seized her suddenly, pinning her arms to her sides. I was conscious again of a faint whirring, somewhere behind us or in the air over our heads. The pitch of the sound seemed to descend a little, and it became perceptibly weaker, as though some electrical machine were gradually dying down. I kissed the edge of her face, just at the corner of the ear, and then covered her face with kisses.

'Alys,' I heard her whispering. 'Just an instant, an instant, an instant.'

Our mouths, groping for each other, met and locked tightly. As in a dream, or as though lowered on silken ropes, we descended into the grass. I lay on her and fumbled along her back for the row of satin buttons on the gown. The discreet murmur in the air was growing very faint now. It was only because it was very quiet that I could hear it at all. Then it died out entirely. I lost consciousness. It was as though I had fallen into a deep and dreamless sleep, or as though the anesthetist's needle, slipping painlessly into a vein, had infused me with a cool oblivion that filtered through my limbs like an icy nectar, a Nothingness. I knew what it was not to exist.

★   ★   ★

When I came to my senses again I was still lying on the grass behind the false storefront. There was no sign of Moira. I must have slept all night, because the sun was back around in the east now. But time worked very strangely in this world and perhaps it wasn't a real sun at all, only a glowing disk hung up there by special effects. The humming in the air was back to normal now. It was a comforting sound, like that of an air conditioner when you are sleeping in a hot country, or the faint rumble of traffic that reminds you you are safe in your own city where things are going on as normal. It is only when the air conditioner stops, or the sound of traffic is silent, that an ominous feeling comes over you. It seemed to be a nice day. I stood up and filled my lungs with the cool, and clear air.

There was nobody in sight. I walked out into the square enclosed by the false storefronts, but it was deserted. Still feeling energetic and cheerful with the fresh air coursing through my lungs, I went on walking through the empty streets. As I wandered in this way around the lot I continually discovered new sets I had never noticed before. Perhaps they were constantly being put up and taken down, or perhaps I merely took different routes in my way across the lot without being aware of it. Turning left at a corner, I found myself on a Fifth Avenue set, lined with the false fronts of skyscrapers extending two stories up into the air and then ending. A little farther on I came to a courtroom complete with jury box, one wall missing so that I could look directly into it, and next to it a Death Chamber with electric chair, the straps neatly folded back and waiting for its next victim.

Beyond this somewhat creepy spectacle I came out onto the main street of the lot. Looking down toward the office and the entrance gate, I saw that the business of the lot had started for the day; the chain-link gate was open and cars were coming in. The guard was at his usual post, and a few people were standing around on the sidewalk in front of the office.

I turned down the street and walked out to the gate. The guard, his chair leaning back against the wall, was reading a newspaper. He looked up at me and then went back to his reading. I stood for a moment examining him. He was a middle-aged man, a little overweight, wearing a uniform but no hat. He didn't seem to be armed. It seemed to me that I would have no difficulty in outrunning him even if he chose to get up from his chair and attempt to prevent me from going out through the gate.

I walked through the open gate onto the sidewalk beyond. Then, after a moment's hesitation, I went on tentatively down the sidewalk in the direction of the city. The guard didn't even look up from his newspaper. I stopped and looked around me, at the boulevard, at the lot behind me, and at the city in the distance. Off to the north the line of mountains was cleanly outlined against the sky. A few stucco bungalows were scattered among the vacant lots along Washington, with a larger building here and there. A short distance away I could see the intersection with La Cienega. I had an impulse to break into a run and dash on down the sidewalk on the route I knew well now, toward the distant city and the Alhambra Theater.

Then I remembered: Moira. Moira.

I stood for a moment longer watching the traffic passing on the boulevard. A streetcar went by, then a Ford Model T sedan, brand new and polished like a dancing shoe. The sun was beating down intensely now. Everything was clearly outlined and glaring: the pavement was black, the sky was white, the Ford was black, the face of the driver white as he turned and stared at me.

My eyes were beginning to hurt a little from the strong contrasts of light. I went back in through the gate. The guard, looking up from his newspaper, nodded at me in a friendly way.

I drifted slowly back up the main street of the lot, staying in the shade of the buildings as well as I could. Without really realizing where I was going I found myself on the way to the commissary, perhaps with the vague idea that I might find Moira there. I went in and found the place almost deserted. It wasn't time yet for the morning coffee break. I got a cup of coffee at the counter and took a place at an empty table. Almost immediately I caught sight of Nesselrode staring at me from only a few feet away. I hadn't noticed him coming in the door. He sidled into a chair across the table from me, examining me balefully out of his large protruding eyes.

'How are you this morning, Mr. Nesselrode? Will you have a cup of coffee?'

'I don't use caffeine. A glass of orange juice I will have. My young friend, I have a word to bandy with you.'

It occurred to me for the first time that he never called me by my name. Perhaps he couldn't remember it, or perhaps he preferred not to pronounce it because for him, at least, it carried a suggestion of the effeminate, which he probably disapproved of as much as he did drugs and eating dead animals. I waited for him to go on.

'You wanted to be in pictures. So I helped you and now you are in pictures. Fine. But now you should take my advices more. Your head is too strong, just like all young people, and you think you know better than anyone else what to do.'

I sipped my coffee and set it down. 'Very well,' I said cheerfully, 'give me some of your advices.'

'If you listen to me I can make you a star, even,' he went on. 'So far, a star you are not.'

'Mr. Nesselrode, am I free to leave the lot?'

He glanced up, suddenly intent. 'Leave the lot? Why would you want to leave the lot?'

'No particular reason. It's just that I feel confined here, that's all. There's a chain-link fence around it. It's like a prison.'

'A prison!' he said, faking an astonishment he obviously did not feel. 'There are millions—millions!—that would like to get inside here.'

'It's a prison if you can't leave.'

'You left the lot already this morning. You walked out on the boulevard, you looked at a streetcar, and then you came back in.'

'What if I hadn't?'

'I can't discuss hypotenuses. You did come back in. Why?'

I didn't care to go into this, at least for the moment. 'You haven't given me your advices,' I reminded him.

'You need more versatility. You should do different kinds of parts. Especially you should play with other actresses.'

'Very well. Which?'

'Vanessa Nesser, for example.'

'She's not my type.'

'That's what I mean, you're not versatile. A star should be able to play with any type.'

'Besides Vanessa who is there?'

'Well, just at the moment we don't have a lot of other people around,' he conceded. 'There's Claudia Leroy, she plays child parts, a very cute little girl and full of talent, a genius almost.'

I had never had any particular feeling for little girls. It was one of the few vices I hadn't tried. But instead of telling him this I merely remarked that Moira herself seemed a child to me in many ways.

'No, no. Moira is experienced. She makes a specialty of ingenue parts, true, but she has been in pictures a long time. She is experienced,' he repeated, as if he preferred this term to any reference to her age.

'Mr. Nesselrode, can Moira leave the lot?'

At this he really looked alarmed. 'Moira? To go where?'

'Outside.'

He moved sideways in his chair as though he were about to get up and leave. His nose twitched and his shiny, slightly bulging eyes fixed on me. 'Young man, let me tell you a thing. If you want to be a star and make big pictures, don't talk about outside. Talk about making pictures. Everything outside, forget it.'

'A streetcar goes right by the lot. You could get on it and go everywhere.'

'Where? To China? To Paris? Go ahead and try. Here is another advice, young man. If you want to travel around the world, make pictures. Then your pictures will go everywhere in the world. To China, to Paris. You will be known everywhere. You will always be young and handsome. Why does Moira stay so young? Because she sticks to making pictures and doesn't talk foolishness.'

'That's what Ziff says. Art is immortal.'

'Who?'

'My friend Ziff. He studied philosophy at UCLA.'

'Ziff! Ziff! An evil man. A gangster, a hoodlum. I would think that even you, a child, could see that.'

'I'm not a child. And Ziff is not exactly a gangster. I'm not sure what he is. He works for some charitable organization, perhaps.'

'A hoodlum,' he repeated. After a moment he added in a mutter, 'Ziff is not your friend.'

I was enjoying the conversation, now that I seemed to have him on the defensive. 'Maybe you could get him into pictures. He could play gangster parts.'

'We already have plenty of gangsters. Perhaps you would like to work in a gangster picture? I could speak to Reiter.'

'Would Moira be in it?'

He thought he had shaken me off and changed the subject. This time he seemed more angry than alarmed. The scar on his lip stood up suddenly in a knotted line, like a welt on a shoe. 'Moira! Always you are harping on Moira. Young man, remember an advice I gave you. On the lot we don't make . . .'

'I know, attachments. I just feel I play well opposite Moira.'

'You should be more versatile,' he told me again. That ended the conversation.

*   *   *

When I came out the day's work was really under way. The main street of the lot was full of trucks, costume people trundling along racks of clothing, and extras in various bizarre garb. As I went down the street I could see that a large crowd had collected by the artificial ocean with its backdrop of clouds. Extras were standing around in Roman and Egyptian costumes. There were two cameras and a number of reflector screens on dollies. Reiter was striding around slapping his boot with his riding crop and shouting at people. Evidently the Battle of Actium had already taken place; the bow of a sunken Egyptian ship, beaked like a bird, protruded from the water. A fragment of papier-mâche Egyptian palace had been erected at one side. It consisted of a pair of columns, a statue of Anubis, a stone wall with hieroglyphics in bas-relief, and an urn with some papyrus stalks stuck in it. Vanessa Nesser was reclining on a kind of chaise longue with lion-head legs, drawing her fingers through her hair with an expression of grief. Mark Antony had already lost the battle to the Romans and had died by falling on his sword. He was standing behind the camera in a cardboard breastplate and helmet, still holding the sword which was made in sections so that it folded up like a telescope as it disappeared into his breast. Sick with love for her dead paramour, Cleopatra lay facing the camera, clutching her fingers in her long hair and combing it out absentmindedly. This hair-combing was done very slowly. All her movements were slow; it was a dramatic scene.

'Death where is thy sting!' shouted Reiter.

'OH DEATH, WHERE IS THY STING?'

'The asp!' shouted Reiter. 'Who's got the asp?'

A slave hurried up with a bowl of wax fruit with a rubber snake in it.

Vanessa took the snake and applied it to her bosom, which was only half concealed by a pair

211

of chased brass cups supported by golden chains. There was a short wait while the snake made up his mind to bite. Her look of grief intensified. Then she made a sudden spasm as though stung by a bee. She flung away the snake and stretched out her arms, writhing.

'Roll it up!' Reiter yelled. 'Medium close shot!'

The camera moved closer to watch Vanessa dying. Rhythmic contortions like sea-waves began at her shoulders, moved down her torso, and slid over her shapely and rounded hips.

'Center on her tits!' shouted Reiter.

The camera tilted down until it pointed directly at the pair of brass cups. Vanessa writhed even more violently, her head thrown back to reveal the fine and fragile molding of her throat. Her torso heaved up and down. Then she drew up one knee and crossed it over the other leg, a curiously chaste gesture that in some way intensified the sensuality of her half-bare breasts and the writhing of the rest of her body. It was as though, in her last moment, she wished to prevent Death from violating her. She stiffened, her head still thrown back, and extended an arm which fell to the floor. After that she was motionless.

'Cut! Fine! Fine! Print that!'

Reiter took off his hat and wiped the perspiration from his head. The planes of his skull glowed in the sunshine. 'That's great,

212

Van. One of your best. It'll box a million. Okay, everybody, that about wraps it up. Extras can go to accounting for their checks. Come around in the morning and we'll look at the rushes, Van.'

The script-girl closed up her book. Reiter put his hat back on, scratched the back of his neck, and went over to the camera to look at the counter.

'Seventy-five feet,' said the cameraman. 'A long take.'

'We'll cut it a little. It doesn't take a woman that long to die.'

Then he turned and noticed me for the first time standing behind the camera.

'Ah, it's you.'

'Mr. Reiter, did I do all right in *My Lord?*'

He shrugged. 'For a beginner.'

He started off toward the office with the script-girl at his elbow. I tagged along behind him and a little at one side. 'Mr. Reiter, I want to make another picture with Moira.'

'Who? Oh yes. Julius said to watch out for you. You're the kind that tends to form attachments.'

'What's wrong with that?'

'It's not professional, that's all. It distracts you and interferes with the job. Take Vanessa, for example. Those tin cups would make anybody's pecker come to attention. But do you think I am going to get involved with her? No. Why not? Because it wouldn't be professional.

We're here to make pictures, not to chase muff.'

'I can be a professional, Mr. Reiter. It's just that I think I play well opposite Moira.'

'You've still got a few things to learn about falling down.'

'I don't want to be a type-cast in comic parts. That's not what I want to do. I have serious ambitions to be an actor.'

'Ah, serious ambitions.' He smiled a little. 'I'm not sure I understand the word "serious."'

'I would like to play a serious lead opposite Moira. Something dramatic. A love story.'

Here he looked at me again a little more searchingly. He was carrying his riding crop as usual and he began fingering it in an unconscious way; I wondered whether he was going to hit me with it.

'You're not so bad at comedy. Maybe you should stick to it.'

'That's the kind of part you gave me. You haven't tried me at other things.'

We had almost reached the front office. He stopped and contemplated me. He still seemed friendly but distant. I had the impression that he was regarding me not as a human being but as something cut out of celluloid that perhaps might be fitted into a picture, although he still had doubts. Friendly was not really the right word for his attitude. Perhaps he didn't have any friends, the idea struck me. Perhaps the only thing he was interested in was making pictures. Just as he didn't believe in falling in love with the actresses, perhaps he also didn't believe in making friends with the actors, or with anybody else. He was a technician and he expected everybody else to be the same. Unfortunately my feelings toward Moira were not technical.

'Well, you are a good-looking boy,' he said finally. 'Maybe they would go for it. It's the box that decides in the end, Alys. If it pays at the box it's good. If it doesn't pay at the box it's garbage.'

'Why don't you try me.'

'I'll ask Julius what he thinks.'

It seemed to me there was a faint maliciousness in this. 'Don't ask him. He would only—'

'Recommend against forming attachments,' he finished for me. I wasn't sure what his attitude was toward Nesselrode. There was a slightly satirical edge to his voice as he said this. It was even possible that there was an element of hostility in his relations with Nesselrode. It was not clear to me what the hierarchy of the lot was, whether he was superior to Nesselrode or whether Nesselrode was superior to him. If Nesselrode was his superior, that would account for his devious humor on the subject.

'There's nothing wrong with attachments,' he said, 'as long as they're off the lot. Well, come on in the office and we'll talk about it.'

215

We went into the fake Spanish hacienda, through the lobby, and down the corridor. On a hall leading off to one side there was an office marked 'Mr. Reiter.' It was next to the men's room, I noticed. Even if he was a genius, as Nesselrode alleged, he didn't seem to have a very important place for an office.

Inside the small room was an untidy mess of books, shooting scripts, unopened letters, and loose papers. There was a dusty sofa at one side, also piled with papers, and a desk for Reiter with a swivel chair. The script-girl had her own smaller desk with a typewriter. I began to wonder more about the script-girl. Reiter never said anything to her but instructions and questions about the picture they were shooting, but she was always with him and now it seemed she shared his office. Perhaps he concealed his attachment and only expressed it when he was off the lot. I tried to imagine Reiter off the lot, without success. He sat down in the swivel chair, leaving his hat on and still holding the crop, and I sat down before the desk in a folding chair of the kind provided by rental companies for funerals.

'What was that thing we had around about the poison in the tea?' he asked the script-girl.

'*The White Telephone.*'

She went to a file cabinet, searched around for it for a while, and found it and pulled it out.

Reiter took the script and began thumbing

through it. 'What would you do to show your love for me,' he read. 'She gazes at him questioningly. His lips hesitate. He speaks. Anything. She is silent for a long moment. She is dubious. She is not sure of him. She looks at him as though trying to decide. Anything?'

He shut the script up and tossed it onto the desk in the pile of other scripts and papers.

'I don't know if you can do this, Alys. It's very complex. It's full of psychology,' he said, underlining the word a little as if he were not sure I knew what it meant.

'It doesn't sound so difficult.'

'You're pretty sure of yourself, aren't you?'

There was no sarcasm in this, and no hostility. He was simply inquiring if that were, in fact, a quality of my character.

'I think I can do it.'

'Well, maybe we'll give you a try.'

THE SECOND PICTURE

I walked along Fifth Avenue with the portfolio under my arm, wearing a soft velvet coat and a blouse with a loose Byronic tie. A busy throng hurried up and down the sidewalk past me, carrying briefcases and folded newspapers. Looking for an address, I turned into a doorway past a sign 'Beaux-Arts Gallery. London. Paris.

New York.'

In the gallery, I opened my portfolio and showed the drawings to an elegant young man in a well-fitting dark suit, a white shirt, and a conservative necktie. At first, as I explained silently why I had come, he glanced at me in a perfunctory and indifferent way. But as he examined the drawings one by one his manner changed. He took a more careful look at me.

'I WANT MR. BELLINGHAM TO SEE THESE.'

Mr. Bellingham's office was done in Art Deco style, with furniture of polished metal tubing and leather. Mr. Bellingham himself, like the clerk, was dressed conservatively in a dark suit and necktie. His graying hair was carefully brushed over his temples, and his neatly clipped mustache was the same elegant gray. He had a mannerism of touching the ends of this mustache before he spoke. While the clerk looked on from a respectful distance, he took out the drawings from the portfolio and turned them over one by one. For a long time he said nothing. Then he looked at me and touched the end of his mustache.

'YOU HAVE A GENUINE TALENT, YOUNG MAN.'

The camera cut back to me. I made a faint smile.

218

'Come on, come on, start acting!' Reiter shouted at me from the edge of the set. 'Don't stand there like a dummy! You can't believe what he is saying! You want to believe it, but it hardly seems possible!'

My smile vanished. I looked uncertain. A little of my smile came back again. I glanced from Mr. Bellingham to the portfolio and then back to his face. He touched his mustache.

'IF YOU HAVE MORE WORK LIKE THIS, I CAN MAKE YOU INTO A FAMOUS ARTIST.

Another shot of me looking pleased but uncertain. 'Good! Good!' yelled Reiter. 'Cut. That's not bad, except you've got to get more psychology into it. Okay, now he invites you home for dinner.' We all tramped off to the next set.

★　　★　　★

On we went, I trying to get more psychology into it, and Reiter bawling at me from behind the camera. It was evening in the Bellinghams' penthouse overlooking Central Park. A few lights glittered through little holes in the blown-up photograph of Manhattan behind the window. The living room was empty for a few seconds, then a maid in a black uniform with a white collar crossed the room and opened the

219

door. Mr. Bellingham and I walked in. I no longer had my portfolio but I was still wearing my velvet jacket.

'WHERE ARE YOU, DEAR?'

Moira appeared wearing a long white gown that fitted her closely, clinging to her legs and bursting out at the ankles into a froth of white chiffon. Tiny silver sparkles in the gown caught the light as she turned. Her only adornments were a long pearl necklace that came to her waist and a pearl bracelet encircling one wrist. She stopped and looked at me with a sibylline glance, her chin raised slightly. I had never seen her dressed in such elegance. It was a new Moira. My limbs felt weak and I stood there as though rooted to the spot. I endeavored to show nothing.

But now Reiter began yelling at me to simulate the very emotion I was trying to conceal. 'Look love-struck!' he shouted. 'This is your first glimpse of the woman who is going to be your grand passion! Look as though somebody hit you over the head! That's what love is! Open your mouth a little! Raise your hand to your throat!'

He didn't have to tell me. My lips parted. They felt dry. My hand rose up and the fingers closed around my throat. I was unable to take my eyes away from Moira in the white gown.

'DEAR, THIS IS MR. DARTY. HE IS THE
PROMISING YOUNG ARTIST I TOLD YOU ABOUT.'

Moira extended her hand. When I felt the touch of her long cool fingers it was all I could do to restrain myself from taking her into my arms. I held the hand a little longer than necessary.

'Fine! Fine!' yelled Reiter.

Mr. Bellingham gazed at me curiously. The shadow of a frown appeared in his forehead. Luckily at that moment the maid appeared carrying a tray with three glasses on it, the pale amber fluid in them clinking with ice cubes.

'THIS IS THE VERY BEST STUFF. I GET
IT FROM MY SUPPLIER IN CANADA.'

Mr. Bellingham's premonitions vanished. The frown disappeared and he resumed his former air of slightly patronizing friendliness. We sipped at the bootleg highballs, then we went in to dinner. The dining room was as luxurious as the rest of the penthouse. It looked out past a landscaped terrace to a view over the Hudson. The long table, gleaming with white linen and silver, was set for three. I glanced at Mr. Bellingham, uncertain where to sit.

'Keep looking at Moira! Never mind the husband! You're struck dumb with love! All

221

you can look at is her!'

Our glances were locked. I stared at her as
though enchanted. She looked back at me with a
mysterious, faintly ironic promise at the corners
of her lips. Then she spoke.

'SIT HERE BY ME, MR. DARTY.'

Fadeout. The camera stopped and the kliegs
went off with a snap. I came to myself and found
that I was sitting alone at the table with a foolish
smile.

*　　*　　*

'Scene Three, Take One. Darty's rented room
in Greenwich Village.'

We all trooped over to the next set, which
consisted of three sides of a squalid rented room
left over from a picture about an East Side
tenement. On the windowsill was a cloth flower
in a milk bottle. There was an iron bed with a
cheap calico spread.

'Okay. Alys, sit on the bed and bite your lip.'

I sat on the edge of the bed, biting my lip and
thinking.

'Okay, that's enough. You've decided.
Clench your fists in resolve. Get up and go
phone her.'

I got up and opened the prop door, making
the flat quiver slightly. Outside in the hallway I

took the black receiver off the hook, hesitated for a moment, and spoke some words into the mouthpiece.

'Moira's answering it at the other end!' bawled Reiter. 'We'll shoot that later! You talk and then she talks! She says yes! She says come right over! She says her husband won't be home until six! You nod, Alys! Look serious! You are asking yourself is this a good idea or not? You aren't sure.'

I nodded into the phone, looking very pale. I hung up the receiver and stared into the air at a point just to one side of the camera, with an expression of mingled uncertainty and surmise on my face.

'Good, good! Cut! The kid's learning! He's still got a long way to go, but he's learning!'

*   *   *

The penthouse again. The doorbell rang as before and the maid crossed the room. I entered in my velvet coat, rather awkwardly and hesitantly. Moira, coming up behind the maid, made a conventional smile.

'WHY, MR. DARTY. WHAT A PLEASANT SURPRISE.'

She extended her hand, I took it briefly, and we sat down on the sofa. She was wearing a white negligee and had only flung on a flimsy peignoir over it. Turning her head away from me, she spoke something into the air. The maid appeared almost instantly with two cocktails in wide conical glasses, something white with froth on top. We sipped these, our glances fixed on each other over the rims of the glasses. 'It's real booze,' she told me in a low tone. 'I had them fix it. I'm a . . .'

'TELL ME SOMETHING ABOUT YOUR WORK.'

'. . . little nervous, aren't you?'

'That's fine!' shouted Reiter. 'Go on chatting! It's what's called double entendre! You're saying one thing but you really mean another!'

'At least we can be together this way,' she told me in an undertone.

'So look cryptic, Alys! Look like you're saying one thing but you really mean something else!'

I formed my face into an expression of innuendo, meanwhile trying to keep my mind on these two things at once, the lines I was supposed to be reciting and what I was really feeling.

'But every time I touch you . . .'

'Yes, I know,' she murmured, still smiling. 'Everything stops. There's nothing we can do about it.'

'Oh, it doesn't amount to much!' Reiter shouted.

I shrugged.

'OH, IT DOESN'T AMOUNT TO MUCH.'

Now Moira assumed her own expression of innuendo. She examined me intently, as though she were attempting to penetrate into something private and personal that lay beneath my outward semblance.

'I'M SURE YOU'RE GOING TO BE A GREAT
ARTIST SOME DAY.'

She gazed at me meaningfully out of her dark eyes. She set the empty cocktail glass down, and I did the same. After a moment a new idea struck her. Her smile changed. It became faintly conspiratorial, suggestive.

'PERHAPS I COULD HELP YOU. I COULD
BE YOUR INSPIRATION.'

Just at that moment the doorbell rang. The maid crossed the room again. Mr. Bellingham entered, carrying his fedora in one hand and a cane in the other.

Moira half rose from the sofa. She looked at me and then at her husband.

'BUT YOU'RE HOME EARLY, DEAR.'

225

Mr. Bellingham gave the hat and cane to the maid. He stood uncertainly in the entryway for a few seconds, then he advanced into the room. He looked from me to Moira.

'I CAME . . .'

He glanced at me again and thought.

'BECAUSE I HAVE SOMETHING TO TAKE
UP WITH MR. DARTY.'

Moira and I glanced at each other. But how could he have known I was here? The question hung unanswered in the air. We were playing a dangerous game. I got up and went off with Mr. Bellingham into his study.

He had my portfolio in there. He looked again at the drawings. Then he turned to me.

'IF YOU WANT TO BE A SUCCESSFUL ARTIST,
YOU WILL HAVE TO TURN FROM DRAWINGS TO
OIL PAINTINGS.'

We both gazed without conviction at the very bad oil painting on the wall of the study. It depicted some waves beating on some rocks in Laguna Beach. A pine tree bent over the cliff, looking as though it were about to fall into the sea.

'Look guilty, for God's sake, Alys! He's

caught you practically with your paws on his wife!'

I swallowed, inserted my fingers into my collar, and looked slightly away as Bellingham stared at me.

'Glower a little!' Reiter shouted at the husband. 'You suspect the son of a bitch!'

Mr. Bellingham glowered a little. He gazed at me with two separate expressions mingled in his glance, suspicion and paternal friendliness toward a young artist. He was an excellent actor.

'BUT YOU WILL HAVE TO WORK HARD, AND
KEEP YOUR MIND ON YOUR ART.'

'A heavy innuendo!' Reiter shouted. Bellingham stared at me for perhaps four seconds with heavy innuendo. 'Cut! Great! Print that!' said Reiter. The cameraman took off his cap and turned the visor around to the front. The grips lit cigarettes.

★　　★　　★

I was in the Bellinghams' penthouse again. It was another afternoon a few days later. The maid showed me in and then turned to her mistress.

'YOU MAY HAVE THE AFTERNOON OFF,
JEANETTE.'

227

The maid disappeared discreetly. Moira (in the picture her name was Charmian) went to the window and stood looking out at the view of the park and the Bronx. Since it was daylight now there were no little pinpoints of light showing through the photograph behind the window. She seemed pensive. She turned, and her pale white hand came up and touched the velvet of my jacket.

'MR. DARTY . . . LOUIS.'

'You don't say anything! But you feel like grabbing her!'
An eloquent but mute look of earnestness showed in my face. My hands stirred at my sides, but I didn't dare to lift them. My lips worked. Finally I managed to pronounce a word.

'CHARMIAN . . .'

To this, with a little smile, Moira turned away to the window again. Then she reached up, almost indifferently, to fasten a pin in her hair. I looked at her questioningly.

'BUT YOUR HUSBAND?'

'You needn't be so shy,' she told me in an

undertone. 'You can kiss me if you like. There are some . . .'

'HE IS ODIOUS TO ME.'

'. . . things we can do and some we can't.'

I restrained an impulse to turn around and see if the camera was still watching. 'Can we go into the bedroom?'

'Oh yes.'

'And lie down?'

'Yes. But all we can do is kiss.'

'What would you do to show your love for me!' shouted Reiter.

Turning back to me, she fixed me in a powerful and steady gaze, her mouth tightening over her teeth. She seemed to study me. It was as though her eyes pierced deeply into my soul, into my private thoughts.

'WHAT WOULD YOU DO TO SHOW YOUR LOVE FOR ME?'

The camera turned to me. At first my face showed doubt. But then a resolve spread through me, a reckless abandon. My expression darkened; the muscles of my face hardened.

'ANYTHING.'

At this she smiled again, but it was a new,

hard, and cynical smile. She fixed me in her glance. I couldn't look away. I was transfixed and unable to move, like the victim of a serpent.

'ANYTHING?'

I nodded. She touched her lips to mine, only briefly so that I had a fleeting sensation of their soft parted coolness.

'She'll go to bed, but for a price! The two of you discuss it in low voices!'

'Now can we . . .'

'What?'

'Go into the bedroom.'

'It doesn't sound like much fun, does it?'

'It doesn't matter. If it's all I can have . . .'

'Anyhow we don't do that now. Now you leave me to buy the poison.'

'You realize what she's asking, Alys! You're horrified! But you imagine your life together! You'll do it for her anyhow!'

I went through the required gamut of expressions: first a shock of horror, then a moment of dreamy thought, and finally my look of resolve returned. I nodded wordlessly.

'Cut!' yelled Reiter. 'Well, that's not bad, Alys. The thing is, you're in love with this dame but at the same time you realize it's wrong. You show two expressions at once. It's psychology, see.'

230

When I came back to the penthouse she herself
let me in. I stole through the door with my hand
in my pocket, looking cautiously about me.
Then I turned to her, and she asked me
something in a low voice audible only to me.

'Still feel like kissing me?'

With a faintly troubled look, I nodded.
Slowly and deliberately I took my hand from my
pocket. There was a small glass vial in it. Our
bodies were very close together; only a few
inches separated us. My hand moved slowly
toward hers and she took the vial.

The camera moved to her face. Slowly it
formed into an expression of complicity, with a
hard and knowing smile. 'Don't forget, you
can't...'

'I KNEW YOU WOULD DO IT.'

'...monkey with my clothing.'

A closeup of my face. Guilt, resolve, and
desire were mingled in my expression. Then
abruptly I gripped her in my arms. Her head
turned away, and I buried my face in her hair.
The camera rolled on this for perhaps five
seconds.

'Good! Good! Good!' bawled Reiter. 'Okay,
everybody, into the bedroom.'

We moved on to the next set, while the camera, the cameraman, the electricians, the script-girl, and Reiter followed along behind. The bedroom was a large room with everything in white: the walls, the carpet, the bedspread, even the telephone. A glare of simulated sunlight came through the filmy curtain over the window. Moira went to the window and then turned around and faced directly toward me. The camera started buzzing again. I could see the outline of her face and body silhouetted in the window, with a bright silver halo around her hair and a knifeblade of light between her legs. In the strong light from behind the negligee and peignoir were almost transparent. I felt the warm honey of desire trickling through my veins again. As though pulled by a magnet I moved toward her.

'Not too fast! Take your time! You're only a kid! You're just a young artist! You don't have too much experience with women! You're a little bit uncertain whether you can perform with this dame!'

I stopped and stood stock-still, my hands at my sides. My mouth worked a little. I was hardly aware of what Reiter was saying. It didn't matter. I was transfixed by the sensuous shadow hanging before me in the lucid white air.

'Okay, Moira, he's standing there like a dummy, so *you* move forward! The klieg on her just as she reaches him. That one there.' He pointed to the light he wanted. 'Go, Moira, go! Slink forward!'

She passed into the glare from the klieg and her face became visible again, her eyes unnaturally widened as though with belladona.

'Take her in your arms, Alys! You may be only a kid, but you're a man after all. She's waiting. Careful—keep your hands off her boobs or we'll have to reshoot the whole scene.'

Moira's face was suffused with desire. 'You can put your hands *some* places,' she whispered without changing her expression.

The shifting and elusive levels of reality around me blurred, and I was no longer sure what I was doing. 'Moira . . .'

'Her name is Charmian! It has three syllables!'

'He *can* hear us.'

'No, he was just reading lips.'

'CHARMIAN . . .'

With one hand on her cheek, I bent to kiss her. Then I hesitated, my face eloquent with the struggle going on inside me.

'IF I THOUGHT THAT IT WAS BECAUSE . . .'

Her glance still locked on mine, faintly smiling, she shook her head slowly back and forth. 'If you think this is hard, wait till you . . .'

'NO, I LOVE YOU. WE WILL ALWAYS BE TOGETHER.'

'. . . have to lie on top of me on the bed.'

'If only they would all go away,' I murmured, 'Reiter, the cameraman, all of them, and leave us here alone.'

I bent forward and our lips touched. I turned my head sideways to press my mouth tightly against hers. Her entire body, from shoulders to knees, was touching mine through the thin negligee.

'Cut! Fine! Okay! Print that!' yelled Reiter. 'Cut the lights now or Moira's going to melt. Where are we now?' he asked the script-girl.

'Take Thirty-one. The lovers fall on the bed.'

* * *

'Now you kids, see,' said Reiter, 'you're writhing around here on the bed, and meanwhile Bellingham from the office is trying to get his wife. He suspects something. But the phone is off the hook because you've kicked it, although you didn't notice. So you just go right on writhing, and later we'll cut in the shot of

Bellingham trying to phone from the office, getting madder and madder. Okay, try the lights over here on the bed. Camera medium close, about ten feet. You got your satin filter on?' he asked the cameraman.

'Yep.'

'The idea with the lights is, we keep them a little to one side so the lovers are in shadow. That way we can get away with more than if we lighted them directly.'

He had one of the grips lie down on the bed. The electricians pushed the lights around until the figure on the bed was shadowed the way Reiter wanted it. 'Good, good. Now Moira, you see the depression the guy left in the bed? You've got to fall right into that or the lights won't be right. And Alys, watch yourself. Hands off her boobs and nothing below the waist.'

I nodded.

'Can he slip his knee in between my legs?'

'Okay, if it seems natural. He can't just jam it in there like he's hammering nails. Okay, everybody? Let's roll. Moira, you stand there, and Alys there. You're still in each other's arms. After a while you just sort of naturally float down on the bed. You don't notice what you're doing. All ready? Lights—camera. Action!'

He began roaming around behind the camera like a tiger, slapping his boot with his crop. 'Get your hand up there on her face! You just

235

finished kissing her, remember, Alys? Now you sort of swirl around and finally land on the bed. But you start writhing while you're still standing up! Haven't you ever done this before? You're acting like a high school boy at a prom. You're going to be sticking it in her in only a minute. You want her! You can hardly stand it!'

My hand still rested on Moira's cheek. From a few inches away I could see her only in a kind of blur. Her dark eyes swam, slightly out of focus. I moved my lips forward to kiss her again, but she floated away from me, pulling me gently but insistently with her arms. Her face hung just out of reach, and I followed it. Then, as though we were suspended in an invisible and viscous fluid, we sank slowly through the lucid air down onto the bed.

'Right on the dent where the guy was lying! A little more to the left!'

I managed to shift Moira a little farther to the left. I found that my knee had somehow slipped between her legs, which parted slightly to make room for it. My elbow, or hers, struck the white telephone on the nightstand. It fell to the floor with a thump, the wire dangling.

Now I really had three things to think about. I pretended to make love to Moira, and I lay on top of her in a perfect agony of unrequited and impossible desire. Meanwhile, in a third part of my mind, I imagined Mr. Bellingham in his office endeavoring to call his home number. He waited, but there was only a busy signal. He held the old-fashioned black telephone with one hand and pressed the receiver to his ear with the other, shaking the telephone and frowning.

'Camera in! Center on the lovers on the bed! The two of you talk in whispers! You say something and she says something! It doesn't matter what!'

'I can't take much more of this. There must be somewhere we can go.'

'There's nowhere, nowhere.'

'Let's try.'

Her head moved spasmodically from side to side. 'It's no use, I tell you.'

'I want to be alone with you. Not here, among these people. Somewhere else. Alone.'

'I know, Alys. It's what I want too. But we can't...'

'We can just go out through the gate and run. There's a whole world...'

'You keep saying that, but I'm telling you it's no use.'

'I'll find some way or other.'

'Say her name, Alys!'

'CHARMIAN...'

I lifted my head slightly so that I was gazing into her eyes. Her head moving slowly back and forth, her lips parting slightly in the anguish of desire.

'Now you say his name!'

'LOUIS . . .'

With a spasmodic impulse she reached up and pulled my face down onto hers. Our lips crushed together again and I felt the hardness of her small sharp teeth, the trembling nervousness of the searching tongue between them. This made a dagger of flame leap through my nerves. Frantically my hands roamed over her negligee. I hardly knew what I was dong.

'Good! Cut!' I heard Reiter shouting. 'Print that! Okay, Alys, you can stop now. The scene is over.'

I sat up dazed on the bed. Behind me Moira was sitting up too, adjusting the negligee over her hips and touching her disarranged hair. My temples pounded and I felt hot and cold at the same time; a tight knot of desire was still clenched at the center of my body. I stared as though half deranged into the darkness off beyond the camera. At last I stood up and wandered away from the bed.

'That's just great,' said Reiter, taking off his hat and mopping his head. 'One of your best, Moira. Alys, what have you got there in your pants, a coat hanger? Better go take a shower and cool off.'

★   ★   ★

238

Take Thirty-two. The breakfast scene. I wasn't in this take and so I stood in the shadows at one side of the camera, watching the others work. Reiter paced back and forth, slapping his bull chest and going around to look through the viewfinder of the camera. 'Bring up the klieg behind the window. It's morning. Sunlight streaming in. On set everybody. Are we ready?'

Moira, that is Charmian, and her husband were having breakfast in the breakfast room. The furniture was chrome tubing and white leather, much like that in Mr. Bellingham's office. The maid was seen through the doorway doing something in the kitchen. Mr. Bellingham was seated at the breakfast table, and Moira was standing at the buffet behind him. On the table was an object I recognized: a nickel-plated toaster on four Bakelite legs. Mr. Bellingham, without taking his eyes off the newspaper, opened the door on the side and put in a slice of bread. Moira, facing the camera, watched him intently. She was wearing a morning dress in a printed fabric with two pockets in the front. Without looking down, she slipped her hand slowly into the pocket and removed the vial. Still keeping her eyes fixed on her husband, she opened the vial and shook two tablets into the teacup on the buffet beside her. Then she lifted the teapot and filled the cup. All this without looking at what she was doing, as though she were blind, so to speak; she never took her eyes off her husband. Only once did her glance rise a little to look over his head, and she caught sight of me in the shadows behind the camera. Her glance fixed on me for an instant or two, with a look of calm but portentous significance.

She set the teacup and saucer on the table.

'YOUR TEA, DEAR.'

He nodded without raising his eyes from the paper. Lifting the cup, he drank half its contents and set it down again.

'THE WORKERS ARE STRIKING AGAIN. THEY SHOULD BE PUT DOWN RUTHLESSLY.'

He drank the rest of the cup of tea.

'Camera up!' yelled Reiter. 'Roll it right up to the table! Closeup on the toaster!'

The dolly rolled up, so close that the words 'Omega Homemaker' were clearly visible on the toaster. A thread of smoke appeared over it and spiraled slowly in the air. Then it began emitting smoke heavily.

*   *   *

Take Thirty-three. The courtroom scene. Here we had to move to another studio and everything was trundled across the main street of the lot: the camera on its dolly, the klicgs trailing cables, and the script-girl with her book following behind. A whole crowd of extras was herded onto the set: twelve jurors, a lot of spectators, a bailiff, and a few more to spare in case they were needed. Charles Morton, looking like Lincoln without his beard, played the judge. Moira sat in the courtroom in the front row of the spectator section in a prim tailored suit and a white blouse, without makeup. The entire take consisted of my examination by the district attorney, who was a suave young man with an insinuating way of glancing at the jury between questions.

'WERE YOU AWARE THAT A POISONOUS SUBSTANCE, TO WIT TWO FIVE-MILLIGRAM TABLETS OF POTASSIUM CYANIDE, WAS PUT INTO MR. BELLINGHAM'S TEA?'

I caught Moira's eye. Her expression as she gazed back at me was searching and intent. I turned back to the district attorney, said something, and nodded.

'DO YOU KNOW WHO THE PERSON WAS WHO PUT THAT POISONOUS SUBSTANCE INTO MR. BELLINGHAM'S TEA?'

I hesitated, Reiter, from behind the camera, shouted, 'Look at Moira again! You look at

241

Moira between every question!'

She and I exchanged another long and significant glance. She said something too faint to hear, but her lips formed the words, 'I ... love ... you.' The camera took all this in. I turned back to the district attorney and spoke.

'YES, I DO.'

The jurors stirred in their seats. The district attorney glanced at them from under his brows, as though calling on them to pay close attention, and then he faced me again.

'WHO WAS THAT PERSON?'

'Don't answer too quickly! Keep up the suspense! Look around the courtroom! Let the audience sweat! What are you going to say? They don't know!'

My glance traveled slowly around the courtroom: to the judge, across the row of jurors in their box, to the bailiff, then the spectators, and finally fixed on Moira's face. I turned back to the district attorney.

'IT WAS MYSELF.'

Sensation in the courtroom. Everyone began buzzing. A few spectators stood up and had to be admonished by the bailiff. The judge, frowning, struck his gavel.

'WAS MRS. BELLINGHAM AWARE THAT YOU PUT
THIS POISONOUS SUBSTANCE IN THE TEA?'

'Camera up on Alys! Medium close on his
face!'

The dolly rolled up. The glass eye stared at
me. Behind the machine was the cameraman
with his cap turned around, reaching up to
adjust something and then watching me intently
with the others.

I drew myself up in the witness chair. I was
pale but resolute. There was no hesitation in my
manner. If I paused for a long and silent
moment before speaking, it was only to be sure
that everyone heard what I said.

'NO, SHE WAS NOT. SHE KNEW NOTHING OF IT.'

Another sensation. More murmurs. 'Cut to
Moira!' yelled Reiter. 'Move it! Get going! Roll
it around for a closeup of Moira's face!'

The camera on the dolly turned at right angles
and rolled across the courtroom, the kliegs
following it trailing cables. It closed in and fixed
on Moira's face. She had never taken her eyes
from me.

★   ★   ★

243

The Death Chamber set was next to the Courtroom, so there was only a short wait while everybody was moved over to it and the camera set up again. The extras who had played the spectators in the courtroom scene were used again as witnesses. The district attorney was there too, the smooth-talking bastard; now he had his chin grimly set and it was clear that he was ready, at the cost of any mental suffering, to see the thing through to the end. The witnesses buzzed. They kept looking around at the door behind them. Finally I came through it, in handcuffs, with a prison guard on either side. I looked for Moira among the witnesses and caught her eye. It was not clear why she was a witness to the execution of her lover, except that the star had to be in on the end of the picture.

'Surge forward, Moira!'

As she caught sight of me Moira surged forward, and hands reached out and held her back. With the hands still restraining her, she watched as the guards led me past the witnesses and up to the crudely made wooden chair with its straps and electrical wires. I was coatless and wearing a white shirt with the collar cut off. They sat me down in the chair and turned back my shirtsleeves.

HE PAYS THE FINAL PRICE.

Now it was I who mouthed 'I . . . love . . .

244

you' silently with my lips. Her dark eyes were fixed on me, her mouth working as though she were about to speak. Don't worry, her expression said. They can't kill you, any more than you can take off my clothes. I stared back at her calmly. A little smile played on my lips. Then it disappeared and I impassively awaited my fate. Fadeout to black.

THE END

CHAPTER FOURTEEN

The white morning sunlight beat down onto the main street of the lot. A truck was parked at one side of the street and workmen were unloading some lath-and-canvas flats from it and carrying them into a studio. Now and then an automobile came down the street and had to thread its way around this truck. I squeezed through the narrow space between the truck and the building. Ahead of me, a hundred yards or so down the street, I saw a brand-new Ford roadster parked at the curb.

I went on down the street and stopped to look at it. It was a new Model T, painted a midnight black, so glossy that I could see my reflection in it. I stood for a while examining it covertly, with particular attention to its mechanical features

245

and controls. The engine in front was concealed under a tiny hood the size of a baby-coffin, with a black radiator. Only the radiator cap with its two handles was nickel-plated. Everything else was black. The upholstery was black horsehide, quilted in a diamond pattern held down by large black buttons. There was a black steering wheel with a pair of levers protruding from the column, a black dashboard with a speedometer as the only instrument, and a number of black iron pedals on the floorboard. The car was so new that the paint had not yet been worn off the pedals by the driver's feet. The windshield was a large upright expanse of glass held in what seemed a rather fragile black frame. There was no top, or more precisely it had disappeared in some way into a compartment behind the seats. The windshield wiper consisted of a rubber squeegee on the outside of the windshield and a hand-operated lever on the inside to work it back and forth.

Everything now depended on my solving this very simple problem. I had to figure out how to drive a Model T Ford. Dirk had been a classic-car fancier and I myself had operated all kinds of exotic cars. It shouldn't be too difficult.

After a furtive glance around to be sure no one was watching, I reached in and turned on the magneto switch. Then I went around to the front. The crank was quite hard to turn, and I seemed to remember that if you didn't retard the spark you could break your arm. I hoped the spark was retarded. The engine coughed and wheezed a couple of times and then started, and the Ford inched forward and nudged gently against my shoulder. I now remembered something else about Model T's, that you had to set the hand brake before starting them. What to do? The car was pushing against me quite strongly and it was all I could do to hold it back. Possibly, I thought, I could let go of the radiator, run around to the side, and get in before it got going too fast for me. But more probably it would outpace me and speed off driverless down the street, perhaps turning the corner of its own volition and going off to join some zany comedy. It was a dilemma. I couldn't let go of the car and I couldn't stand there forever holding it back. Luckily, at that moment the engine gave a wheeze and died.

Breathing a little heavily, I went around and set the hand brake, then I returned to my task at the crank. This time, when it started, the engine took hold in a businesslike way but the car stayed in place. A workman in overalls stared at me curiously from across the street. I opened the tiny side door and got in. The controls were simple. Under ordinary conditions the car was always in high gear. There was a low pedal for starting out in low gear, a reverse pedal for backing up, and a foot brake. The throttle was one of the two levers on the steering column. I didn't know what the other one was. I released the hand brake, pressed down on the low pedal, and away I went.

I quickly found that driving the car was not as easy as I had expected. The thing was that shifting was done with the feet instead of the hands as in ordinary cars. Pushing in succession on the four controls—the throttle lever, the brake, the low pedal, and the reverse pedal—I felt like an incompetent organist trying to deal with Bach's Toccata and Fugue in D Minor. First I had to make a U-turn on the main street of the lot. This was accomplished with several backings and fillings. Then I had to negotiate my way around the parked truck, which seemed to have been left there to test the mettle of anybody who drove a car down the street. The steering wheel was set at a high angle, like that of a bus, and it felt queer. I managed to get around the truck with my right fender clearing it an inch or two. After that it was a simple matter to drive it on up the street and around the corner at the end of the block, where I had imagined the Ford turning and going off by itself to be pursued, perhaps, by some comic cops in baggy pants.

I drove up and down the streets of the lot for some time, looking for Moira. I had no idea where she was and it was only a chance that I would find her out in the street instead of inside some studio shooting a picture, or in the commissary. But it was too risky getting out of the Ford to look for her now that I had possession of it. At one point I caught sight of Nesselrode's overcoat going down the right-hand side of the street ahead of me. As I passed him I glanced to the side. He turned his face and his eyes fixed on me, glittering like two buttons. But he did nothing and made no attempt to stop me; he only twitched his nose.

The streets were cluttered with all kinds of obstacles—they were really broad sidewalks, intended for people walking and for trundling things along on dollies rather than for cars—and I threaded my way through them, somewhat handicapped by the fact that the Ford had no clutch and was always in gear, so that you could slow it down only by pushing the low pedal. By some miracle I saw Moira just coming out of the door of a shooting stage at the far end of the lot. She was only fifty yards or so ahead. I pushed the low pedal and then, as the car slowed down, the foot brake. This was perhaps not the right way to stop it; the engine began lurching and shaking the whole car, and it almost died. Somehow I managed to bring it to a stop.

Moira had caught sight of me almost at the same instant and stopped in the street a few feet from the car. She was wearing riding breeches, a simple blouse like a man's shirt, and a kind of English hunting jacket with pockets on the front. She had slipped her fingers into these

249

pockets, leaving the thumbs outside. She was bareheaded and her hair was loose and free. Without saying anything she looked at me and smiled.

I motioned hurriedly for her to get in, and opened the small door on the passenger's side. She took her place on the leather seat without a word. I pushed on the low pedal and swung around in another U-turn, this one without backing and filling. I was getting the hang of the Ford now and felt more confident.

'You've been working?'

'Yes. A stupid thing about Arabs.'

She was very attractive in the riding breeches and jacket. She had a trim figure and the costume was well-fitting and snug. She turned her face to the breeze streaming around the windshield, which lifted her hair and fluttered it against her cheek. Then, as though she had made preparations in advance for riding in an open car, she pulled out of her pocket a flowered silk scarf, folded it into a band, and tied it around her hair.

I was still a little nervous about having been seen by Nesselrode, even though he had done nothing to stop me when I had driven by him in the car. Perhaps, instead of pursuing me— which would have been ludicrous and impossible anyhow for a man his age—he had simply sent word to the front gate to stop me if I tried to drive the car out through it. Moira

250

seemed to guess my thoughts, or perhaps she only noticed that I was glancing around in a furtive way as I drove through the streets of the lot. Looking straight out through the windshield rather than at me, she said, 'After all, what's the difference? What can he do to you?'

'I don't want to be separated from you.'

She smiled a little, and after a moment took my hand and held it in hers on the leather seat between us. Steering with my left hand, I turned the corner onto the main street of the lot. A hundred yards ahead of us the same truck was still parked at the curb. I steered over to one side to drive around it, but as we approached it the two men dragged another large lath-and-canvas flat out of it, blocking the way. I came to a stop, using the double-pedal technique which I had now mastered to perfection. At that same moment another pair of men came out of the door of the studio across the street, also carrying a flat. The two sets of workmen stopped, looked at one another, and realized that they were carrying identical flats. Each one consisted of a section of wall with a brick fireplace painted on it, including a set of andirons, a mantel, and a flower-pot and a clock on the mantel. They shrugged, turned around, and carried their flats back the way they had come. The two who had come out of the studio disappeared back into it, and the other two began lifting their unwieldy load back into the truck again. I was not sure whether this was an incident in real life, whatever that meant, or a scene in a comedy that somebody was shooting. I looked around for a camera but I couldn't see one. Moira sighed.

*   *   *

Without any particular thought in mind I drove east on Washington Boulevard toward the center of the city. For several miles we drove through an expanse of half-built suburbs with many empty streets. Moira asked no questions about where I was taking her. She seemed to be in a pensive mood, as if she were reflecting about something, although on the surface she was cheerful as usual. I was in excellent spirits, in spite of the fact that I had no clear idea about what I was going to do or where we were going. It was enough to be out of the lot and on the open boulevard, at the wheel of the small car that would take us anywhere we wanted to go. And no one seemed to be pursuing us. It was a warm clear day and a fresh breeze streamed around the windshield and over our faces. Moira lifted her chin and smiled as the breeze played in the curls that protruded from under the scarf. Ahead of us I could see the line of skyscrapers along Broadway.

'Have you ever been downtown?'
'Oh yes. Many times.'

'We could stop and have lunch at Clifton's.'

'I'm not hungry.'

For some reason I had imagined myself holding hands with her beside the waterfall, while we ate Salisbury steak with mashed potatoes, or perhaps a Waldorf salad.

'Besides,' she said, 'we don't have time. We'd be late.'

I didn't know what she meant by this. A little twinge of apprehension passed through me. I glanced at her but she was exactly the same, looking out through the windshield with her placid expression. I didn't say anything more and turned my attention back to my driving. At Broadway I turned left into a busy stream of traffic, including taxis, streetcars, and a large number of shiny black cars like our own. It was a curious sensation. The downtown district was exactly as I had always known it, except that now it was new and it was the center of the city. There were no bums or street evangelists; the sidewalks were thronged with well-dressed shoppers and businessmen in black suits and hats. There was Clifton's, there was Bullock's, there was the Security Bank building where a well-known goggled comedian had clung by his fingertips to a clock hand seven stories above the street. The yellowish haze of the city was gone. The air was clear and sparkling, with only a slight smell of ozone from the streetcars.

'Do you want to stop for anything?'

'No. Or wait, yes.'

I stopped the car at the curb, and she went into Woolworth's and came out wearing a ring with a cut-glass diamond on it as big as a pigeon's egg. She held it out to show me with a flamboyant gesture. Our eyes met—mine puzzled, hers mirthful.

'Is that our engagement ring?'

'If you like. Of course,' she added after a moment, 'you have to win me.'

She got in and I reached over across her to shut the door. As I did this my hand inadvertently brushed across her riding breeches, and this made me desire her so strongly that I almost stopped the car again and looked around to see if there wasn't a hotel in sight. I mastered myself, drove on down Broadway, and turned right on Sixth Street.

'Now where?'

'To the seaside!' she said in a theatrical tone, still with an air as though she knew something I didn't. She held the ring up before her and turned it so that the glass glittered in the sunshine.

*   *   *

Sixth Street crossed the riverbed, a dry arroyo at this time of the year, on a rickety wooden bridge. On the other side of the river it turned into Whittier Boulevard, which led off into the fashionable east-side suburb of Boyle Heights. After winding its way through the hills for a while it left the houses behind and came out into the open countryside. There were dairy farms, alfalfa fields, and an occasional grove of eucalyptus or sycamores along a streambed. There was almost no traffic; now and then we passed a wagon with a load of hay, or another Model T coming in the other direction. After a quarter of an hour or so of driving down the country road we came to Whittier, a pleasant middle-sized town with bungalows and white clapboard houses set in neatly clipped lawns.

'We could live here,' I said, 'after we're married.'

'I have my career as an actress. Can you see me washing dishes?'

'Well, just for fun.'

'You could dry them.'

'Then we could quarrel and have a fight.'

'Slapping each other with the dishtowel. Then we could kiss and make up.'

'And it would end in the bedroom.'

But here she stopped and didn't go on with the game. She went back to looking out through the windshield with her childish air of knowing a secret she wasn't going to tell. I drove on down the narrow country road lined with eucalyptus trees. Beyond Whittier the dairy farms began to give way to orange and walnut groves, with occasional fields of sugar beets. Norwalk and

255

Buena Park were just crossroads, small farm towns with a single cross street, a few white houses, and a general store.

On the outskirts of Buena Park the Ford faltered once or twice, then began coughing and after a block or two died entirely. I pulled over to the side of the road as it rolled to a stop and sat there with my hands still on the steering wheel, looking out at the radiator cap with its two shiny handles. In the silence the dead engine clicked faintly.

'Do we have a flat tire?'

I shook my head.

'Perhaps we're out of gas.'

I sat there for some time, feeling oddly content. It was a pleasant sylvan scene. There was an orange grove over on the right with some bees buzzing around the blossoms. Occasionally a car came down the road toward us, went by with a swish, and disappeared off in the other direction. In the intervals between it was very quiet. Then I became aware that for some time now, ever since the car had stopped, there had been a low and almost inaudible humming in the air, seeming to come from overhead and behind us, that could not be accounted for by the bees in the orchard or anything mechanical like the passing cars.

I glanced at Moira. I knew that she heard it too.

'I wish that thing would stop.'

'You'd better hope that it doesn't.'

'I thought we were alone.'

'We're alone. Don't worry. It's Nobody.'

I wished Nobody would go away. I looked furtively around behind me up into the air, knowing that there was nothing there to see.

I turned back to her, and it was a moment or two before I spoke.

'We're still behind the Screen,' I said. 'Even here. Out in the countryside. With nobody around. Nobody to see us.'

'Of course. What did you think?'

'I thought we could get away from them and be happy together. Alone.'

'They own us,' she told me as she had told me once before. 'Once we're in pictures we belong to them.'

I felt a little twinge of anxiety again, as I had when she had told me, *We don't have time. We'd be late.* I began to suspect now what she meant. Yet the feeling wasn't really unpleasant. It was just a small shadow, of the kind that makes the sunshine seem brighter by contrast. After all I *was* alone with her, even if Nobody was following us. I came out of my trance and turned my attention back to the immediate problem, the fact that the car had stopped for some reason. Moira was no mechanic, but perhaps she was right and it had run out of gas. I began searching around on the instrument panel for a gasoline gauge. There was nothing, only

257

the speedometer and the switch for the magneto. I got out of the car and walked around it, inspecting it more carefully than I had on the lot when I was nervous about being observed. The gas tank was a cylindrical affair mounted behind the seats. Sticking up from it was a narrow filler pipe, and next to it was a gauge. It was a very simple contrivance, worked by a floating cork down inside the tank which turned a ring behind a small glass lens. Right now 'E' was showing in the glass.

I got back in the car and sat down. 'We're out of gas,' I told her.

Without a word she pointed to a filling station a hundred yards or so down the road. Once again I began to feel a sense of metaphysical anxiety. How had this all happened anyhow? The whole business—my stealing the Model T Ford, our setting out in this direction, the car running out of gas. It was a situation out of a classic picture, slightly comic, and the joke was on me. I looked around to see if there was a small boy who was about to shout, 'Get a horse!' but the road was deserted except for the filling station ahead, where the attendant was leaning against the pump with his ankles crossed, looking with mild interest in my direction. I got out, went around to the back, and started pushing on the spare tire.

I soon began to perspire. But the light car moved easily and I was able to get it going at a good pace—enough, I hoped, to mount up the slight slope into the filling station. Moira, in the passenger seat, deigned to stretch over her left hand and turn the steering wheel back and forth as needed. The filling station man, still leaning against the pump with his arms crossed, observed this scene with interest. Finally I got the car up to the pump, panting, and took out my handkerchief to wipe my forehead.

'Brand-new one, eh?'

'Yep.'

'Fill 'er up?'

I nodded.

He stuck the hose into the tank, pressed the handle, and watched while the liquid gurgled down through the glass cylinder on top of the pump. It too was a very simple contrivance, with lines painted on it to mark the gallons. When the level got down to ten the gasoline splashed out of the filler-pipe and there was a heavy etherlike odor.

'Dollar twenty,' he said.

As it happened I had picked up my pay envelope at the front office the day before and I had plenty of money. I counted it out dime by dime. While he waited he glanced back at the car. The two of us were standing in the unpaved dirt yard of the station, in front of the small office.

He looked at Moira again and then back at me.

'Nice lookin' lady-friend you got there.'

I said nothing to this.

He went on. 'I'll bet she's one o' them Hollywood stars.' He mused some more, scratching his chin, while he alternated his glances between Moira and the money I was counting out. 'Seems to me I've seen her before.' Another thoughtful look and more chin-scratching. 'That's Moira Silver, ain't it?'

At this I only smiled. I felt secretly pleased though. I gave him the dollar twenty along with a ten-cent tip, which seemed to cheer him up, although he didn't offer to crank the car for me or in any other way help to start it. All he said was, 'Retard the spark on that thing or you'll break your arm.' It finally struck me what the second lever on the steering column was. I retarded the spark, went back to the front, and cranked. It started with a confident clatter, and the radiator immediately began pushing against my shoulder. 'You forgot to set the hand brake!' he shouted at me. Ignoring him, I stepped briskly away from the front of the car, waited for it to accelerate past me, and then vaulted into the driver's seat over the top of the door without opening it. I soon had the thing under control and headed down the country road again under the eucalyptus trees. For this athletic feat, Moira kissed me.

★   ★   ★

Santa Ana was a sleepy little county seat. Everything was covered with dust and only one street was paved, a few black cars parked on it with their noses in toward the curb. There were awnings stretched out over the shops and the few loafers in sight were trying to stay in the shade of them as best they could. A dog lay in the middle of Main Street and we drove around him. There was a single movie house, a block or so from the business district and next to a Chinese laundry; it was called the Electric Theater. We were out of town and in the open country again in five minutes.

From here it was only ten miles or so to the beach. Over to the left were some brown hills, and ahead, as we went on, the sea gradually came into view with the sunlight sparkling on it like a thousand tiny diamonds. We went through Costa Mesa, the last town before the beach, and wound down a hill past a rather disreputable-looking roadhouse. Here we came out on a bay, and beyond it were the Newport dunes stretching along the coast as far as the eye could see. We crossed an arm of the bay on a narrow bridge and set off across the dunes, an endless expanse of sand carved by the wind into elaborate mounds and hillocks, with clusters of weeds growing here and there in crevices where the rainwater collected.

After we crossed the bridge the road turned

into a pair of wheel tracks and then dwindled away entirely. The expanse of sand was unbroken except for the tops of some trees showing over the dunes in the distance. As we came closer I could see they were palms. I drove toward them over the dunes, the loose sand scrunching and shifting under the narrow tires of the Ford. I imagined stopping the car and getting out and resting with Moira in the shade of the palms. If there were trees there must be water too, and there would be grass and it would be cool. As though I were recalling a distant and almost forgotten happiness from another life I remembered sitting with Moira on the grass by the Old Mill Stream. I pulled down on the hand throttle to make the Ford go a little faster.

Then we came up over the top of a rise in the sand and we could see the palms only a short distance ahead of us. There was a small crowd in the shade of the trees and scattered around on the dunes near them. The camera was set up on its dolly, with boards for it to roll around on so it wouldn't get stuck in the sand, and there was a folding chair for the script-girl. Everybody else was standing around smoking cigarettes.

I pushed the throttle back up and the Ford slowed almost to a walking pace, wallowing and pitching as it crawled over the uneven surface. But I had to keep it moving a little or the wheels would sink into the sand. I stared out through the windshield, watching the scene ahead of me grow larger until it almost filled the scrccn of glass in its metal frame. I didn't look at Moira. Finally I heard her saying, 'You couldn't turn around in this sand anyhow.'

I stopped the car near the trees and shut off the magneto switch. In the silence I was aware of the murmur of voices and of the faint crepitation of sand as people walked back and forth on it. Moira got out of the car, untied the scarf around her head, and shook her hair free. I went on sitting there in the driver's seat for a while, and then I got out too.

The grips were setting up a tent that seemed to be made out of old scarves and Persian carpets, a long elaborate affair higher at one end than the other. I noticed for the first time that there were a dozen or so mangy-looking camels standing on the other side of the trees, where they had been out of sight as we came across the dunes in the car. The reflector-screen men were setting up their screens to point into the tent, which had its front drawn up and folded back so that you could see into the interior. Near it was a prop well with a wooden bucket in it, worked by a primitive windlass. The extras were all standing around in Bedouin garb. Well, here we were. It was the stupid thing about Arabs, as Moira had put it.

Reiter, who was standing by the camera, took off his hat and wiped his head with his handkerchief. The planes of his skull, gleaming with moisture, shone in the sunshine. He put the hat back on and strode around waving everybody toward the set with his riding-crop, as though he were shooing geese. 'Okay, let's go!' he shouted.

I started to turn back toward the car, but Reiter gave me a light blow across the back of the legs with the crop—just a friendly tap. 'Over this way, Alys. Come on, come on, everybody. We've got to get moving on this thing! What's the holdup?'

'*Pirate of the Dunes*, Take Four,' said the script-girl, looking at her book. 'The Expedition stops at the Oasis.'

Reiter looked around through the crowd and caught sight of Moira. 'Where've you been anyhow? Get your ass over there and climb on a camel. Where's her pith helmet?'

'Pith on you, Reiter,' said Moira under her breath.

The costume-girl fitted a topi onto Moira's head and bent down to apply a quick touch of the comb to the curls that emerged from it.

'Fine, fine,' said Reiter. He turned to a couple of grips standing next to him. 'You guys get out there with the rakes and smooth out the tracks of that Ford. The only thing worse than shooting in sand,' he said, 'is shooting in snow.'

THE THIRD PICTURE

I lay on the couch in my tent, listlessly smoking and gazing out through the opening at the heat shimmering on the sand in the distance. The air in the tent was almost motionless; the smoke from the cigarette hung in lazy coils over my head, drifting away only slowly. The sand inside the tent was spread with fine Persian carpets. There were rifles stacked in one corner, and a primitive cookstove. Lying near me on the carpet were the only sources of entertainment in the oasis: a guitar and an oil-stained French novel which I had just set down with a bored expression. Ahmed, thin and brown, appeared before the opening of the tent and beckoned to me with a knowing expression.

I got up reluctantly and went out to look in the direction he was pointing. Over the shimmering sands in the distance a line of camels was crawling slowly towards us. Three of them were loaded with packsaddles and the other three had people on them. Three Egyptians in long white nightgowns were following along on foot, urging the pack camels on with sticks. The people mounted on the camels ahead of them seemed to be westerners, to judge from their clothing. Ahmed made his sinister smile, his eyes fixed on my face.

'ENGLISH, MASTER.'

I shrugged. We went on watching as the caravan wound its way slowly toward us. At last they stopped, only a few yards from the oasis, and gazed at us curiously. The man on the first camel was Roland Lightfoot, clad in riding breeches, a loose white hunting jacket, and a topi. Next was Moira, in a feminine version of the same garb. The third rider was a heavyset mustached Englishman in a campaign hat, evidently a guide. His face had been burned by the sun and repeatedly peeled so that it resembled a piece of half-cooked beef. After a while Lightfoot, with a glance back at the guide, turned to us again and spoke.

'SALAAM.'

I deliberately said nothing, staring back at them. Ahmed at my elbow smiled encouragement. It was impossible for Ahmed not to look sinister, no matter whether he was smiling or frowning. It was his specialty. He made a good living out of it as a character actor. He whispered something to me. I lifted my chin arrogantly in the direction of the English.

'WHO ARE YOU, ANYHOW?'

266

Lightfoot looked at me speculatively. He seemed to examine me carefully for the first time.

'THEN YOU SPEAK ENGLISH.'

It was a while before I replied to this. I stared back at him, a slightly contemptuous expression on my face. Finally my lips parted.

'I SPEAK MANY LANGUAGES.'

'Stare at the girl!' shouted Reiter. 'You're interested in her, but don't let Ahmed notice!'
Deliberately I turned to examine Moira. I narrowed my eyes slightly, and my lips closed and tightened a little. Except for that nothing showed on my face. Lightfoot spoke again.

'WE'RE AN ENGLISH EXPLORATION PARTY. MAY WE CAMP HERE FOR THE NIGHT?'

Ahmed pulled at the hem of my burnoose and whispered to me. The three English, including the girl, were all armed; there were two light Martini rifles in saddle holsters on the camels. The guide had a pair of binoculars hanging around his neck and Lightfoot an expensive German camera. There also seemed to be scientific instruments, including a theodolite and a barometer, piled on the pack camels in the rear. One of my Bedouins came out of the tent with two of our own Lee-Enfields and slipped one to me and one to Ahmed. After I stared back at the Englishman for a while longer I shook my head.

He turned to his companions doubtfully. They conferred together. They had noticed the Lee-Enfields. The guide, in a low voice, counseled going on and finding some other place to spend the night. Lightfoot turned back to me.

'THEN MAY WE AT LEAST HAVE SOME WATER?'

I still had my eyes fixed on Moira. She looked back at me, perfectly calm. She shifted her hand on the pommel of the camel saddle, and the diamond ring on her finger caught the sunlight and flared like a star. Her lips moved faintly. Was it a smile? It was impossible to say in the glare of the sunlight; perhaps it was only a grimace of discomfort from the heat and the long day in the saddle. I took my eyes away from her reluctantly and turned back to Lightfoot. I nodded. Turning to one side, I spoke to my servant Hassan. He ran off quickly to draw up the well bucket with its primitive windlass. The guide dismounted rather warily, and he and Hassan refilled the sheepskins in which the English carried their water.

'Keep staring at the girl!' shouted Reiter.

I turned back toward Moira and gave her a long look. After a moment I ran my tongue lightly over my lips. She shifted slightly in her saddle and, because of the heat, pushed back the hunting jacket to her side, a gesture that threw her breasts in the light linen shirt into prominence. Lightfoot seemed to notice that our glances were fixed on each other. He frowned.

'Offer him the money!' yelled Reiter.

Lightfoot seemed hesitant. He glanced from me to Moira, and then at the Lee-Enfields that Ahmed and I held with seeming carelessness in our left hands. Reaching into the pocket of his hunting jacket, he took out a purse. From this he removed a gold sovereign and held it out in my direction. Hassan started forward to take it, but I gripped him by his clothing. Turning to Lightfoot with a contemptuous expression, I dismissed the offer of the coin with a sweeping motion of my hand.

Lightfoot shrugged. He struck the camel lightly with his crop—for the first time I noticed that Reiter had evidently lent him his riding crop for this scene, or perhaps for the whole picture—and his camel set into motion. The others followed him. Moira turned once to look back at me. There was a fixed and intent expression on the pale face under the topi. I watched the expedition disappear off across the dunes, only the wrinkle in my brow indicating

269

the turmoil taking place inside me.

★   ★   ★

'Night scene. Blue filter. Shine the reflectors inside the tent. Is that enough light, Sid?'

The cameraman looked into his viewfinder. He got out a light meter and pointed it into the tent. 'I think so.'

My band of Bedouins was gathered in the tent. We had finished our primitive supper of couscous and mutton and the dishes were lying around on the carpets. I was thoughtful, lying on the couch, drawing restlessly on my cigarette and then setting it down again. Hassan offered me a plate of sweetmeats. I shook my head. Ahmed smiled at this in his knowing way.

'MASTER IS TROUBLED IN HIS MIND TONIGHT.'

I met his glance and stared back at him. Then I drew again at my cigarette, imperturbable, and went on watching him while I exhaled the smoke slowly between my teeth.

'IT IS BECAUSE OF THE ENGLISH, IS IT NOT SO? . . . AND ESPECIALLY THE GIRL.'

I got to my feet slowly. He was standing too. We confronted each other across the tent. Ahmed glanced in a meaningful way at the

270

others and then back to me. He made one of his longer speeches. Generally he was not a talkative person.

'THEY CARRY WITH THEM MANY VALUABLE THINGS. BINOCULARS. SCIENTIFIC INSTRUMENTS. THE WEAPONS. AND . . . THE WHITE EFFENDI'S PURSE OF COINS.'

I smiled. A distant and contemplative expression came over my face, as though I were examining some image in my memory. Finally I spoke.

'THAT IS NOT THE ONLY VALUABLE THING THEY CARRY WITH THEM.'

Ahmed made a kind of contemptuous snort. He looked at the others. They exchanged glances, nodding. They knew what it was that the Master was thinking of. Ahmed turned back to me and his face hardened.

'WE MUST SLAY THEM ALL. THERE MUST BE NO SURVIVORS.'

Inconspicuously my hand rose toward my belt where my weapon lay ready, concealed in a fold of the burnoose. It was an elaborately chased paper knife with Arabic inscriptions on the handle, the one that Nesselrode had stolen from

271

the house. Staring back at Ahmed without fear, I spoke a single word.

'NO.'

Ahmed made another of his long speeches. He was certainly developing as an orator. He spoke well too, with just the right touch of sarcasm.

'MASTER IS WEAK. HE HAS LOST HIS HEAD OVER A GIRL. HE IS A GIRL HIMSELF. FROM NOW ON, I AM THE LEADER OF THIS BAND.'

At that he got out his own weapon, a rusty and unsanitary-looking stiletto twice as long as my own knife. The others cleared a space for us in the tent and we wound scarves around our left arms. My own scarf, I noticed, was the one with the flowered pattern that Moira had wrapped around her head in the car. Ahmed made a lunge at me. I stepped back and parried his blow skillfully. His blade glanced off the scarf and slashed it slightly, but I was unscathed. We clashed again. This time I seized the wrist that held the knife, and he clutched my wrist in a similar grasp. Our teeth clenched, our muscles strained. Then I flung myself loose from him and, in a single motion, bent low and sprang upward at him like a tiger with the blade outstretched in my hand. He attempted a counterblow, which grazed my shoulder, but the paper knife struck him to the heart. He gasped a long 'Aaaaah ...' and sank to the carpet, his eyes glazed, dropping the knife. With a shrug I told the others to throw his body to the jackals.

★   ★   ★

We left the oasis at dawn, after watering our camels and fitting bandoleers of ammunition for the Lee-Enfields around our shoulders. As I reached up to the camel saddle to mount I noticed an inscription on the leather: 'Cairo. 1928.' Fitting myself easily into the saddle with the grace of an expert rider, I looked around to see if the others were ready. There were seven or eight of them, all experienced and capable men. Only Hassan would be left behind to guard the camp. Our Lee-Enfields were fitted in the holsters under the camel saddles. I tossed my head, half-hidden in the cape of the burnoose.

'FORWARD!'

We set off at a trot across the dunes. It was not long until we descried the English party in the distance. They had stopped to camp before nightfall, and I knew they could not have gone far with their drivers leading the pack camels on foot.

'Look into the distance! Point to show the others!' Reiter yelled.

Reiter, the camera and the cameraman, the script-girl, and all the others were swaying along on a flatbed truck, a short distance to one side and behind us. The driver at the wheel of the truck was Charles Morton, who was playing nobody but himself, that is, he had been recruited as a truck driver because there was nothing for him to play in this picture. I found this a little disorienting. It was an element of distortion that helped to blend together and confuse, more and more, the unreality of the Picture and the more expansive unreality of the whole world behind the Screen. For, I reasoned, if Morton was real—that is, if he had any existence apart from his characterizations on the screen—then perhaps the others were too— Lightfoot, the beefy English guide, and possibly even Reiter and the script-girl. And if they were real, then Moira and I were real too, and it might be possible for us to lead an existence quite apart from this flimsy and improbable farrago in which we found ourselves at the moment. This encouraged me. I smiled to myself through my clenched teeth, a bit of acting perfectly suited to the script at this moment.

Following the yelled instructions from the truck, I raised my hand to shield my eyes from the sun and looked off into the distance. I

274

turned in my saddle and pointed to show the others. They nodded, and we spurred our mounts to a slightly faster pace.

The English had broken camp and were proceeding slowly over the dunes about a mile in the distance. We overtook them rapidly, cutting in diagonally to intersect their course across the sands. The camels were making their way along a ridge in the dunes, silhouetted against the morning sunshine. Even at a distance, I could make out Lightfoot on the lead camel, then Moira's slighter form, and then the bulky outline of the guide. One by one the Egyptians leading the pack camels came up from behind a dune and joined in behind them in the line. It was a beautiful ocmposition, one of Reiter's most successful shots. The six camels, back-lighted in the sunshine, made their way along the ridge in the distance, and the camera shot them through our own band in the foreground, where we had stopped on a slight elevation to appraise the situation.

I looked around at the others. They were ready. I nodded and flogged my own camel into a gallop. The truck started up again, slithering over the loose sand of the dunes in an effort to keep up with us. I could hear Reiter yelling to Morton to get over to one side so he could go on shooting the English expedition and still have our band in the foreground. Morton was doing his best, but neither of them had counted on the fact that a camel under ideal conditions can make better time over sand than a flatbed truck.

'Alys! Don't be in such a goddam hurry! Slow down until we catch up with you!'

I slowed my camel to a trot. Lightfoot had caught sight of us now. He spurred his own camel to a trot and urged on the others; the three mounted camels drew ahead, leaving the pack camels and the Egyptian drivers behind. The two lines of camels were almost parallel now; my own was converging gradually on the others. I unslung my Lee-Enfield from the holster, and my Bedouins did the same. My face shadowed in the hood of the burnoose and my expression invisible, I shouted across the hot sand.

'WE WANT THE GOLD . . . AND THE GIRL.'

At this the guide raised his Martini and fired. There was a small pop and a puff of sand sprang up a few yards ahead of us. I curled my lip contemptuously. The Martinis were light hunting rifles and not very dangerous. Lightfoot was raising his own rifle now. I could see Moira's pale face turned toward me, the eyes watchful but showing no trace of fear. I fired, and behind me I heard the multiple crackle of the Lee-Enfields of my Bedouins. The two shot camels, those of Lightfoot and the guide, galloped on awkwardly for a few yards and then

276

fell like broken toys. The guide scrambled for his rifle and Lightfoot raised his hands in surrender. We shot them both. In the distance the three Egyptians scampered away leading the pack camels. We ignored them. The flatbed truck tore up behind us and skidded to a stop in the sand. Reiter was shouting at us as usual.

'Great! Great! Alys, tie up the girl! You lead her back to the oasis! You tell your Arabs to go off and chase the Egyptians, so you can be alone with the girl!'

Flogging my camel, I cut off Moira's mount skillfully and brought it to a stop. Without a word, even though our knees were touching, I snapped out a length of rawhide from under my saddle and bound her hands behind her. She offered no resistance, only looking back at me with a seraphic calm, and I carried out my feat of tying her wrists without taking my eyes from hers. I couldn't have looked away even if Reiter had shouted at me to do so; I was hypnotized by my desire for her and by the excruciating magnetism of the moment. Finally I managed to govern myself and turned to shout at my Bedouins.

'AFTER THE PACK CAMELS! THEY ARE VALUABLE!'

They galloped away, grinning and brandishing their Lee-Enfields. I turned back to Moira, ready to attach a rope to her camel and

277

lead it away to the oasis.

'Hold it!' shouted Reiter. I turned to see his thick eye-glasses glinting in the sunshine. 'Roll it up, Sid! This is a medium closeup! About twenty-five feet! Wait! Cut! Stop the camera! Moira's camel is a mess. Is it shedding or what? Why doesn't somebody else take care of these details? Why do I have to think of everything? Get a comb, somebody! Comb the camel!'

The costume-girl came running up with a comb. Everybody was getting down off the flatbed truck. I took a clip from the bandoleer around my shoulder and reloaded the Lee-Enfield, then I shot Reiter at point-blank range. He fell with an astonished look, his glasses breaking and scattering like tiny diamonds over the sand. I swung around and fired in succession at the camera, the cameraman, and the grips who were unloading reflector-screens from the truck. I missed the cameraman, who developed an unexpected adroitness at ducking, and it took me three shots to bring him down. The clip was expended and I reloaded again. The costume-girl went down with grace and crumpled on the sand, as though she were a trained actress. I wheeled around and noticed the script-girl fleeing away over the sand, rising up and down over the convolutions of the dunes, the book still in her hands. I galloped after her and dropped her with a single shot. She fell sprawling, the leaves of the book spilling out over the sand around her.

I came back and shot Morton, the two reflector-screen men, and the rest of the grips. Then I rode back to Moira and attached her camel to mine with a length of rope. Reiter, the cameraman, and the others had all fallen down in various conventional postures of agony. Now they got up, brushing the sand off themselves, and stood looking after us rather foolishly as we rode off toward the oasis.

'This isn't going to work, Alys,' said Moira.

★   ★   ★

In the tent I treated her with great correctness, even with deference. I untied her hands and invited her to remove her jacket. This she did, looking around for something to set it on, but there was no furniture in the tent except for the couch with a pile of cushions on it in the corner. She dropped it onto the carpet, and I threw back the hood of my burnoose. In some way it had become almost evening now; the inside of the tent was a gray and indistinct gloom.

I clapped my hands. Hassan the noiseless servant appeared with pastel drinks, clinking with ice, and oriental sweetmeats. Moira ignored these. Instead she watched me fixedly, withdrawing a little and holding her hands behind her. I noticed that the top button of her blouse had become unbuttoned, perhaps in the gallop over the dunes or in some other violence of the episode. She seemed to be aware of the direction of my glance, although she never took her eyes from my face. Mechanically we went through our lines. Her lips moved and she spoke in a faint voice.

'WHAT DO YOU WANT FROM ME?'

With infinite slowness, like the hand of a clock, she raised her arm and extended it with the palm down. The glass jewel in the ring caught the light and flared. I looked first at the ring and then back at her pale and intent face. Then I moved slowly toward her, bent, and applied my lips to the outstretched hand.

At the touch of her fingers against my lips the rush of desire overwhelmed me again. I hardly knew what I was doing and I realized I had forgotten my line. For a short time, perhaps only a second or two, I struggled to remember it. I released her hand, which sank in the dim air, and glanced at her meaningfully.

'IT IS NOT THE RING.'

She backed slowly away from me across the tent in the direction of the couch. Mechanically, and with a professional competence, we carried out the gestures of our roles: she her knowing and slightly ambiguous fear, I the narrowed eyes

280

and bared teeth of my lust. At the edge of the couch she stopped. Even though my face was still frozen in its conventional grimace of desire, I contemplated her with calm. It seemed to me that the moment was a terribly significant one, and I struggled to grasp why this was. Then with the suddenness of a revelation the answer fled up to me out of my memory: it was the exact moment of the still from *Pictureland,* the one I had cut out and put in the silver frame in my house in St. Albans Place. The lips in the papery-white face seemed on the point at last of pronouncing the word significant with richest expectation, a word that up to this moment had remained concealed in the microdots of the magazine page and now was to be revealed at last. Her mouth tremored a little at the corners and her lips parted. With her dark eyes fixed on me, she spoke.

'YES.'

This word too was written for us. Everything was written; and yet, even as I performed the conventional gestures and grimaces, in another part of me I struggled against these roles that other wills had commanded for us, roles we were obliged to play and yet confined us to a flimsy and shabby artificial existence in which all the depth, all the suffering and intensity of human experience was denied, a world in which violence was unreal and corpses rose up from the sand to dust themselves off, in which love ended with a tremulous kiss like two flowers touching and all else was forbidden, in which an impenetrable barrier, like a screen of pitiless and resilient gray plastic, interposed between one body and another. In this will to rebellion I sought above all to define whether I myself was a creature of flesh and blood or only a shadow and play of light, whether the promise of bliss that hung before us in this moment was a thing of substance or only a black-and-white dance of mute ghosts.

The blood pulsing in me was real, and so was my desire. I stepped forward and she was in my arms. I felt the hardness of the two delicate bones behind her shoulders, my hands touched the pale eloquent face, they slipped pulsing with desire down the blouse and the sides of the snugly cut riding breeches. Her own arms around my shoulders seemed to pull me backward and downward. Weightlessly and magically we floated down onto the heap of silken cushions. She lay with her eyes closed and lips slightly parted, her head moving back and forth like a slow pendulum with the urgence of her desire. 'Alys, Alys,' I heard her murmuring. 'Quickly, quickly.'

From overhead, as though it were coming from the stuff of scarves and carpets that hung over us and shielded us from the world, I was aware of a subdued and insistent humming. I grasped at the blouse and fumbled with the buttons, but my fingers were too slow, the buttons too tiny and intricate. 'Quickly, quickly.' I pressed my hand over the soft convexity of a breast, feeling the point at the center harden under my touch, then I seized at the seam of the blouse and jerked it impatiently. The buttons flew away and there was a sound of tearing cloth. I had a glimpse of a perfect pale hemisphere, like a tiny moon, with a delicate upright aureole in its center. Then the murmur overhead gradually grew fainter until it stopped altogether. The body lying under me seemed to dissolve, and a kind of darkness fell over my eyes, growing deeper and deeper until everything was black and there was nothing.

CHAPTER SIXTEEN

Moira said very little on the drive back toward the city. After our long swoon in the tent— which had perhaps lasted all night, since we had come back to the oasis at nightfall and now it seemed to be morning with the sun shining brightly—we got into the Ford and started off without very much conversation. The dunes were deserted; there was nobody in sight. The traffic on the country road was light and the

Ford buzzed along making good time. As we passed through Whittier there was no more talk of our settling down in a little bungalow and washing the dishes together. Moira had put the hunting jacket back on over her torn blouse and fastened it tightly so that nothing showed. She looked steadily out through the windshield at the black road winding its way toward us. She seemed subdued and a little depressed.

After a while I said, looking not at her but out through the windshield at the road ahead, 'I'll think of some way.'

'Will you?' she said with false brightness.

'Once,' I said, 'I went back out through the Screen with Nesselrode and then came back in. We have to talk to Nesselrode. He can take us out if he wants to.'

'Yes,' she said rather vaguely. I wasn't sure she was following what I was saying. Or perhaps she simply felt that everything I was telling her was futile, but didn't want to say so. After a while she said just as brightly, 'Of course he's a . . . pervert. You know that.'

At first I was about to remark that mutilating paper dolls seemed to be a fairly harmless sport. Then I remembered the riding crop. After all she had been his mistress and knew a good deal more about his private nature than I did.

'Did he ever really . . .'

'What?'

'Hurt you?'

284

'That depends,' she said, 'on whether you would say that a prisoner is being hurt.'

'As I said. If we talk to him, maybe he would . . .'

'Yes,' she said again. It seemed she was greatly addicted to saying yes this morning. I remembered her pronouncing the word the night before as she had stared at me fixedly in the tent. Now, for some reason, it didn't produce my usual reflex of purely animal lust. Instead I felt a warm rush of protectiveness for her; I wanted to steal her away to some rose-covered cottage or other and take care of her and live there with her for the rest of my life, to be with her every day and make toast with her in the morning and go to bed with her at night, where I would be skillful and tender and solicitous and think about her pleasure instead of always thinking about myself.

'Moira.'

'Yes.'

'I know another way. Without Nesselrode. At least it's worth trying.'

'Yes,' she said, looking out through the windshield and lifting her chin with something, at least, of her old confidence and flair.

★   ★   ★

When the downtown traffic was behind us I continued out west on Washington Boulevard, dodging around an occasional parked truck or a pedestrian making his way blithely across the street in the middle of a block. But when I came to La Cienega, instead of continuing on toward the lot a mile or so ahead I turned right abruptly, skidding around the corner so that Moira had to grab the door for support. She looked at me with an air of slight puzzlement, or perhaps, since her aplomb was unmarred even now, surmise would be a more precise term. After that she never took her eyes from my face, as though she hoped to read there some answer to her unspoken question. We didn't have far to go. At the corner of Pickford, without slackening my speed, I made another violent turn and swung around in a circle to stop in front of the Alhambra Theater. Moira clutched at the windshield in order not to be thrown out. Then, after we had come to a stop, she looked at me calmly to see what I was going to do next.

I went around the car and opened the door and she got out. The stucco of the theater was fresh and new, and the playbills in their glass frames announced a new picture with Vanessa Nesser. 'That tart,' said Moira mildly. This reassured me a little; she seemed her old self again. The front doors of the theater were of course locked, since it was only ten o'clock in the morning. Everything was phenomenally quiet. There was hardly any traffic on the streets; now and then a black car buzzed by, or a

286

square truck with the name of a bakery or a furniture store on it. The sidewalk was deserted in both directions as far as the eye could see.

Then, several blocks away, I made out a small gray figure bobbing up and down slightly as it came up the sidewalk toward us. It was too small to make out any details, but the rhythm of the motion was unmistakable. Almost at the same moment Nesselrode seemed to catch sight of us, or perhaps of the Ford parked at the curb. The bobbing stopped, the figure straightened and elevated a little, and then set into motion again at a brisker pace.

I took Moira's hand and pulled her after me around the theater to the rear door. It was unlocked and we slipped in quickly. I had no key to lock the door and could only fasten it with the flimsy wire hook. We mounted up the steps to the stage, where the usual junk was standing around: a stepladder, piles of lumber, crates. But all these things seemed newer now, as though they had been recently used, and there was no more dust on them than there was in the backstage area of an ordinary theater. I looked around. At the same instant I heard a kind of scratching or grating from the latched door behind us.

To pass through the Screen on previous occasions it had been necessary for me to hold Nesselrode's hand, or so he had given me the impression. I remembered the creepy feeling of

287

intimacy, a kind of inversion or perversion of human companionship, that this had given me. I took her hand and we moved forward. Our bodies struck limply, with a kind of bounce, onto the Screen. It had a slick surface that felt like rubber, but it was tough and strong. It hardly gave under the impact of our bodies at all.

'It's no use, Alys.'

Releasing her hand, I stepped back a few feet and flung myself at it with all my force. I bounced off it and ricocheted back onto the pile of lumber, collapsing in a sprawl.

'It's no good. It's no good. It won't work, I tell you.'

I inspected the pile of lumber more carefully. One timber in particular seemed suited to my purposes. It was heavy and strong, probably a four-by-four, and it had been cut off diagonally at one end for some reason so that it ended in a kind of chisel-point. Lifting the timber, I pushed this sharp end against the bottom of the Screen. Even though the grayish material was tough it had a certain elasticity. I heaved at the end of the timber with all my strength. The diagonal end slipped under the Screen, lifting it a little. After more pushing, and some waggling of the timber back and forth, I was able to work its entire thickness under the bottom of the Screen so that two feet or so of the timber projected out onto the forestage. Then I attempted to lift the other end of the timber to pry up the Screen.

It was an extraordinary substance. It seemed as tough as steel, even though to a certain point it had the elasticity of rubber. Beyond that point—the point where I managed to lift my end of the timber to the height of my waist—the resistance intensified so that it was all I could do to hold the timber up, let alone lift it any higher. I had now prised the bottom of the Screen six inches or so from the stage, nowhere near enough for us to crawl under. In any case, I couldn't let go of the end to crawl through, or the timber would have slammed down onto the stage with the violence of a Roman catapult. The perspiration broke out on my face and prickled under my arms. I looked around to see if perhaps there wasn't another timber or something, about three feet long, that Moira could hand me to brace up the end of the timber at least temporarily while I took a breath and thought what to do.

At this point Moira, without a word, tugged at my sleeve. I turned and she pointed out through the gray luminescent Screen into the theater. Although the light was dim, my eyes had adjusted now and I could make out the rows of seats and the projection booth above. Something was happening out there. A figure stole along behind the last row of seats and turned to look behind him. Two more figures

289

followed.

The three Chicano boys were dressed almost alike, in tight-fitting black pants, shiny shoes, and flowered shirts. They hurried on down the aisle at the side of the theater, still looking behind over their shoulders. At the rear of the theater a pair of policemen in black uniforms came into view, and then another, this last one evidently a motorcyclist since he was in boots and a white helmet. All three of them had their guns out. Their eyes were still adjusting to the darkness and they stood for a moment at the rear of the theater, keeping close to the wall behind the projection booth.

I lowered the beam to the floor, with an excruciating strain as though my backbone was about to split. Taking Moira by the hand, I drew her behind the pile of lumber where we were half hidden but could look over the top and see what was happening. We could see only dimly through the Screen, but we could hear every sound clearly as though magnified.

'Pendejo, tira la arma.'

The boy in the lead, glancing around at his companion, took something from his belt and slung it away in a single adroit gesture. A small snub-nosed revolver struck the stage with a clink and came to rest against the Screen, near the point where I had been trying to pry it up.

The three officers had caught sight of the boys now. 'Okay, hold it right there,' said one of

290

them in an offhand tone. They still had their guns out but in a way as though they didn't expect to use them. They were all very professional, both the cops and the boys. Nobody got excited. The boys were neatly cornered and they saw it. They made no real effort to find other exits from the theater.

'All right, boys, on the wall. Are there just the three of you?'

'That's right, just the three of us.'

As though they were repeating a game they had played many times, the boys faced the wall and put their hands on it while the cops patted their pockets. When they heard the clink of the handcuffs coming out they meekly put their wrists together behind them. One turned to the other and shrugged, with a little grin. Like all boys, they enjoyed playing cops and robbers. There was not much else to do in this part of town. As for police brutality, the cops gave the impression that they were too overworked to hit anybody. They probably had three or four other things to do that morning.

'Okay, I guess we can go now,' said the one in charge.

They all went out together, disappeared into the darkness of the foyer. The theater was very quiet. Moira started to get up, and I pushed her down again. She looked at me questioningly but I said nothing. When I listened carefully I could hear it again: a kind of snuffling noise from the rear of the building, and a scratching as though someone was prying at the door with some kind of tool. There was a small sound of splitting wood, followed by a silence. Then I heard the creak of the door opening and the sound of Nesselrode's feet mounting the steps at the side of the stage.

For a moment Moira and I crouched there silently looking at each other. Then I crawled out on my hands and knees, lay down next to the wooden timber, and stuck my arm under the Screen at the place where the timber had lifted it a little. By stretching the arm as far as I could, and flattening my cheek against the gray rubbery surface, I managed to get two fingers onto the revolver and edge it over to the point where I could grasp it. Then I quickly crawled back and took my place beside Moira. She looked down at my hand and realized for the first time what I had in it. I turned the revolver over in my hand and fingered it curiously: an object from the real world.

At that precise moment Nesselrode appeared, dimly visible in the gray light of the stage. His wisps of hair were awry and his overcoat was hanging open. I could see the small protruding eyes gleaming in the semidarkness. He turned his head back and forth in little jerks, inspecting every corner of the stage. Then he caught sight of us; even when we were crouching down as low as we could the pile of lumber only concealed us to the shoulders.

I stood up and pulled Moira after me. Since she was on my right I shifted the revolver to my left hand. The two of us confronted him across the pile of lumber. I was uncertain what was going to happen. I didn't think it was likely that Nesselrode would use his power to help us out through the Screen, and in any case I didn't feel like asking him for any favors. To help us through the Screen he would have to take our hands, and I had a horror of his touching Moira. I was determined not to let this happen.

After he stared beadily at us for a moment or two he started to make his way around the pile of lumber. He was only a few feet from Moira now. I said, 'Don't touch her.'

At that moment I transferred the revolver to my right hand, and he seemed to take notice of it for the first time. He looked alarmed. His nose twitched and his mouth worked.

'What's that? No. Real is not allowed.'

But he kept sidling around the pile of lumber toward Moira, perhaps only mechanically now and unaware of what he was doing.

I lifted my arm toward him, sticking it out at a stiff and stilted angle, and pulled the trigger. Nothing happened; it seemed to be stuck. I found the safety, pushed it off, and tried again. This time the gun fired with an ear-splitting detonation inside the confined space. There was an acrid smell and a veil of smoke that for an instant hid the view in front of me. When it cleared I wasn't sure at first whether my shot had taken effect. Then I saw that Nesselrode was down on the floor of the stage groping around as though he were looking for something. He rolled over like a trained dog, got his knees up under him, and began crawling toward us again.

'Come on.'

I tried to pull Moira after me. But she lingered with her hand on the pile of lumber, staring at Nesselrode as though hypnotized. Before I could unwind her fingers from the boards Nesselrode had crawled up and seized my pants cuff; I could feel a heavy weight whenever I moved my right leg. I bent down to detach his hand, but it clung tenaciously. Dragging the both of them after me, I struggled my way inch by inch toward the Screen at the edge of the stage. When I came to it I realized that the reason I had no free hand was that I was still holding the gun. I transferred it to my back pocket and reached out toward the Screen.

My fingers passed through it as though it were a veil of smoke. Nesselrode lost his grip on my cuff, but as soon as I moved the leg he managed somehow to clutch onto the other one. I found myself standing on one foot, trying to dislodge him from the other as though he were a piece of chewing gum. It was no good; he clung to me with fingers like iron and in the end I had to pull the three of us through the Screen together, in a clump of entangled bodies. A film like a grayish spiderweb seemed to cling to our shoulders for an instant. When Moira and I were through I gave an irritated kick and Nesselrode at last let go of my leg. I looked back and saw him lying prone over the frame of the Screen, his four limbs groping in an uncoordinated way. I dragged Moira away by the hand, off the stage and up the aisle through the dusty rows of seats. When I looked around again I saw that Nesselrode was still pursuing us, although he wasn't making much progress. When he came to the stairs at the edge of the stage he fell prone again, with a sigh I could hear from the other end of the theater, and began slithering down them like a snake.

'Hurry.'

'I'm afraid,' she said.

'It's all right.'

In the foyer, ahead of us and a little to one side, I could see an angular gleam of light. As I drew closer I saw what it was: the Chicano boys had broken the glass door and left a piece of plywood sagging down where they had pried their way through it. They had gone out, with the cops leading them, in the same way. The plywood was only hanging by a couple of nails and there was broken glass on the carpet.

The opening was small and we had to stoop a little to go through it. Moira seemed reluctant. I went out first, drawing her after me by the hand, and then turned to help her through.

'Watch out for the broken glass.'

'Alys, Alys, I can't go out there.'

'Come on,' I urged her.

With a gentle pressure I urged her through, one limb at a time, as though I were an obstetrician carefully and skillfully pulling a child from the womb. She came out with a sigh and straightened up, putting her hand to her head to smooth her disarranged hair. Then the two of us turned to the street in front of the theater.

It was a typical hot summer day in Los Angeles. I had forgotten what it was like and at first the colors struck me with a shock. Bright reds, blues, greens, violets, and yellows glared in the sunshine. It didn't seem real; it gave the impression of a world brightened with cheap chemical dyes, or a television screen with the color intensity turned up too high. The atmosphere too contributed to the effect of strangeness; there was a thin saffron-colored haze over the street and the air had a sweetish molasses taste in the mouth.

I looked at Moira. She was unchanged, exactly as before; everything about her was black and white. There was hardly any color in her face. Her skin was white, her clothing white or very light beige; only her hair and her large expressive eyes were dark. She stood with a little

296

smile looking out at the street before her.

'It *is* awfully hot, isn't it?' she said with a falsely bright cheerfulness.

We were both reluctant to leave the shade of the marquee. But when I looked over my shoulder I seized her arm again and pulled her away after me. She turned to see what I was looking at and gave a little gasp. Painfully, inch by inch, Nesselrode was working his way out through the broken glass door. He was still on his hands and knees and he lifted first one limb and then the other as he oozed out through the broken glass and slithered to the sidewalk. He brought his second leg through and stretched out flat, his hands clutching at the concrete as though he were trying to pull himself forward with his fingernails. He looked up and swiveled his head until he caught sight of us. Then somehow he got into motion again and crawled slowly along on his belly toward us.

We hurried away across the sidewalk. I caught sight of a taxi coming up the boulevard, and I stepped out onto the curb and raised my hand. It came to a stop with a squeal of rubber.

As I opened the door and shoved Moira inside I turned and caught a last glimpse of Nesselrode. He had managed to cross the sidewalk now and had reached a bus bench at the curb. He crawled halfway up on this and groped out with his hands, as though he hoped to clutch at us from a distance of fifty feet. But

297

this effort was too much for him; he toppled sideways and collapsed until his forehead was resting on the bench.

We got in and slammed the door after us. The driver was a black wearing a knitted cap pulled down over his ears in spite of the heat. The sides of his wrap-around sunglasses were stuck in under the cap. He said nothing and didn't even bother to turn his head. The car went off with a squeal of tires, accelerating until the stores along La Cienega flashed by dizzily. The figure up ahead in the knitted cap bent over his wheel as though he were paying no attention to us.

After a block or so, instead of speaking, he looked up and caught my eye in the rear-vision mirror.

'Sunset Strip,' I told him.

'Motel?'

I could see his face in the mirror. I nodded.

'I got a good one. Waikiki Palms.'

'They give you a cut, I imagine.'

'It's a good one.'

Moira, smiling and looking past the driver out the windshield, said, 'I wish he wouldn't drive so fast.'

CHAPTER SEVENTEEN

The palms were real, not plastic as I had expected. Once we were in the room with the door shut I found that it too was somewhat less squalid than I had anticipated. There was a large queen-sized bed—this, I imagined, was what the driver had meant by saying it was a 'good one.' Everything was pink, including the absolutely opaque window curtains and the bedspread. It was true there was a mural of Waikiki on the wallpaper covering one whole wall, but it was in pastels and not intrusive. The other amenities included a pair of fuzzy armchairs, a color TV, an immaculate bathroom, a 'Do not disturb' sign to hang outside, and a chain on the door heavy enough to stop a medieval army with a battering ram. The carpet, of the same pink as the bedspread, was so thick that it came up to our ankles. The room was a little close and stuffy and I went to the window and turned on the air conditioner.

Moira gazed around without curiosity. Almost absentmindedy, as though she were not aware of what she was doing, she took off her jacket and dropped it on the floor. When I saw her torn blouse with the buttons ripped off I was reminded of the violence of my desire the night before in the tent, and immediately it returned.

We took up exactly where we had left off, as though the scene had stopped for a moment while the cameraman adjusted his camera or the lighting was changed. She undid the sole remaining button of the blouse and stood looking at me placidly and yet intently out of her dark eyes. I took her in my arms and she gripped me with a sudden and unexpected intensity, like a small wild animal; it was difficult for me to breathe. Then, just as abruptly, she released me and turned away. First she drew back the bedclothes, folding back the spread and the sheet exactly to the middle of the bed. Then she disrobed and lay down on the bed.

In the bright light from overhead the whiteness of her body was dazzling. It extended to every part of her body, even the fingernails and toenails. The only exceptions were the large and shadowy eyes, the dark hair flung out over the pillow, and the small and inconspicuous triangle at the base of the pubic mound, itself as delicately fashioned as a Balinese sculpture in ivory. Her body seemed unexpectedly small when it was unclothed; the hands and feet might have been those of a child. The curves of her body were discreet, more boyish than exaggeratedly feminine. I switched off the overhead light leaving only the subdued glow of the bedside lamp. Then I lay down beside her, as though we were two children taking an

300

afternoon nap.

It was very quiet. Now and then I could hear the swish of a car going by on Sunset Boulevard. The only other sound was the subdued hum of the air conditioner, which was now sending out a flow of cool air that played refreshingly over our bodies. At first I found this sound vaguely disturbing, and after a while I remembered why. But since it didn't stop when Moira took off her clothes, and since I retained the lucid intensity of my consciousness even now that I was naked myself, I ignored the sound and soon forgot it.

Moira seemed tired. Even though she showed unmistakable signs of pleasure as I caressed her, she lay passively without moving her limbs or caressing me in return. In spite of the smallness of her body, of everything about her, I had no difficulty in carrying out my wishes with her. In fact it happened almost without my knowing it, as though her own desire drew me into her with the quick and gentle force of a sea anemone. Time passed. I was aware of it slipping away, minute after minute, stealing from us tiny fragments of our existence. Before me fragments of Moira's face appeared, a pale and unfocused surface moving restlessly from side to side under my caresses. Everything was white; even when I closed my eyes there was nothing but whiteness. And when our pleasure at last rippled out and broke into waves, it too was white, as though a pure and perfect surface of snow was suddenly broken by the surging-up of a white violent animal. A snowquake: it convulsed, shivered, and died away slowly into a trail of tiny tremors. At that exact moment, while I was still lying in her arms, the air conditioner, having cooled the room enough to trip the thermostat, shut itself off and the humming stopped.

★   ★   ★

I got out of bed, glanced at the clock on the nightstand, and went to the TV and switched it on. Then I stood before it, still naked, waiting for it to warm up, while she watched me from the bed. 'Alys. Alys,' she said in a curiously matter-of-fact tone. 'You're beautiful.' And after a moment, just as the gray screen before me flickered and broke into dull jabs of light, she added, 'And very skillful.'

It was six o'clock and I switched on the Channel 2 news. There was a war in the Middle East, and a congressman had been indicted for bribery. Two female twins in the San Fernando Valley were bringing a charge of rape against two male twins they had met at a twin convention. There was nothing about Nesselrode. After fifteen minutes I switched to Channel 4. It was much the same.

'Perhaps they haven't found him yet,' she said with her false brightness, still from the bed.

302

I turned the TV off and began putting on my clothes folded over the chair. Moira's own clothes—the jacket, the blouse, the riding breeches, and a scrap or two of underwear— were scattered over the carpet, one garment here and another there.

She watched me. 'Do you always put your trousers on last?' she asked with a bright curiosity.

It struck me that she had never had any other real lover except Nesselrode, and he perhaps was a little odd in his habits.

'Yes. Except for the shoes.'

I pulled up the pants and fastened them. A trace of Nesselrode's smell still lingered in the cuff where he had seized it; it had a rancid gamy odor like spoiled meat. There was a dark spot that looked as though it might be blood too, but perhaps it was only a smear of grease. I buckled the belt, then at my feet I noticed the small snub-nosed revolver, which had fallen out of my pocket when I undressed.

I took it into the bathroom. There was a container marked 'For razor blades only' but the opening was far too narrow. No chance of flushing it away down the toilet. After looking around for a while I found a small bag of waxy paper like those provided to throw up in on airplanes. It said on it, 'For your convenience for sanitary napkins only.' Thinking that no one was likely to open this to inspect its contents, I

303

put the gun in it and dropped it into the wastebasket. Then I went back into the bedroom.

'I'll be back in a few minutes.'

'All right, Alys dear.'

She made no move to get out of bed or to put on her own clothes. She seemed content just to stay there propped up in bed looking at everything, with her small pale breasts just showing over the edge of the bedspread. I took the key and went out. It was dusk, with a Turner-like sunset flaring in the sky to the west.

On the sidewalk in front of the motel I got an evening paper from the coin rack, and then after a moment's thought I went down the boulevard to a fast-food outlet and bought some chicken and french fries. With a glance around—I had developed all the instincts of a hunted criminal—I let myself back into the motel room. Moira was still in bed, following me with her little smile as I set the food on the Formica counter and sat down to look at the paper.

The only space large enough to unfold the paper completely was on the bed. I pulled up the chair and spread the paper over the pink bedspread. Moira's slender legs, stretched out straight before her, hardly made a bump in the middle. I spent a quarter of an hour or so carefully searching through the paper. There was nothing, not even in the rubric of a dozen or so minor crimes buried in the middle of the

304

second section. Most of the stories were the same ones we had seen on TV. There was a photograph of the twins gazing at each other in profile, one glancing coyly sideways at the camera. Moira crawled out from under the bedspread and looked at it curiously over my shoulder. 'They probably just want to get into pictures,' she said. I went through the paper again, this time even searching through the sports and the financial section. There was not even one murder, which was unusual for Los Angeles. I folded it up and stuck it into the shelf under the nightstand.

'Do you want something to eat?'

'No.'

I opened the box and began picking at the chicken and french fries. There was also cole slaw in a paper cup which was to be eaten with a small plastic fork. I ate a piece or two of the chicken but I wasn't really hungry either. After a while I turned my attention back to the TV. I noticed for the first time that there was a printed decal fixed to the front of the TV over the screen. It said, 'This set equipped with private TeleCable service. For your enjoyment adult films are presented on Channel 46. For viewing by persons over 21 years of age only.'

'What's a Channel, Alys dear?'

'It's like a theater. There are all these theaters, and you can see them one after the other just by turning the knob.'

'How nice.'

I turned on the TV again, waited for it to warm up, and switched it to Channel 46. Then I slumped down into the chair beside the bed and we watched the so-called adult films. They were divided into various categories, and there was something for all tastes. Each category ran for about twenty minutes, and then there would be a title—white and shaky against a black background as in a silent film—and the next category would begin. In fact the pictures *were* silent, except for a toneless and vaguely sensuous music of the kind played in elevators. I soon had the categories memorized.

BONDAGE & DOMINATION
MIXED WRESTLING
SPANKING
GROUP LOVE
GAY

The whole thing took about an hour and forty minutes, and then it would start all over again:

BONDAGE & DOMINATION
MIXED WRESTLING

and so on. There was a fascination to it, mainly because the images that passed across the screen were so unreal. Writhing and ghostly shapes twisted themselves into improbable

306

concatenations, separated, merged into clusters, and oozed in pink tentacles from one side of the screen to the other. Everything was in color, and the intensity of the colors seemed too bright, even when I got up to adjust the set. Before our eyes appeared organs that gave the appearance of having been taken from the inside of a human body by a surgeon rather than attached to the outside of it. I was surprised at the poor quality of the photography. You would think that something so attractive, and so illegal, would be more profitable.

After a while I found the chair was uncomfortable, and I took my clothes off again and got back in bed with Moira. We sat there propped against the headboard watching the films for most of the night. She didn't seem to be sleepy; she kept her eyes fixed on the screen with a watchful, slightly amused expression. After the films had run through their sequence three or four times I glanced at my watch and was surprised to find it was three o'clock in the morning. I got out of bed and reached for my clothing again.

'Get dressed,' I told her.

'Why?'

'We're going out.'

'I only have *this* to wear,' she said primly, getting out of bed stark naked and holding up the riding breeches by one leg.

Everything was dark outside and the office was locked up. The motel manager had given up trying to rent the rest of his rooms, even to casual fornicators like us, and he had turned on the neon 'NO' in his No Vacancy sign and gone to bed. We went out to the front and stood on the curb waiting for a taxi. In the orange glare of the streetlight in front of the motel she seemed very tired and drawn. A fine network of lines was visible around her eyes, even though she had her face lifted up into a semblance of cheerfulness. I was familiar enough with the feminine temperament to realize that she would probably like to put on some makeup, and also to change her clothes. There was nothing I could do about this and I said nothing. I saw a taxi coming around the curve on Sunset and I stepped out and flagged it down.

The driver had a Chicago accent, and he was wearing a cloth cap with a button on it that said, 'Nuke the Ayatollah.' I told him to take us to Olympic between Crenshaw and Arlington.

'Where exactly, buddy?'

'I'll show you when we get there.'

We went off, not quite so violently as we had with the black driver. 'Sunset Boulevard is my favorite street,' said Moira. 'All these beautiful signs.'

Slabs of tin with bright polychrome letters

glaring from them flashed by the car in endless succession. She went on looking at them with her happy expression, and seemed a little disappointed when we turned onto La Brea and left most of the signs behind. Olympic, on the part of it where the taxi stopped, was almost entirely residential and it was quite dark. The nearest streetlight was several hundred yards away. There was no moon and a thin starlight shone on the pavement, glittering here and there on a pebble imbedded in the asphalt.

'This all right?'

'Fine.'

I gave him a bill that I couldn't see very well in the dim light, but evidently it was a five because he took it and drove off without a word. We were about a block away from the chained entrance to St. Albans Place. I hadn't wanted the taxi to stop too close to the gate. There wasn't much traffic here on Olympic; an occasional car went by with its headlights boring into the darkness. We set off down the sidewalk. Moira kept lagging behind me, and I had to slow down a little so that she could keep up. At the gate I got out my keys, which I had carefully transferred from pocket to pocket each time that I had changed costume in the past few weeks, and unlocked the rusty iron door. We slipped through it and I locked it again. Then we made our way through the deep shadows under the trees toward the house.

'What a nice street,' she whispered.

'Shhh.'

She went on turning to look at the houses, on one side of the street and the other, as I led her along by the hand. She whispered again, 'If you have to have a key to get in, they can't find us here.'

'There's another entrance.'

She hardly seemed to pay attention to what I was saying. She seemed lost in her own thoughts, as though entranced, and yet as far as I could tell perfectly content.

When we arrived at a point a hundred yards or so from the house I stopped and inspected it carefully. The wndows were dark and there were no cars parked anywhere near it. That didn't mean much; they wouldn't park their car in front of the house. Leaving the sidewalk, I crossed the lawn of the house next door and approached cautiously under the shrubbery, drawing Moira after me. From a position behind the hedge I could see there was no one on the porch. There might be someone waiting inside but that was a chance we would have to take. We stole on tiptoe across the lawn and up the wooden stairs of the porch. Moira suppressed a smile, as though it were all a game. I didn't need a key here because I had left the door unlocked when I had dashed out after Nesselrode—it seemed an eternity ago. I stood there for a few moments on the porch. There was no sound

310

from inside.

We went in. The rooms were dimly visible in the starlight that came in through the windows. I knew the house so well that I could move through it in the dark, but Moira was helpless and I had to draw her after me wherever I went.

'Stay here. I'm going upstairs to look for the car keys.'

'The car keys?'

'We have to get out of here.'

'You have a car?' she said in her usual bright and casual tone.

'I have two.'

'How nice.'

I went upstairs, stepping over the ones that creaked, and made my way to the upstairs study where I kept the keys in a bowl on the desk. I had to decide between the Hudson and the Invicta. Both of them were conspicuous, and I realized now the disadvantages of owning classic cars, as exquisite and elegant as they were. I took the Hudson keys, identifying them by feel as the ones in the oblong leather holder with a miniature Hudson emblem on it. I had just slipped them into my pocket when the telephone on the desk in front of me jangled, so loudly that I jumped like a scalded cat.

I stood there with my nerves leaping every time the thing went off. it rang only three or four times and then it stopped. Standing there in the darkness, I tried to calm myself. The

311

blood was still pounding in my head; I could almost hear it thumping in the darkness. After a while I took a breath and my pulse slowed down.

I went back down the stairs into the living room. The large windows facing to the west were open, and in the starlight I could see Moira standing by the sofa holding the phone to her ear. She was nodding as though she understood something. She said, 'Yes.'

She turned to me and held out the phone. 'It's for you.'

'Why did you . . .' I mouthed at her silently. She only went on holding out the phone to me. I exchanged a look with her. Then slowly I reached out and took it from her.

'Yes?'

'This is Lieutenant Donner of Wilshire Division homicide.'

It was a crisp bureaucratic voice, with an unconvincing politeness laid on over the top of it. I didn't care for the tone of it at all. Moira was watching me expectantly with a little smile hovering at the corners of her mouth. I said nothing and the voice went on.

'Are you acquainted with a person named Julius Nesselrode?'

I hesitated for only a few seconds. Then I said, 'What about him?'

I exchanged another look with Moira. I wasn't sure whether she could hear the voice on the other end of the wire or not.

'We're just checking the case out. It looks like a death from natural causes.'

'A what?'

'They found him on a bus stop bench near La Cienega and Pico. Because it's in our division the coroner notified us, and we're doing a routine on the identity.'

'What . . . what was the . . .'

'Well, he was quite an old gentleman. We don't know yet what the autopsy will show, but I imagine his heart just quit running. Are you still there?' he inquired when I didn't say anything.

'When you said homicide I was afraid somebody might have hurt him. A mugger or somebody.'

'No. There's not a scratch on him. He had an address in his pocket that checks out to a house owned by you in St. Albans Place. Is that right?'

'Yes. He lived with me.'

'A relative?'

'No, just a roomer.'

'I see. Well, we're just trying to identify him and close the file. Does he have a next of kin?'

'I don't know. You're calling me at four in the morning about this?'

'We've been trying to reach you for some time.'

'Come in the morning and take his stuff away if you like,' I said. I hung up.

313

'We don't have to go away after all,' I told Moira.

'That's nice.'

'We can stay here.'

'It's a lovely house, Alys. It's the kind of house I've always wanted.'

'Are you sleepy?'

'Yes, a little.'

'Shall we go upstairs?'

She trailed her hand over the sofa, and then sat down on it. 'No, I'll just lie down here.'

I didn't ask her why. I could hardly make out her face in the gloom. After she spoke she turned away from me. I had the impression that it was not that she didn't want to make love, but that she thought I might turn a light on upstairs and she didn't want me to look at her now. I went up to the bedroom, lay down on the double bed, and pulled the spread over me. After a while I fell into a sleep so deep and dreamless that I might have been on another planet, or anesthetized.

CHAPTER EIGHTEEN

When I woke up a bright sun was shining through the window. It was ten in the morning. I got out of bed, finding that I was fully clothed except for my shoes, and I put these on. Out of a kind of reflex, just as though it were any other ordinary day in my life, I went into the bathroom, shaved, washed myself, and came back out and changed into a clean shirt. Then, still behaving more or less mechanically, I went downstairs to see about some breakfast.

To reach the kitchen I had to walk through the living room. At first I didn't recognize Moira and wondered who the person lying on the sofa was. Evidently she was not asleep but only lying with her eyes closed, because when she heard me she opened her eyes and sat up slowly, smiling.

Her face was a mass of wrinkles which covered it from her brow to the base of her throat where they disappeared into her blouse. Her hands too were strangely convoluted, as though someone had crisscrossed them with pencil marks, and the backs of the hands were covered with brown liver spots. Her hair was white, a halo so fine and fragile that it looked as though it could have been blown away with a puff. When she raised her chin there were two little white pouches at the corners of it, like the wattles of some exotic albino bird. Only her eyes were the same: dark, shadowy and expressive, watching me with a faintly uneasy expression that nevertheless contained an admixture of irony. The wrinkles were deepest around her eyes, forming an intricate lacework that radiated out from them in all directions over the face.

For some moments I stared at her without speaking. I felt chill and my skin prickled; it was a sensation as though insects were slowly working their way up my back under the shirt. I didn't know what to say or do and I could only stand there examining every detail of her face, her hair, and her hands, the parts of her that protruded from her clothing. She remained motionless and said nothing, allowing me to examine her. After the first moment of shock was over, I examined my deepest and most private thoughts and realized that I was not really surprised. I reflected that what had happened to Moira was no more horrible than what happened to every human being, except that it had taken place more abruptly and therefore struck the senses with a greater shock. If the reactions it provoked in me were unpleasant, it was simply because it was an analogue of my own eventual fate. If this was so it might be salubrious to my own mental health or help me to a better understanding of the human condition, perhaps. Still something inside me felt heavy, as though some organ had died or I were carrying a small dead animal in my chest.

The hunting jacket and breeches were still immaculate, even though she had slept in them. Unlike me she had gone to sleep without taking off her shoes, stout British walking boots. When I said nothing she got up slowly from the sofa, pushing herself with one hand. She came up to me and folded me in her arms.

'You will be faithful to me, won't you, Alys?'

She made a kind of parody of her former fascinating smile. The wrinkles around her mouth gathered into a curve and then settled again. I allowed her to embrace me for a few moments, and then I drew away.

'Would you like some breakfast?'

'That would be nice.'

I went into the kitchen and made some coffee. There was some bread in the freezer and I toasted two pieces of it by holding them over the gas flame with a fork, since I still hadn't replaced the toaster. I never expected to get the old one back now. I found butter and some jam. We sat down at the small breakfast table.

'I'm sorry there's no cream.'

'I always take it black.'

We went on for the rest of the breakfast making banal remarks like an old married pair. When she had finished her second cup of coffee she went off to the bathroom, and after a while I heard a thin tinkling through the door, an odd and secret feminine sound that I hadn't heard since the days when Astrée lived in the house. There followed the little Niagara of the old-fashioned apparatus—the patent for which, I had almost forgotten, had brought all the money into the family. Then she turned the water on and off several times. Evidently she was

317

washing. For a moment there was silence, and then the door opened. Through it I could see her standing before the mirror combing her white hair with a slightly palsied hand. She turned to me and smiled.

'Alys dear, I *do* have to buy some clothes.'

'All right.'

'I usually go to Robinson's,' she said. 'They have the nicest things.'

★   ★   ★

I decided to take the Invicta instead of the Hudson, since it was an authentic artifact from Moira's epoch. I backed it out of the garage, then I got out and opened the right-hand door for her. She settled into the leather seat with a little sigh, lowering herself with one hand. I got in and we drove away, the well-adjusted engine making a steady chucking sound. At the exit from the park on Wilshire I turned left, deciding not to take her to the old Robinson's at Seventh and Grand downtown but to the branch in Beverly Hills. She didn't seem to notice. She gazed out placidly through the windshield at the long hood with its shiny persimmon enamel, the nickel-plated radiator, and the round dial of the temperature gauge on top of it.

'What a nice car,' she said.

It was possible that she couldn't see very well at a distance and so commented mostly on things that were closest to her eyes. She asked no questions and had nothing to say about the jungle of flashy stores and offices along the Miracle Mile, or about the sleek modern cars streaming past on the boulevard in both directions. But then I was interested in cars and she wasn't. The remark about the Invicta had been merely polite conversation. She was quite cheerful and after a while told me, with the impulsive candor of a child, 'It's such fun going out to buy clothes.'

We stopped for the light at Beverly Drive and a cluster of pedestrians crossed in front of the car, most of them shoppers. One of them turned to look at the Invicta with its persimmon paint and its nickel-plated goggle headlights. It was a blond girl with a khaki bag on a strap over her shoulder, and after a moment I realized it was Belinda. I failed to recognize her at first because she had adopted a new style of clothing: designer jeans, a raw-cotton Mexican shirt which she left hanging out, and silver jewelry. Our eyes met through the windshield. It was clear that she recognized me, and in any case the car was unmistakable. She took in the octogenarian at my side, and for an instant her lips tightened in a quite contrived smile, one with more than a trace of irony in it. Then she disappeared in the crowd. The light changed and I drove on.

Moira sat straight in the seat, looking out

through the glass. She had never turned her head. 'Who was that young woman, dear?'

'A radio announcer.'

'How odd,' she said placidly.

★　　★　　★

I hurriedly parked the car in the Robinson's lot and went around to open the door for Moira. She got out only very slowly, while I waited. Finally she took my arm. 'You know, Alys, as you get on, your joints start to creak a little,' she told me, still cheerful.

I pushed open the glass door of the store for her. Inside everything was air-conditioned, expensive, and elegant. The racks were full of bright-colored clothes. She looked around with a pleased smile. 'Robinson's *is* the best,' she said.

'You'll be all right here for awhile?'

'What's that, Alys dear?'

'I have something . . . I'll only be a few minutes.'

She hardly paid attention. 'You go ahead, dear, I'll just look around for a bit and see what I need.'

She had already turned away to take a dress from a rack and hold it up against her at a mirror. I pushed out through the glass door onto Wilshire and hurried the four or five blocks back to Rodeo. I knew where I would find her:

in a specialty record shop called the Hautboy & Sackbut where we had often gone to look for records together. It was just around the corner on Charleville. As soon as I came in I saw her going through the Deutsche Gramophon records at the rear of the shop. I went back slowly until I was standing at her elbow.

'Belinda.'

'How nice to see you. Have you been out of town?' She smiled and went on looking through the records.

'You might say that.'

'You *do* lead a mysterious life, you know.'

'How about a cup of coffee somewhere?'

'I've only got a minute or two and then I have an appointment.'

'Perhaps I could—come around to see you. Do you still live at the same place?'

'I'm getting kicked out of the apartment. They're converting to condos, and I can't afford to buy mine.' Here she stopped, and glanced up at me only briefly. Then she went back to looking through the records. 'And you. Are you still living in that spooky old house all by yourself?'

Now it was time for me to make my own little smile.

'Usually the man is the one that puts the propositions. You sound like one of those modern girls we read about in magazines.'

'That's right.'

'It's a little embarrassing. Just now I . . .'

'I saw someone with you. Are you in the escort business?'

'It's just that—one isn't always free. I have . . . promises to keep.'

'And miles to go before you sleep? Well, sweet dreams.'

She found the record she wanted and pulled it out and took it off to pay for it at the desk, with a final smile over her shoulder. For an instant she was framed in the doorway: the blond hair, the suntanned face with the pale lipstick, the long slim legs in the jeans below the shirttail. With a bittersweet tug of regret I remembered the body inside the clothes, tanned all over. So we ended, quoting Robert Frost to each other, like two high school kids.

★   ★   ★

When I got back to Robinson's I found that Moira had bought about seven hundred dollars' worth of clothes in the half hour I was gone. Her purchases were in several different departments, so they added it all up and I had to go to the credit desk to write a check for it. I gave the bill to Moira to keep. She put it away in her purse, a kind of paisley affair with a clasp that snapped at the top. She was wearing a nylon dress in a colorful flowered pattern, hose, aubergine pumps with heels, and a large picture hat.

Everything else she had had sent to the house in St. Albans Place. She had evidently bought some cosmetics too and applied them in the ladies' room while I was dealing with the credit clerk, because she was made up like a mime with a white face, dark mascara eyes, and dark-red lipstick.

I asked her if she would like to have lunch. She agreed cheerfully, and we walked back on Wilshire and up Cañon Drive to the Bistro. It was cool and shadowy inside. The captain recognized me as soon as we were seated at the table. 'A Shirley Temple?' he asked me.

*   *   *

It was odd how Moira and I settled into the old house, almost as though we had lived there all our lives. She took one of the small rooms upstairs for a dressing room, but we slept together in the large bedroom with its walls and ceiling covered with mirrors. I bought a new toaster, but I didn't replace anything else; I didn't really feel we needed a camel saddle or an oaken table with ball-and-claw feet. Moira and I eat in the breakfast room for the most part; if it is a special dinner we set up a card table in the dining room. These special dinners, with good wine and a candle on the table, are what she calls our 'parties'; at the end we go upstairs and I do her bidding on the large double bed, while the mirrors on the walls examine us pitilessly from all sides. Basically she is an affectionate and generous person and she appreciates my attentions. We don't go out very much, except that now and then I get out the Invicta to take her shopping to Beverly Hills or Century Plaza. She buys a good many clothes and also spends quite a lot on cosmetics, but there is still plenty of money to spare. I myself buy almost nothing but a few books and records; we can't spend anywhere near the monthly allowance that accumulates at the bank. It's very quiet in St. Albans Place. When the breeze comes up in the afternoon it sighs faintly in the trees outside the windows, as though it were whispering something to itself. Late at night, after we have made love in the mirrored room and lie side by side on the bed, we can hear over the treetops the subdued and distant, almost inaudible roar of the city.

I find that I have fallen into this new life with scarcely any feeling of strangeness, or any sense that it is different from the life I led before. The short period in my life that I spent behind the Screen might not have happened. Everything is the way it is when you return from a foreign country, or when you come out of a movie into the afternoon sunlight. The old reality is just as it always was, and the place you have been seems unreal and only half remembered. You have to make an effort of the will to recall the details, and everything takes up as it was before the brief interlude you spent in the theater of your fantasies.

Now and then, perhaps when Moira is taking a nap in the afternoon, I slip out of the house and wander around the city on foot, in the way that I imagine Nesselrode used to. She doesn't like me to leave her alone in the house, and the sound of a car starting up would waken her; like many old people she sleeps lightly. The city is much as it always was: the stucco storefronts, the forest of neon signs, the bright polychrome graffiti on the walls. Only a few things change from time to time: a store goes out of business or a new shopping center is built. The other day I went back to the Alhambra Theater and found it wasn't there anymore. The wreckers had torn it down to the foundations, leaving their bulldozer standing in the heaps of rubble they had made. You could see right across it to the alley, and there was nothing particularly special about the place where the theater had been; it was just like every other part of the daily and ordinary city. Facing the sidewalk there was a sign firmly imbedded into the ground on two legs: 'Coming Soon. For Your Convenience a New Branch of the Sunset Bank Will Be Erected on This Site.'

This reminded me that for some time I had been half expecting a telephone call from Ziff, but it never came. The only indication that he was still aware of my existence was a rather curious card that arrived in the mail a few weeks ago. It was a large lilac-colored affair that looked like a greeting card, but it was also a business card too, because at the top it bore the legend 'Ziff & Ruben. Surveillance—Investigation—Protection.' There was an address in West Hollywood but no phone number. Framing this inscription, like cherubs in an Annunciation, was a pair of figures rather bizarrely clad in modern urban clothing, but provided with gossamer wings enabling them to hover in the upper left and right corners of the card respectively. The one on the left was unmistakably Ziff, and the other, more portly, was evidently Ruben, who perhaps took care of the more sedentary side of the enterprise. Down at the bottom—not in longhand but printed in flowery letters with daisies growing out of the capitals—were the words 'Happy Birthday.' This was a rather interesting document and I considered keeping it as a memento, but after a second thought I dropped it into the wastebasket.

'What is that, dear?'

'A greeting card from a friend.'

'How nice.'

As a matter of fact it wasn't my birthday. Since then I've heard nothing from him. Evidently he approves of my present way of life, or has lost interest in me. The phone never rings, and no one follows me around, on my walks, in a car with an antenna sticking up. However he may still be hovering around, making sure I am not unfaithful to Moira or that I don't try to go back through the Screen, which would be impossible anyhow because the Alhambra Theater no longer exists. And perhaps it never existed, perhaps it was all in my mind, as Ziff & Ruben's psychiatric consultant so shrewdly suggested. However I can hardly believe that; it was so concrete and vivid. And Moira is really here beside me, although it's true that she's not really very concrete; she is rather phantasmogoric and sometimes gives the impression that she is, perhaps, only an impression on a badly fading film. To be sure she is still there, I go into the bedroom and speak to her. 'I love you, Moira.' She folds me in her arms. 'Alys.'

It's odd that she has never told me that she loves me. But women are like that; for us it's enough if they go to bed with us, but they need constant reassurance. I tell her, 'I love you, Moira' three or four times a day, or whenever she seems to be looking at me questioningly. I ask myself: is this true? Of course it is true, I reply to myself in this inner dialogue, I have always loved her, from the moment I first saw her face through a crowd of people in the commissary. And nothing that has happened since can change that. Why should it? If an octogenarian husband can still love his octogenarian wife, why can't a young husband love a wife who has suddenly become an octogenarian? Suppose a young wife remained young but was stricken with a disfiguring skin disease. Couldn't the young husband go on loving her? Wouldn't he feel an obligation to stay and take care of her and be faithful to her? And wouldn't he even, perhaps, be capable of having sexual relations with her, even though she was no longer sexually attractive? That is what it means to love, and that is how I love Moira—I conclude, satisfied with my arguments to myself.

So the days pass, identical, indistinguishable the one from the other. I have the feeling that something else is going to happen, but the feeling is really only a hope, because nothing else will. It will be just like this. Ghosts walk through the old house, both at night and in the daytime, making the old boards creak, tittering at some private joke or humming scraps of music. For the rest, the city seems to have forgotten me. I don't go to the movies anymore. I don't know anybody and I don't have any friends except Moira. I tell her, 'You know, I've always loved you. Ever since we were in pictures together.'

'Yes,' she says brightly, lifting her wrinkles up into a placid smile. 'That was fun. But this is better, isn't it?'

I don't know what to say to this. After some

328

thought, and an effort to generate a profound comment on the situation, all I can think of is, 'It's more real.'

'Yes. That's what I mean.'

I have my books and my music, and she has her clothes, her cosmetics, and the large mirrors in the bedroom in which she never tires of looking at herself in different costumes or makeups. The way it has happened is best for her, I am sure of that. At least she believes it. She has someone who loves her and is faithful to her, and she is happy to have escaped from behind the Screen, even at the price of her mortality. She takes a particular pleasure in the shopping trips, and our parties at the card table. Only a few days ago she told me, 'I'm enjoying myself tremendously. Everything's so colorful. I want it to go on forever.' Of course, as I watch her closely—and there is nothing else in particular to look at in the house, at least nothing that changes—I can see that she grows perceptibly weaker and more fragile month by month, so that she will die in a few years at the most. So will I of course, sooner or later; but there will be no particular hurry about that.

Photoset, printed and bound in Great Britain by
REDWOOD BURN LIMITED, Trowbridge, Wiltshire